# The Wings of Woolcot

## Mary Frances

New Generation Publishing

# THE FAMILY TREES

| THE KENTS | | | THE CROFTS | | | THE FOLEYS | |
|---|---|---|---|---|---|---|---|

Joseph Kineally m Winifred      **Squire William** m Belinda Hope      Benjamin m Mary

I      I      I

| John m Margaret | Julia | m | Rupert | Julian m Celia | Isabelle | m | Thomas | Ted m Susan |
|---|---|---|---|---|---|---|---|---|

I      I      I      I      I

| Daniel m Elizabeth | Gerald m Rachel | | Bernard m Eileen | Billy | Rosie m Matt Dube | Annie m John Simmons |
|---|---|---|---|---|---|---|

I      I

| Michael m Ruth | Sarah m Neil Chalmers | Jack | Gemma | Andy m Janet |
|---|---|---|---|---|

I      I

Peter      Lee Anne

**For Norah
who loves angels**

# Acknowledgements

My very grateful thanks go first to my two wonderful proof-readers, Cathy Butler and Julia Foxwell, whose utterly different perception of the same book gave me truly valuable insight. Also, thanks to my wonderful friends and family, especially Ron vanderHolt, who kept me writing the book, despite many setbacks, while at the same time writing his own - and who shares my love of words. Thank you to Joan Eggmore who, as a redhead herself, was able to describe some of its drawbacks. And my thanks go to all my acquaintances who were patient enough to accept being ignored and neglected by the hermit crab I became for many months. Thanks to all of you, this hermit crab will now be emerging from its battered shell to blink once again at the brightness of real life, love and beauty.

Most of all, my eternal gratitude goes to God, who inspired this fantasy and kept it alive and well.

# CHAPTER ONE

"Tell me a story," I demanded. I was sitting cross-legged on the floor, my back against an armchair. My grandmother was, as usual, seated comfortably in her recliner, looking not at all put out by my demand.

"Fact or fiction?"

"Oh, fact I think. I write enough fiction for the paper, disguised of course. "

My grandmother regarded me, eyebrows lowered questioningly. "Do I detect a note of disenchantment here? "

"Maybe a bit, but where is my story? You promised."

"Did I? I don't recall promising, but you shall have one all the same."

I lifted my knees so I could cross my arms over them and grinned at her over my elbows. "It's your own fault. You shouldn't be so good at it."

"In that case, are you sitting comfortably?"

"I am agog!." I nodded. I really was agog. My grandmother knows how to tell a good tale and she never disappoints. "Is it really and truly true?"

"Of course." Her long, never really beautiful but always interesting face registered surprise that I should harbour even a sniff of a doubt. "I was there."

I nodded. "Oh well, In that case....!"

"In that case I'll begin." And she did.

But before relating her story I should mention that my name is Gemma Croft. I am a redhead, known as one of the Red Crofts, grand-daughter of Squire William and a reporter for a well known London daily. I write stories often carrying my by-line. I live in London, near to my work, and race across to Somerset twice or three times a year, or whenever an opportunity presents itself, to stay with my grandmother in her elegant apartment in Little Woolcot, where the scenes and smells of nearby

1

countryside woo my senses and draw me back again whenever I try to leave. I love my grandmother and consider to be her the wisest and serenest lady of my acquaintance, but neither of us suspected even for a whiff of a heartbeat that the tale she was about to tell in true raconteur style that Spring afternoon was irrevocably going to change all our lives.

"As you know," she began, "a long time ago when I was young - and I mean very young - in the 1930s before the war, Woolcot wasn't the town it is now but two villages, Woolcot Raegis and Little Woolcot. They were known everywhere as "The Woollies". Little Woollie was very little indeed and, only about a mile away from its bigger neighbour where the school and the village shop were. We children walked that mile every day to school and back, but in those days we didn't know anything else and we enjoyed it anyway. It was fun. There were always things to see and check up on and horses used to push their heads over the fences to have their noses rubbed.

"The Big House, Woolcot Hall, was quite near to us at Little Woollie, much nearer than it was to Big Woollie, so we felt it belonged to us and we often knew what was going on there before anyone else did. it was common knowledge in our village that Isabelle, the squire's daughter, was secretly walking out with the gamekeeper. The villagers were sorry for them because the squire was a red-haired Croft with a temper on him you could light your fire with and he wouldn't like her even knowing Jim Foley let alone courting him, so they never talked about it except amongst themselves and then it was in whispers. If they saw the two together they looked the other way. Not that Jim wasn't a nice young boy and extremely handsome, as all the village girls appreciated, and she was as pretty a girl as anyone could wish to see - lovely rich red-gold curls and bright blue eyes. A true Croft, everyone said. She had her father's colouring for sure, and maybe his temper too, though no-one ever saw any sign of that in her. She was far too well brought up for public tantrums. On the whole, the village quietly wished the couple well, even though they didn't expect them to get it. That was before I was born but my mother told me the story, as far as she knew it at the time.

"Eventually, of course, Isabelle's father found out. You couldn't keep secrets like that indefinitely in the Woollies, big or little. But one day the news broke that Jim Foley had been summoned and given the sack right there on the spot. Everyone was sorry, however expected it might have been. Gamekeeping was his livelihood and there was a tied cottage, which meant his mother and brother were thrown out as well. Not that those two suffered much. Ted was already the village carpenter and handyman. He simply married Susan Watkins, whose father ran the local bakery, and managed to rent a cottage not far from us. What the squire thought of this we neither knew nor cared. What made the situation worse, though, was that Isabelle announced that she was pregnant and told her father she was going to marry Jim, whether he, Squire William ,liked it or not."

"Good for her!" I said.

"Well, no, it wasn't because her father told her she had to have the baby adopted and if she saw Jim again she would be turned out as well. In fact he absolutely forbade any more contact and threatened to lock her in her room. My cousin was upper housemaid at the hall at the time and she told me afterwards that they'd never seen the old man so angry. They were afraid he would have a heart attack or a stroke, or at least fall off his horse and break his stubborn neck. Not that any of them would have been too upset if he had. They didn't like him."

"Not surprised," I murmured and waited for the riches I knew were still to come.

"Well anyway, what did the two do but run away together? That very night. No-one knew where they went or what they did for money, because I'm willing to bet her father never gave them a penny. But vanish they did, until Jim Foley returned one night with a baby boy to say that Isabelle had died in childbirth. He stayed just long enough to hand the baby over to his brother Ted and Ted's wife Susan before vanishing once more into outer space. Nobody ever saw him again."

"Unfortunately little Billy grew up with a speech impediment. It was only slight and he could talk but he wasn't always easy to understand. So - very unjustly my mother thought – he earned the name of village idiot. It wasn't until a year or so later that we learnt the truth – that Jim was in fact Squire William's natural son, born secretly to one of his servants, who was of course turned off without a reference. So Jim's marriage to Isabelle had in fact been incestuous. No wonder the squire was so angry. Horror would not have been too strong a word. He was a changed man afterwards.

"Jim's brother Ted, who was now Little Billy's foster father whether he, Ted, liked it or not, was so angry when he learnt the truth that he, so say, dropped (accidentally or on purpose) the baby so hard he damaged his little spine. He never walked again, poor little soul. His childhood was spent being abused by both his foster parents for it goes without saying that Susan hated him - hated him because he was more or less foistered on her and hated him because of the shame of his birth. The fact that he was now severely disabled didn't help, of course."

I was silent, full of thoughts.

Then I asked: "How about the villagers? Did they abuse him too?"

"No. They were especially kind to him as it happened, although the children behaved as children always will and called him names and teased him, but by then he could talk a little, even if what he said wasn't always very understandable, and he learned how to defend himself. And it became very clear that he wasn't the village idiot they had labelled him. Far from it. He grew clever at giving the right answer to every insult and he was good at making people laugh. In fact everyone liked him and, as soon as he could manage it, someone – and we never discovered who – bought him a run-about wheelchair, the sort with huge wheels that you propel with your arms. After that he was never at home. He just spent the rest of his short life scooting around the village chatting to anyone who had time to stop and listen."

"His short life? He didn't live long then? Hardly surprising. What did he die of?"

"He died when he was eight. I was exactly the same age so we more or less grew up together. In fact we became good friends. But the story given was that he died of pneumonia." My grandmother paused, frowning and with angry eyes. She helped herself to a chocolate from the box in front of her. "That's what *they* chose to call it anyway, but my parents and we children knew otherwise. It was neglect of course, but the circumstances of his dying almost over- shadowed the event itself and of what had led up to it. They are the real meat in this story" She fell silent and I waited. If I hadn't known better I would have said there were tears, but her face was towards the window. Somehow the prompting I was about to give to carry on with her story was never given. Instead she turned her head to smile at me and said that an hour's story-telling was more than enough for any 85-year-old and this one now proposed to indulge in her usual afternoon nap.

I smiled back but pointed an accusing finger. "You are *mean!*" I frowned, "leaving me hanging on for the best part. But because you are my aged relative and my hostess I shall forgive you and leave you to nap in peace. However, Mrs Croft, I must have the rest or I'll never visit you again. I shall now go exploring, but *I'll be back.*"

Grandmother chuckled, closed her eyes, folded her hands on her chest and waved me languidly away. "See you at supper time," she murmured.

With a warning frown and a shake of my forefinger, I stepped through her front door, across the foyer and out into afternoon sunshine. "You're not fobbing me off that easily, my dearest grandmother" I thought. "The best is yet to come and I'm having it."

It was and I did.

# CHAPTER TWO

Coming in as I was going out was Mrs Simmons, whose father-in-law, Ted Foley, ran the bakery. She was the lady who cooked Grandmother's main meal of the day, made the bed and kept the flat much like the new pin she herself resembled – except that her basic structure was more akin to pin-cushion than pin. She asked if I were to be present for supper which I assured her I was but that for overnight stay I had a room booked at the Lamb, Little Woollie's ancient but agreeable local inn. Mrs Simmons gave no reply but I suspected an unspoken disapproval, so added that if my grandmother wished for my company overnight I would of course cancel the inn booking, but that so far she had insisted on my freedom to come and go as I pleased.

"I am not entirely decrepit, Gemma," Gran had said, "requiring overnight assistance, so please don't insult me by offering it."

With a smile and a "See you later," to Mrs Simmons and adding that Gran was having her afternoon sleep, which Mrs Simmons would certainly know anyway, I ventured down the flight of elegant stone steps into the dreamy peace of Croft Court's well-kept gardens.

Down the drive towards the gate I turned to look at what only a few years ago had been the Squire's residence, a scene of such illicit and incestuous romance, rage, abuse, death and misery that its story cried out for recognition in print. All my instincts were to hear the end of this apparently true tale and then to research it and write it. Whether my grandmother would allow this was another matter and I proposed leaving the final decision to her.

Meanwhile I regarded the house and garden with fresh eyes. It seemed somehow to have changed in perspective. The mansion, for that is definitely what it was and still is, rose in graceful Georgian elegance with long windows and

7

an imposing entrance with its pillars atop its curve of ten steps. It must have looked much the same when it was still a family home, I thought, only now it was what in other locations would have been merely a block of luxury apartments. .

As Celia Croft and a member of the old squire's family, even if only by marriage, my grandmother had been given first choice of apartment and had elected to live in Suite 1, at the front of the house and on the ground floor. It was still graced with beautiful moulded cornices, high ceilings and, while divested of some panelling here and there, walls which had been tastefully papered in soft regency shades. It overlooked the lawns and flowerbeds and the circular drive which had been purposely kept and was beautifully maintained.

These were, of course, expensive residences for the wealthy and therefore of necessity had what elsewhere would have been known as 'kerb appeal'. They were also invariably advertised as 'suites'. Anything less elegant would not, of course, have been considered.

A mixture of luck and sheer financial flair had finally saved the hall from disaster. The squire's eldest son, Rupert, had been wise enough and lucky enough to "marry money". Julia Kent was the daughter of the hugely successful JK Kent Engineering, the fortunes of which suddenly began to prosper even more with the birth and rise of electronics, so that by the time Rupert's own eldest son, Danny, was old enough to join the family firm Kent Electronics was a well known name in the computer and mobile phone industry. Danny was not only an electronics wizard himself, he had a remarkable talent not only for making money but for investing it all in unusual ways and with astonishing success. So when he realised that his grandfather's noble pile was falling into decay without hope of redemption, he stepped ahead of the National Trust and bought the place himself. He then transformed what had been his grandfather's family home into twenty sumptuous apartments.

These were snapped up in no time, with a waiting list of well-heeled and often well- known celebrity seekers after status. And status was certainly to be had at the newly named Croft Court. William, the original squire, whose prime motivation had been "family pride" had suffered the ultimate humiliation of a runaway daughter in a shameful marriage. He would have been half pleased, half wounded to see his beloved home's new eminence.

Unfortunately both he and his wife Belinda had died within a month of each other five years after the death of their disgraced little grandson.

Deep in thought, I halted at the gate. A right turn would lead me into the heart of what had been Little Woollie and the inn where I would spend the first night of my three week break from toil, noise and the sweat of my brow. A left turn, though, would take me into Woolcot Raaegis itself, the town which was growing so fast that although I had been visiting the Woollies regularly over the past few years, they were always so changed each time that I hardly recognised them.

I had driven from London that morning in time for coffee followed by one of Mrs Simmons' excellent lunches, and should have been tired. But I was young (29 in point of fact) and filled with curiosity (a vital requisite for any reporter) so I turned left and made my way into the town I had watched grow from leafy lanes and farm cottages, cows and cowslips, into a new home for Macdonald's, Marks & Spencer, Sainsbury's and the ubiquitous cafe/restaurants which lined the streets.

The road was leafy enough, if one counted the well kept gardens and kerbside trees of the desirable houses bordering it, but the nearer one approached the town centre one found that yet more buildings had been turned into blocks of retirement homes and town houses, American-style shopping malls and, eventually, into more malls with furniture stores and estate agents and the ever-present antique shops.

I wandered on, fascinated. At a bus stop two people stood alert as a green Number 53 bus drew into the kerb, a young man wearing black trousers and a grey anorak with black stripes skipped easily up the step followed by a middle-aged woman with an empty plaid shopping trolley which she laboriously folded up before boarding. The heads in the bus windows were intent on their own thoughts, except for one or two who gave me a passing glance and promptly forgot me.

The town centre was the least changed, with its clock tower and narrow streets, but even those were now filled, building to building, with dress shops, cafes and poundshops selling cards and gifts and household goods, most of which seemed to be out on the pavement. I browsed here and there, finding a bookshop where I treated myself to a copy of the latest Sue Grafton mystery before wandering into the nearest likely-looking cafe for tea and cake.

I had found a window table and was comfortably ensconced there, idly counting the pram-pushing young women strolling from shop window to shop window, when I noticed the young couple not far from me. The girl was attractive without being poster- pretty, but the young man with her was the most beautiful male I had ever seen. I know I blinked but suspect I also stared in the rudest way, only removing my eyes quickly when the man, obviously aware of someone's gaze, turned his head to look at me.

Beautiful he may have been, but my self-respect did not allow for being caught staring at anyone, let alone at a man so obviously aware of his own image. I was saved by the waitress who stood beside me, notebook expectantly poised. I ordered tea and a slice of coffee cake and reapplied myself to gazing nonchalantly out of the window. When I did finally turn my eyes back to the room I noticed that the girl was sitting in a wheelchair, and finally recalled seeing her before. She was my grandmother's neighbour at Croft Court.

And at the precise moment that I recognised her, she recognised me. She waved.

The die was now cast. Although none of us knew it, another piece of an astonishing jigsaw fitted itself quietly into its allotted space.

With great dexterity, the neighbour whose name I had either forgotten or had never known wheeled herself neatly between the tables and reached mine, holding out her hand and smiling.

"I hope you don't mind, but I know your grandmother. She's told me all about you. My name is Sarah and that's my husband Neil over there. We live in the opposite flat to your grandmother's, the one to the left of the front door."

Another ground floor front, I thought, and then smiled. The designer would not have been pleased with my labelling.

"I saw you arrive," she explained. "I'm afraid life confined to a wheelchair can turn one into a real curtain-twitcher. Sorry about that."

I grinned and decided I liked this girl. "Don't be. I had already demoted your apartments from suites to flats, so am up to my neck in it already."

By this time the beautiful husband had gathered their belongings and joined us. He held out his hand. "Neil Chalmers" he said, and his smile lived up to his name. I couldn't resist a comment. "Chalmers? A name to conjure with. I imagine you had a sticky time with it at school?"

The charming Neil dimpled at me. "I can't begin to tell you," he said, "but 'Charmless' was probably the easiest to deal with, although there were others a great deal worse."

I wrinkled my nose in sympathy. With a face like his, he would be a marked boy in all possible ways. I was sorry for him, although he would probably feel insulted if he knew.

We discovered that eventually we were all aiming homewards, so Neil and I accompanied the swiftly moving wheelchair back the way I had come not long before. Whatever was wrong with Sarah Chalmers she could certainly move. Sarah in particular enthusiastically told me all she could about the road and the villages it once connected. She had been born in Little Woolcot and knew its story intimately. Her husband seemed preoccupied and contributed little, although the charming smile flashed at me occasionally. Half way home, however, he excused himself, saying that he had an appointment which he simply must keep, so would I mind accompanying his wife while he nipped back to town and he'd see us both later.

I agreed, of course, if anything relieved that Sarah and I could continue our journey in peaceful, male-free conversation. I asked what Neil did, and what was his profession?

For the first time Sarah hesitated, then she explained that her husband worked for her father's electronics firm as an account executive. A classy car went with the job, so Neil spent a considerable time away visiting clients – hence her wheelchair. "My father bought it for me," she said, "because it didn't seem right for Neil to have a car while I was stuck at home knitting. Not that I do knit, but I do make things and I love walking around the garden or just staring at it out of the window. It's bigger than you think at first and it's my inspiration. You'd be amazed at the wildlife you can see if you happen to be in the right place at the right time."

"I'm surprised your father didn't buy you a proper mobility scooter while he was about it. They're all the trend now. You see them whizzing around the pavements all the time."

For such a forthright person, Sarah seemed surprisingly embarrassed by my question. She answered it all too quickly.

"Oh he did, but I turned it down, at least for the present. I like the exercise. You should see my arm muscles. And Neil said that if I reached the stage of needing one he would buy it for me himself." Then, as the gates to Croft Court appeared before us, she changed the subject. "Will you call and see me?" she asked. "I've enjoyed your company and would be really happy to have more of it. You cheer me up and life can get a bit lonely at times."

I agreed with pleasure and accompanied her to her own side entrance where a ramp had been placed for her to manipulate her wheelchair, which she did with ease and speed, waving goodbye as she disappeared. I waved back and watched her go, then proceeded up the steps to the communal and rather magnificent front door. A few steps across the imposingly spacious entrance hall brought me back to my grandmother's own front door.

I went first to the kitchen where Mrs Simmons was chopping vegetables. The air was fragrant with cookery smells. I was surprised.

"Two proper meals today? I won't have room for another, or is this for tomorrow?"

"Both", she smiled. "I'm leaving something for your supper but this is prepping for tomorrow".

"You look after my Gran beautifully. I can't thank you enough."

Mrs Simmons didn't look up but her cheeks showed the tiniest spot of pink. "Ah, she deserves it. I'm happy to do it". Looking slightly less pin-neat now that she was dusted up to her armpits with flour, she looked up eventually and smiled. "Had a good afternoon?" she asked. "Where did you get to in the end?"

I replied that I had revisited the town, which had grown even more in my six months absence. I was told about the new houses being built closer to Little Woollie "although they can't just do what they want here because a lot of the old village is listed."

I said "Good," and asked if my grandmother was awake from her nap.

"Oh my goodness yes, she's been in here making a cake. Not one for sitting still, that one! Supper will be in half an hour. Would you like a cuppa to keep you going?" I thanked her but refused the offer, having something rather more alcoholic in mind. I was anxious now to get my grandmother talking. I wished to oil her memories with drink, and tea would be a poor substitute for a glass of her excellent sherry.

She owed me a full story and I was going to get it.

# CHAPTER THREE

Having left the garlicky pincushion to her prepping, I made my to the high-ceilinged, elegant and beautifully proportioned room which was, in the estate agents' advertisements, designated as the drawing room. I had smiled at the description, amused at the image it conjured up. To me it was either a sitting room or a lounge, depending on one's perspectives. After all, the days of ladies being obliged to leave the dinner table and withdraw, discreetly leaving coarser males to enjoy their coarser conversation without sullying any tender little ears, were now long gone and better left where they belonged – safely in our social history books, except for the tiniest suspicion at the back of my thoughts that maybe our 21$^{st}$ century had lost its sense of graciousness. We had gadgets in plenty and state-of-the-art kitchens and bathrooms, but somehow delicacy and grace had been mislaid or even lost to us. I hoped not forever, but if were true were we perhaps the poorer for it? maybe our 21$^{st}$ century had lost its sense of graciousness.

My grandmother was sitting in her recliner chair, a glass of something that looked hopeful in one hand. With the other she waved me in and pointed to the bottle sitting on the small table beside her.

"Help yourself," she said.

I helped myself. I had been right about the sherry.

"Have a good sleep?" I asked.

She nodded and asked where my roaming had taken me. I told her, then added the question uppermost in my mind at that moment. "I met the couple next door. I like her. Not so sure of him. Why is she in a wheelchair? It didn't seem appropriate to ask her at his early stage. "

"Multiple Sclerosis. Diagnosed not all that long ago but apparently it's the aggressive sort. And you're right about the husband. Too handsome by half. He knows it of course, since he only has to look in the mirror. He's vain, naturally, but I suppose one can't blame a chap for his looks."

"So who is she? I know he works for her father, which makes her what? A Kent?"

My grandmother took another sip, nodded and said "Yep! She was Sarah Kent. That's why she has the flat. Courtesy of wealthy Daddy."

I smiled. "And how lucky for Neil, though I don't suppose he reckoned on M.S. when he married his nice little heiress. She obviously adores him, though, which must make up a good bit for any wheelchair duties." I frowned and thought for a moment, then added: "I hope he's kind to her."

At that point Mrs Simmons appeared in the doorway to say supper was now on the table so would we please come before it spoiled.

We went, like obedient children, to enjoy a totally unspoilt and very delectable supper of mushroom soup with croutons and fresh white rolls, in the tacit understanding that after it would come the denouement of the tale of Billy Foley, for which I now had definite, private, plans of my own.

There was, however, little I could do about it at the moment except wait so, murmuring "Into the breach, Gemma, into the breach," I followed her into the sitting room and possessed my soul in patience. Happily I didn't have to wait for long.

My grandmother tilted her head to savour the last drops of the coffee we had brought with us from the dining room. "How far had I got?"

I seated myself in my favourite position on the floor, legs crossed under me. I gazed up expectantly. "Billy died when you were both eight," I prompted, "and you said things had started to happen a long time before."

"Amazing stuff. We didn't tell because we didn't think anyone would believe us. And before I tell you the rest I want to know what you'll do with the story. No News of the World or photos in The Sun, please."

"Certainly not," I replied, "Well, certainly not the Sun or the News of the World anyway. They wouldn't even read it, let alone print it. I'll write it up and see how it looks, but I promise not to do anything without consulting you. After all, I haven't driven all the way here just for copy. I'm on holiday. But please do carry on."

There was quite a long pause, as if she were uncertain, or even unwilling to continue.

"I'm going to ask you to suspend your disbelief," she said finally. "I saw all this for myself, as did most of the village at the time, and although it was written off by some as mass hallucination, I can assure you there was too much evidence to simply dismiss it out of hand."

I nodded my agreement. Grannie suddenly smiled. "It was a single feather at first which just appeared one day in Billy's hair, which grew to two feathers next day. Everyone laughed and asked him if he'd been sticking his head in the hen coop. But next day there were three more, not in his hair but on his bedroom floor. We still didn't take much notice. Billy was wild about all animals and they sort of gathered around him. Followed after him sometimes like children following the Pied Piper.

"Then someone remarked that all the feathers were white, which provoked another comment that white feathers signified that an angel had been visiting. Billy laughed and looked delighted when the number of feathers grew and grew until they were floating around the floor in Ted's cottage. At that point Susan began to be seriously annoyed. She told Billy enough was enough, she was sick of sweeping his feathers out of everywhere so whatever he

17

was doing would he please stop or he would be severely punished.

"But he or they didn't stop. In fact the number of feathers grew day by day until Billy himself was covered all the time. They were in his hair and on his clothes and wheelchair and even followed his progress around the village. People had noticed two white pigeons among the many in the gardens and on rooftops,, but these were not only still alive but walking around with what looked like their normal quantity of home-grown plumage which didn't seem to be depleted in any way.

"The swans on the village pond were also among the chief suspects, despite the fact that there was no way in which Billy in his wheelchair could have enticed and de-feathered them himself. They were vicious, those swans, and would have pecked him to death given half a chance. So Billy's feather storm remained a mystery, and his foster mother grew angrier and angrier. So did Ted, the uncle he called his father, who threatened to lock him up in his room if he didn't stop.

"But it seemed that poor little Billy couldn't stop. He wasn't a disobedient boy, as I knew well, because he fascinated me and I spent a lot of time pushing him around and showing him things and just having fun. Because that's what he was. A fun child. He made me laugh and he saw the funny side of everything. I couldn't bear to see him punished like he was by his so-called parents, and occasionally made myself unpopular with Ted and Susan by sticking up for him. Not that they would have dared to punish me. My father was the local doctor and had too much standing in the village – which was no doubt why I was allowed to marry Julian, the squire's younger son. The 'spare' to Rupert's' 'heir.'

"Anyway, true to their threats, Ted and Susan had locked Billy in his room, which became as full of white feathers as if he had upended all his pillows and his eiderdown and everyone else's as well. But they weren't duck feathers any more than they had been pigeon or swan feathers. They were all the wrong size. Billy's were smaller and curlier. Besides, the bedding was all still the same shape and as full and fluffy as it had always been.

"It was while he was locked in his room that he mysterious woman called. She was very specific in what she wanted and obviously determined to get it. She was looking for Billy Foley and wasn't going to leave without seeing him. This she couldn't of course be allowed to do while he was in his room looking as if he'd been caught in a snowstorm. So Ted and Susan had, feathers and all, been forced to clean Billy up and let him out. Denying him was not working. They couldn't say he wasn't there because everyone in the village had been asked where he was by the mystery woman and had told the truth

"The visitor was young and very beautiful in a quiet, serene sort of way, neatly but nicely dressed in what even at that early age I recognised as good and well chosen. I can remember the moment when she met him, and remember crying because she was crying. I think I cried partly because I was afraid she might be taking him away, but on the whole I cried because the whole thing was so moving. However, after talking together outside in the garden, the woman hugged Billy and gave him a kiss and a bag of sweets.

"What happened next?" I demanded.

"When Billy saw me he called me over and she shook my hand as if I was a proper grown up person. She told me she had been married to Billy's dad, Tom, but he was busy flying commercial aeroplanes and she had promised to look for his little boy and make sure he was happy and well cared for. "I've been trying to find him," she explained, "but Tom never told me much about his past, except that he had married a girl called Isabelle who had died when little Billy was born. He wanted Billy to know who his real father was. My grandmother paused and looked out of the window. This time I was certain that her cheeks were wet. I was silent. There was nothing I could say.

Then she took a deep breath and began again. "The woman said her name was Joan, and asked if he had been well treated. She gave me a card with her name, address and telephone number printed on it and said she had promised Billy's father that she would look for his little son and tell him he had never stopped loving him, and that the only reason he hadn't sent for him was because his own life was so precarious he thought Billy would be safer in the country, where he was. "And he was right wasn't he?" she smiled. Tom was in danger every single day, even before the war, flying for commercial firms in old planes made of cardboard and string."

"Joan promised to keep in touch and that she'd be back to check on Billy whenever she could."

"And did she?"

My grandmother shook her head, looking sad. "No," she said, "Not until after the war, but by then Billy had died and she was too late. She didn't have Tom long herself. He was a squadron leader by then, flying spitfires, and he was shot down in the battle of Britain."

This time Joan sought me out. She told me she had brought Billy something very special but wanted to give it to someone who would love it and treat it with care and respect. She suggested Billy's foster parents, but I pulled a face. "Please don't give things to Billy or Ted because Ted will swipe them and I'm not sure what he'd do with them. If you give them to me I'll keep 'em safe for him."

"Joan didn't question the advice. I felt she probably knew already from her researches that Ted had always been too hard on the little boy so when she handed them to me I accepted them and made a personal vow to keep them safe as long as I lived. It was a very serious vow.

"I still have them," said my grandmother.

"What are they?"

Gran rose from her chair and vanished into her bedroom, returning with a blue bag. Inside it was an RAF cap, complete with wings, and a DFC medal in a velvet-lined box.

"I have treasured them," she told me, "but it was his life that ended before time, not mine. When he was just coming up to 9, the same age as me, he died of pneumonia, quite quickly. He'd been undernourished for so long his little body couldn't fight it, and everybody in the village was at the funeral. I'd never seen so many people and they all saw what I saw."

This time I knew for sure that she was weeping.

"The little pint-sized coffin was covered, every inch of it, with white feathers. The grass too, and the churchyard. Even the inside of the church had its own white carpet. It was like snow only it fluttered when anyone moved. And when the coffin was lowered into the ground and we'd said our final farewells, there was the most dramatic moment of all.

"As we all turned to leave, the feathers seemed to gather themselves together, floating here and there and changing shape all the time, then finally taking off like a cloud, only the cloud formed itself into a pair of wings and soared away into the sky exactly like you see starlings do, moving to and fro in wonderful curves only they didn't change shape but kept together.

"We all saw it, Gemma, but no-one dared talk about it afterwards. We knew we would be laughed at and disbelieved as gullible villagers back in the days of witch hunts and fairy stories. But we all saw it. And I don't think any of us ever forgot it. In fact I think a few of the older ones were superstitious about it, as if some kind of spell would fall on us if we told the outside world."

My grandmother sighed. She had been talking for a long time and looked impossibly weary.

"I've tired you out, "I said at last. "I hadn't realised how the time had gone by, so I'm going to let you go to bed while I find my Lamb Inn and dream about feathers. But please promise not stay up dozing in your chair."

She didn't argue but nodded and rose, still gracefully, to limp her way to bed, only to halt at the door to look back at me. "There's one more thing," she said. "I know I should have given Ted Foley the cap and medals, but I didn't. He might have sold them or thrown them away and I couldn't have borne that, so I kept them.. It didn't feel wrong at the time and it still doesn't. I just couldn't bear to let them disappear and Ted certainly wouldn't have given them to me. Losing them would have been as if Billy had never existed."

I rose from my place on the carpet and went to put my arms around her. "You did absolutely the right thing," I told her, then I kissed her on the forehead, said "Good night, sleep tight," and left. Outside It was still daylight, but with the dusky glimmer of the countryside, so, too full of thoughts of today to think about tomorrow, I found my car and drove away.

I was in no hurry to arrive. Easing the car into one of the spaces provided for such as me, I found that the evening seemed to have grown even more delicious, enchanting me with its softly tinted greys and greens and with fragrances so intoxicating I could hardly bear to leave them. Just as I was about to move reluctantly towards the inn door, Neil Chalmers emerged from it and we stared at each other. I wasn't sure which of us was the more surprised, but after the first shock Neil was the first to recover. He became all instant charm, smiling as though I were the one person in the whole world he most wished to see.

"Are you coming in? I took it for granted you'd be staying with your grandmother, I don't know why, but if you would like to come into the bar I'd be delighted to offer you a drink."

I thanked him but suggested that as he was probably on his way home I wouldn't keep him any longer, though at another time of course I would accept with pleasure.

His was a face hard to read, but I felt rather than saw that 'relief' was written there somewhere. Relief with a tiny trace of – could it be? – embarrassment? The one thing I could be sure about was that he had not expected to see me.

With that we went our separate ways and I proceeded alone into the bar for a much needed night-cap. The lounge was pleasantly full, but not so full that I didn't immediately capture the attention of the slightly exotic but comfortable-looking woman behind the counter. She was wearing a tight fitting black top with a sequinned V neck that hinted at riches beneath, and she was industriously plying a damp cloth to the counter top. Her name, as I knew from previous visits, was Amy. That she was amiable was apparent for all to see. She beamed at me. I asked for a single brandy and remained where I was, sipping it and looking around me.

"Nice to see you again, Gemma," Amy said, still beaming. "Up to see your Grannie? How is she? We don't get to see her in here much these days."

I explained that although she was well and happy, she was after all in her eighties and preferred to do her drinking in the comfort of her own home. "Not that she does tipple much, but when she does, I think she likes to do it in peace and quiet."

Amy nodded as vigorously as she did everything else. "Quite right too," she agreed. "If you can't do things how you want when you're eighty plus, when can you? That's what I ask myself."

I smiled my agreement, took another sip and said: "She's been telling me the story of Little Billy and the feathers. I knew vaguely that there was a Little Billy but I got all the details today and I'm intrigued."

Amy lost some of her vigour and stopping wiping the bar. "Yeah, there was a story but I only got half of it myself, not being old enough to have been there at the time, like your Gran. I know there was some sort of secret," she stopped and frowned, "Not secret so much as everyone seemed a bit embarrassed and stopped talking whenever the subject came up. If you want to know more, you'd have to speak to some of the older ones here. Like him, for instance," and she nodded in the direction of a dapper little man with a clipped white beard and bushy moustache who was sitting by himself in a corner reading the paper.

"The younger ones wouldn't know the first thing," she continued, "like that little lot over there." She nodded this time at the small group of young men chatting, heads together, at a table along the far wall. "Your gran's neighbour, that Neil, was one of them until a minute ago. He left just before you came in. It's a wonder you didn't bump into him."

"I did. He offered to come back in and buy me a drink."

"Did he? That was nice of him." Amy spoke noncommittally but her very lack of expression gave her away.

Deciding that although I was almost too tired to care, my day was not quite finished after all, I made my way towards the dapper man with the beard and stopped beside his table. He lowered his newspaper to regard me through half-spectacles. I smiled, apologised for disturbing him but explained that I was doing some research on the Little Bill story of the 1930s. "I'm pretty sure you're not old enough to have been around at the time," I lied, "but maybe your parents told you about it and you might have opinions of your own."

The man stared at me for a second or two before saying "Poppycock!" Shaking his newspaper. He raised it to eyelevel again. I was dismissed.

"So much for that," I thought, deciding at last that enough was enough for one day and that one more secret would be have been one too many anyway after a day of travelling and discovery. I finished my brandy, stood up and said goodnight.

Amy smiled at me from behind the bar. "Guessed you wouldn't get much out of him, flattery or no flattery," she said. "You know the way to your room? It's the same one you had last time. And what about your luggage?"

I pointed to the backpack by my side, hefted it over my shoulders, smiled and went willingly to bed. Some unravelling of my day was urgently required. There was plenty for me to unravel and lying between clean sheets seemed the only possible place for doing it. Unfortunately, that theory turned out to be faulty since although I might wrestle with the details, the plot of the Little Billy story remained what it always was – a puzzle. Who belonged to what and to whom could be worked out through research. It was the Why that defeated me, as it had defeated a whole village seventy-plus years ago. Why feathers and where had they come from? And why had they only come to Billy? In a question-tormented wakefulness I went over it all again, considering an emptied pillow-case or an old-fashioned eiderdown or even a proper feather bed, but conceded that the last option was unlikely. I didn't see Ted Foley providing a disliked foster son with such a luxury item. Some sacking and a horse blanket seemed more likely. In the end, however, I had to stop guessing, for where could Billy find so many pillows or eiderdowns to cover as much ground as his feathers had done? And what happened to the empty pillow cases? It would need more than one pillow, for sure, and the loss of it would have been noticed – and certainly punished. I smiled at the thought of how many items would have to be found, emptied and distributed, in secret, in order to create such a gigantic featherstorm. He would certainly have been rumbled and the puzzle solved there and then. Logically none of it could have happened as my grandmother had described. Yet not only had she been alive but present and a witness to the whole thing - and my grandmother was not given to telling lies, least of all with tears in her eyes.

Even allowing for artistic exaggeration there was no doubt she had been moved. .

At that point thought gave way to oblivion and I fell asleep. Tomorrow I would take action.    But not before. Certainly not before.

# CHAPTER FOUR

I awoke to sunshine and birdsong and the sounds of a small town, only just emerging from its village status, waking up and preparing for duty. I stepped from my bed to open the window, and for a very few seconds my eyes and ears prepared for the more familiar sounds of London traffic and flying aircraft, the clip, clip of shoe-leather as thousand upon thousand pairs of shoes trod the pavement below my window. But this image was instantly lost and replaced by sheer, joyful thankfulness for the delectable whiffs of fresh air, the little town itself and for the smell of frying bacon that was wafting up to me from the hotel kitchens. There was no doubt in my mind that The Lamb Inn's bacon was the best this side of paradise. Within minutes, it seemed, I had cleaned my teeth, showered and shampooed my short, auburn drip-dry curly cap, (though if I am to be truly honest I confess to being as out-and-out a redhead as one can possibly be), had pulled on jeans and a cotton shirt and was leaping down the stairs towards the dining room, where the tables were scrupulously set with crisp white cloths, and the toaster and preserves were laid neatly, ready to hand. The room was familiar but the walls were now a tasteful shade of mint green, with their original beams still holding the place together after its several hundred year old history.

There were few residents about and even those appeared to be mainly of the passing-through kind, so as the day was showing signs of being a seriously beautiful one, I rose replete and ready for whatever fate or myself decided upon. A dishful of bacon, eggs and fried bread followed by two rounds of toast and marmalade would, I thought, have sent my grandmother instantly to sleep, but instead I wandered out into what felt to me like earthly paradise with renewed energy and ambition. The air was soft and scented. The sky was that wonderfully pale blue of new day and the sun was playing on the stone walls and Tudor windows which made Little Woollie what it was – a place of unusual natural beauty. One to be treasured and preserved.

Words, I thought, could not adequately describe the charm this place held for me.

"London?" I asked the tubs of varying shades of begonias and pansies burgeoning each side of the inn door. "Who needs it?"

Well, of course I knew that I needed it, simply to allow me to live in a tidily furnished flat and enjoy the delights of London's social fast track. Not for nothing had I worked my way up from tea-girl, trainee and rooky reporter to the position where I found myself at present – a journalist of no small repute whose stories often made the front pages and even influenced the occasional editorial. With my 30th birthday knocking closely at the door, I was a lucky girl and knew it. I was also free of encumbrances, having, it seems, a thousand friends but no *friend* and certainly no lover. Many had tried but no-one had as yet breached my defences.

I also knew, of course, that I was unusual, being a still single almost-30-something, a position that was no longer the anomaly it would have seemed a few years earlier - without a world war and the passionate campaigning of two generations of women for Liberation and Girl Power. It was as *ok* to be single at 30 now as it was certainly *not ok* in my grandmother's time. I smiled. "She must feel I've come straight out of science fiction," I murmured, but that image didn't fit. My grandmother may have been two generations away in years but she was now very surely up with the society she had watched grow.

I went to retrieve my car from its 'residents only' parking space and drove happily back to Croft Court. The lions on the two pillars guarding the gate welcomed me in, albeit a bit grudgingly, I thought, as if they would as soon eat me as not. But as I steered unchewed around the circular gravel drive I saw Sarah approaching me from across the grass. Attached to the wheelchair on a long, extendable lead, was a very young and very unruly Labrador puppy.

I was surprised, not only by the sight of a dog, obviously too strong for its owner, but by the fact that she, the dog and the wheelchair seemed to have emerged from some mystical nowhere land. I hadn't seen her coming.

"Hello" I called through my opened driver's window, "Have you got the gift of levitation or do you just say 'Beam me up Scotty' when you want to go anywhere?"

Sarah waved and came towards me, "Sorry?" she laughed. "Did you just say something about levitation?"

"I was wondering how on earth you managed to appear as if by magic from a new kind of fairyland."

"Oh I have. Don't you recognise chariots and pumpkins when you see them? And my coachman too, of course, though he's a bit unreliable I'm afraid."

"I've noted the coachman, but you are not in the least like a pumpkin and anyway where are your wings?"

"I didn't know pumpkins had wings."

"There are no rules in fairyland, didn't you know? And your dog looks a bit young for his coachman's job. By the way he's behaving, he'd rather tip you over than drive you."

"Yes, bless him. But he's only a pup so you have to forgive him".

I had my own opinions on the matter, but smiled and reached down to stroke the puppy's head as he rushed up to the car, panting and filled to the last ounce with doggy excitement. He kicked up his little back legs, trying vainly to leap through the open window.

"I'm sorry, he's being a nuisance. He loves strangers. Jake get down, Gemma doesn't want your slobber all over her nice car," and she shortened the lead and pulled hard on it. The dog took no notice.

"He's lovely, but isn't he a bit too strong for you," I frowned. "How long have you had him? I don't remember seeing a dog about the place."

"He's new. T only got him yesterday. Neil brought him home after we met you. That's where he was going when he left us. He didn't want to spoil the surprise. Jake is a birthday present and because he's away so often. I'm just having to learn a new skill, that's all."

"Kind of him," I conceded, privately adding yet one more tick to my 'Neil Chalmers' black list. "How big will Jake get? And will you be having any help with walking and training him?"

Sarah gazed long and hard at Jake, who had given up hope of joining me and was now straining and choking on his lead, obviously longing to get back to his desperate search for the source of some seductive smells that were beyond our poor capacity to enjoy. He somehow managed to look both eager and pathetic at the same time. I smiled, wondering how dogs did it and wishing I had the same gift.

Sarah explained: "We haven't done anything about it yet, but we must very soon"

"Well I don't mind walking him for you now and again while I'm here. The trouble is I'm only on leave for three weeks, then I have to depart back to smelly old London."

I was on the point of asking whether Sarah had been consulted in the matter of dogs and their walkers, but didn't, suspecting I might not approve of the answer even had it not been too personal a question on such short acquaintance Instead I suggested perhaps contacting a pet-caring agency. "There are plenty of adverts in the local paper, and I imagine Little Woollie has a kind of newsletter or puts posters on a newsboard or something. I'm sure I've seen one or two around the place."

Sarah beamed. "Thanks. I'll tell Neil," she said, "but thank you so much for your offer. I might even take you up on it. Meanwhile I'm keeping you from your grandmother. She must be dying to see you by now, and here I am holding you up, talking about dog-walking."

I was certainly looking forward to seeing Gran, who must, I thought, be wondering why I was late, but I was just as worried about leaving Sarah alone to manage a heavy wheelchair and a very strong puppy. I fished in my bag to find my business card and handed it to her, pointing to the mobile phone number. "Any trouble of any kind," I told her, "and will you please phone me. If I take Grannie out somewhere we won't be going far and my phone is always on."

Sarah nodded her thanks and raised an arm in salute. . I drove to the parking space at the back of the building where, I imagined, the carriages would have been kept and expensive horses stabled. There I locked the car and trotted round the corner and up the steps to the front door. My grandmother was in the kitchen putting two mugs on the table and reaching for coffee jars and the sugar bowl. On a plate beside them lay a newly baked cake still warm and smelling of cinnamon and dried fruit.

"You smelt the coffee," she smiled.

"And you're telepathic."

"Not really. I saw your car come up the drive. What in the world is Sarah doing with that puppy? Neil is crazy to allow it."

"It was Neil's idea. I'm not sure she had much say in the matter. I might of course be wrong."

Grannie raised her eyes to the ceiling and sighed. "Hardly a surprise," she murmured, pouring hot water into the mugs. "Why can't that boy get anything right? Now let's forget them and make ourselves comfortable. Perhaps you could bring the mugs while I carry the cake?"

I did and we sat in our usual positions to enjoy the coffee sipping and the nibbling at small savoury-smelling biscuits from a tin that had apparently appeared from a secret corner somewhere. .

I asked if she would mind very much if I wrote the story, for fun but also for possible publication somewhere local. "It's the sort of local legend that should be recorded for posterity before everyone forgets it."

She gave me what can only be described as an old-fashioned look. "That would depend on what you write and where it would be published. What do you have in mind?"

"Not sure yet" I mused "but whatever I do will be with your full permission and approval, and anyway probably nobody will want it. It's hardly hot news but it's a bit 'fey' and spooky 'fey' stories are popular nowadays. A local magazine might like it, or the local free paper, maybe."

"It would have to be local and small-scale," was the reply. She was, I saw, quite serious. "And I would like to read it first, if you don't mind."

"Of course. That goes without saying. It's just such a perfect little gem of a story with all the right ingredients. It doesn't need embellishments. It stands up on its own. And like I said, it wouldn't make the major papers anyway. I would of course use a pen name. Croft would give too much away."

My grandmother huffed at me. Then she smiled and addressed herself to her mug. "A small local tale sounds just about permissible. So now let's enjoy our coffee and talk of other things."

And that is what we did. Lunch cooked by the indefatigable Mrs Simmons was followed by the happy and familiar reminiscence that only happens when one meets relatives infrequently. Supper of macaroni cheese, the departure of the wonderfully efficient pin cushion herself, apron and all, had been, enjoyed and gone and It was almost eleven o'clock by the time I had escorted my much loved grandmother to her bed, kissed her goodnight and driven away to the Lamb Inn, to sleep soundly with dreams filled with peaceful expectation of pleasure to come.

# CHAPTER FIVE

I didn't see Sarah again for the next two days since I was
spending time driving my grandmother around Little
Woollie, visiting any villagers of roughly her age group
who might have their own memories of Little Billy and his
feathers. We drank copious pints of tea, ate a great many
biscuits but gained little in the way of personal stories.
The few who were still alive were younger than Gran and
to them the tale was misty and remembered only as a
fairytale from childhood. The older ones seemed to prefer
forgetting the incident, almost as if it were mildly
unsavoury and maybe tinged with a not-quite-respectable
flavour of magic.

One or two, however, had views of their own which
they were more than happy to share with us. Mrs Warner
was in her nineties but fully alert and extremely articulate.
She showed us into a small living room crammed from
corner to corner with dark oak furniture and a plethora of
photographs standing in their frames on every available
surface. She offered us tea, which she rather alarmingly
carried in on a battered tray, refusing my offers of help in a
slightly affronted fashion, and told us she remembered the
feathers event as being, to her, a wonderful magical
mystery surrounded by shivery secrets. "It was very
exciting," she said, spilling tea into a capacious lap and
absent-mindedly rubbing the wet patch with the hem of her
skirt. "I saw the feathers flying, but nobody would tell me
where they'd come from. Probably because they didn't
know. Nobody did, did they? He was such an engaging
little chap. I was thirteen when he died but I always
enjoyed seeing him dashing about in his wheelchair and
smiling at things." She stared at me, thoughtful and
puzzled. "That was what intrigued me. He didn't just
smile at people. He smiled at *things*. Almost as if they
weren't really there and he was seeing through them.

People used to say he was soft in the head, but he wasn't, you know. Sharp as a tack and as full of mischief as any lad his age, although mostly nobody told on him because we all knew what his dad would do to him if we blabbed. A nice little boy. I was sad when he died, and everyone blamed his own family. They said he was neglected. He was thin enough in all conscience. It's no wonder he caught peumony, there wasn't enough of him to fight bugs and he had enough of those, believe me. Cold after cold he had, poor mite. Oh well, it's all a long time ago."

Mrs Warner turned to me. "Are you writing a story about him, then?"

I told her yes, I was, and would she mind if I quoted her.

"Not at all my love, you quote away. I'm not ashamed to talk about him, even if lots of people are. More fool them, I say."

Her next door neighbour, though, was not quite as forthcoming. A tall, heavy-set woman in a flowered apron who, one knew, would have no truck with any far-fetched fanciful tales. We smiled as sweetly as we could, but I knew it would be useless and of course it was. She didn't invite us to cross her threshold but merely stood firmly in the doorway, arms folded and lips in a tight, unforgiving line, and stated the story had been a publicity stunt, a load of rubbish that only idiots could seriously believe. "It's all a tale," she said firmly, glancing at her watch. We took the hint and departed.

We only succeeded in tracking down one man fortunate enough to have survived into his mid-eighties. In fact Mr Ayers turned out to be 92, which surprised me as he seemed fit and active. His views were stated simply and briefly, with no fear of misunderstanding.

"Old wives' tale," he pronounced with a smile that managed to be at once patronising and derisive. "Women's rubbish. I would advise you not to waste your time on a small boy's pranks."

We were not, of course, invited to cross his threshold either, so we left, acknowledging with a smile that we were merely on a fact-finding mission and thanking him for his time and opinion. "What a pity," I remarked as we retraced our steps to his immaculately maintained white gate "that statistically, women outlive men. I wonder why that is."

"I've no doubt Mr Ayres here would be pleased to explain this to you."

"I bet. But how?"

"Why, that men do all the hard work and wear themselves out."

"Now, now, Gran. Do I detect a sour note? This is the 21st century. Equal measures for all and hard work must be shared."

"Women's Lib has a lot to answer for, and I should know. I was reared in the age when men opened doors for me and carried parcels and I've seen everything change before my eyes."

I laughed. "You can't possibly tell me that men don't open doors for you now, *and* carry your parcels because I've watched them do it. So Grandmother dear, pull the other one! Besides, which of us would willingly do without our fridge-freezers, washing machines and smartphones?"

"I'm tired, Gemma. Surely we've done enough research. Can we go home for tea now please?"

"I'm really sorry Grannie darling, but I fear we have one more call to make; the most important really, which I've been putting off, mainly because I wanted to hear what other people had to say first. I have an address for the Foleys, but there's no guarantee they'll still be there. Still, I must try. So fingers crossed...."

"...and prayer hats on" my grandmother added resignedly. "You are quite right of course. You can hardly write about them otherwise. But don't forget," she added, giving me her one-eyebrow-lifted, sidelong glance, "that the Foley family own the best bakery in Woolcot.

What's more, they deliver, so for heaven's sake don't upset them or I shall have to go without bread for months, possibly forever. And, of course," she added, "Mrs Simmons is a Foley herself, so don't upset her for heaven's sake. I couldn't possibly cope with an affronted cook, not to mention an absent one."

"I won't and I doubt a news story would put any local business off a valuable customer. Bad business practice."

I drove to the address I'd been given and rang the bell. The house was a rather upmarket detached residence with white exterior and black window and door frames. Mock Tudor black beams decorated the upper half. The front door was opened slowly and obviously with a struggle, revealing a small girl with crinkly black hair and coffee skin who regarded us solemnly with one finger in her mouth and an air of great self confidence. She said nothing but waited expectantly.

"Hello," I said, "Is your mum in, or perhaps your grannie?"

""My *Nan* is asleep," the child rebuked us firmly without removing her finger, "but my mum is here. What do you want her for?"

A voice from within called "Who is it LeeAnne?" and a plump blonde woman whom I guessed to be in her late forties joined us all in the doorway, one hand possessively on the child's shoulder, the other hand ineffectively dusting flour from a bright red checked apron.

I held out my hand. "Sorry to bother you. You're obviously busy. But this is the Foley house, isn't it?"

"Yes and no," the woman replied, ignoring my proffered hand. "Who wants to know?"

"I'm Gemma Croft and I'm a journalist. This lady," I touched my gandmother's arm, "is Mrs Celia Croft." I smiled at LeeAnne, "and she is my Nan." The child nodded. This time I had it right. She blinked and then vanished into the inner sanctum. "My grandmother was the same age as Little Billy Foley, who I rather think was a relative of yours? And she's has been telling me about Billy's feathers. I'd like to write the story, but giving no names except hers and one or two of the villagers who have given their permission. Have you any objection to my writing it, hopefully for publication although right now I'm not sure what in or who would want to print it. Your names would not, of course, be mentioned unless you wished."

The woman stared hard into my face, then said, with implacable finality, "I suppose I can't stop you, but my family refuses to comment, except that you'd better *not* mention the name Foley or we'll have you. It was all a long time ago and nobody cares anyway. We have a business to run. Now I've got a dinner to cook, so I'll say goodbye." With that she shut the door.

My grandmother and I raised our eyebrows and glanced at each other.

I grinned. "I think we can safely take that as a no."

"It certainly looks that way," she replied, before adding a trifle plaintively: "And now please may we go home? I'm tired."

"Of course we can.," I assured her. "I'm a selfish beast."

I enjoyed two cups of tea and a small slice of the Madeira baked only that morning, and apologised in advance for still having some questions for a grandmother who by now was probably wishing she had kept her story to herself. One look at her face, however, persuaded me that now was not the moment. I needed the facts but not at such a cost.

We had completed one exercise in our researches. The hardest part was now up to me. The fact, however, that it would be both eventful and troubled was something I was to discover in fairly short order. Maybe ignorance really is bliss!

After a fairly long nap, my grandmother showed signs of interested life, so I made a pot of tea, poured her a cup, found the cake and continued my questioning.

"Sorry, Grannie darling, but please can you tell me more about the squire?" I asked. "He certainly chose gentrified names for his offspring. Rupert and Julian? Straight out of the best romantic fiction."

My grandmother chuckled into her tea, took another sip and brushed some cake crumbs from her neat navy trousers.

"Well, yes, he certainly had what is usually known as delusions of grandeur. No, that's not quite right. He had no title or anything apart from being the local squire, but he delighted in the fact that we were called 'the Somerset Crofts.' And we *were* 'the Somerset Crofts,' he made sure of that. I was only just eligible as a marriage partner for Julian because my father was the local doctor. Not that that would have stopped us. We'd have gone ahead anyway."

"I'm delighted to hear it."

Here Grannie tapped the side of her nose and winked. "But we didn't have to because World War One had already started the rot by then, so the Gentry world was beginning to fall apart at the seams."

I smiled. "Serves him right, poor noddle. No wonder he was so upset about his daughter. As if marrying a gamekeeper wasn't bad enough for the family image, it turned out to be incestuous anyway. One can't help feeling a bit sorry for him, especially as he never saw her again. How did he take to his little grandson?"

"He didn't."

"Sorry?"

"Didn't want to know."

"What? Not at all?"

"Not in public anyway. We all suspected where Billy's wheelchair came from, but nobody dared ask. He wasn't the sort of man one asked at the best of times, and so far as I can gather Isabelle's name was never mentioned again."

I sniffed and shook my head. "As I said, straight romantic fiction. Apart from turning his daughter out into the snow, he couldn't have behaved more predictably."

"No, but he could have behaved more honourably. More compassionately. More like a grandfather in fact. As it was he just left the child in the doubtful care of an uncle who seemed to loathe the very sight of him."

I was silent for a few moments, then said "How much of this can I write without upsetting the whole Croft family? I suppose I should ask their permission."

"Your father and I are the only Croft representatives left and your father won't care, that's for sure. Your mother, bless her, will probably treasure any newspaper cutting she gets hold of. So provided you change people's names and leave out a few details, I give you my full permission. That is, of course as long as you let me see it first." She added with a stern frown.

I grinned. "I've already promised, "I told her. "I wouldn't do it otherwise. Cross my heart and hope to die!"

There was silence for a few moments then I said I suppose Billy would have been my uncle.

My grandmother nodded,.

"Where is he buried? I'd like to go there."

"In the old churchyard. On the right as you go in." Her eyes were closing. She had been tired enough before and now her eyes were heavy and she was ready for a longer sleep. I had tired her even further. I kissed the cheek which at the age of 85 was still far from withered, and made my way to the door, to the evening sunshine and to my thoughts. My reporter's brain itched to write the story

39

of Billy's feathers, but In some unfathomable way I knew that it would be a difficult piece to write. It would be too easy to put a muddy smudgeprint onto something clean and fresh and endearing.

Yes, I thought, Billy Foley's feathers had touched and intrigued me. I spent the evening typing up my notes, then left for my hotel room, where I would not be seduced by conversation over a glass or two of Chardonnay. And there I added, edited and polished up the story I would present to my grandmother for her approval next morning. What would happen to it thereafter was in the lap of whichever editor should be lucky enough to receive it. Receive? yes. Read? perhaps, but not very likely. I smiled. Such a fanciful little tale, whimsical and out of tune with the culture of the time. At odds with the prevailing cynicism so cultivated by what is now called The Media.

And yet? And yet? There was also the tide of popular fantasy fiction washed through with a desire for something more than the mere acquisition of *things*. My story had all the right ingredients, an abused child, wicked uncles, incest and scandals, with an alluring whiff of magic thrown in. I slung my ever-present and overfilled backpack over my shoulder and sauntered downstairs for a celebratory glass of wine before wandering off to bed, and, with luck, a dreamless sleep.

"At least," I thought, "I can now turn my attention to other things and start to really enjoy my holiday," and with that I raised my glass in a silent toast, enjoyed a brief, friendly sally with the young man behind the bar, and finally retiring to my well deserved rest.

# CHAPTER SIX

## *Gemma's Story for the Woolcot Gazette*

*Do you believe in fairytales?  Then you will like this one.
It is full of incest, pregnant daughters never to be seen
again, lords of the manor, gamekeepers and small
handicapped boys, not to mention a positive snowstorm of
white feathers.  The stuff of legend indeed, the only thing
wrong with this one being that, according to several
reliable eyewitness accounts, it happens to be true.*

*It concerns a small village with a manor house, a
squire, a beautiful daughter and a gamekeeper.  As one
would expect of any good fairytale, and to the horror and
fury of her father, the beautiful daughter runs away with
the gamekeeper, thereby cutting herself off forever from
her family.  There is, however, a dark secret which the
runaway lovers have not been told.  The gamekeeper is the
squire's illegitimate son.  The marriage is incestuous.*

*When the gamekeeper briefly returns he brings a brand
new baby and the news that his brand new wife had died in
childbirth.  The baby, now known as Little Billy, is thrust
upon his dad's highly reluctant brother who has little
option but to bring the boy up. And this is where the story
really begins.  Little Billy is handicapped, hated, bullied
and neglected by both his foster parents and spends most
of his short life propelling himself around the village in his
wheelchair.*

*Despite everything, however, he remains a cheerful,
friendly child, with what seems to be a habit of collecting
white feathers.  Convinced the boy is playing games by
emptying his pillow cases, his foster parents, together with
half the village, set out to find the source of this feather
nonsense.  But warnings and beating only make matters
worse.  Billy is soon followed everywhere by swarms of the*

*mysterious soft, small white wing-like things that seem to drop from nowhere.*

*Finally, at the age of eight, Little Billy dies of pneumonia. His funeral, planned to be a quiet, private affair, turns out to be a phenomenon all by itself, as millions of the beautifully tipped feathers cover the entire ground with what looks like snow, others flying around above the villagers' heads and finally settling on the coffin. As Billy's small casket is lowered, eye-witnesses, including the Squire's daughter-in-law, swear that the feathers gathered themselves into a swirling mass which disappeared over the village in one huge wing-shaped cloud, never to return.*

*Mrs Croft said: "It's all quite true. I was there." Many other villagers, however, were reluctant to talk about it. Mrs Freda Hughes dismisses it all as "a bag of silly moonshine. Nothing but a small boy playing tricks," while Mr Grazeling at the newspaper shop is convinced that the whole business is just "a media setup to sell their papers." The police were never informed. The villagers knew they would not be believed.*

*Billy's foster parents were unavailable for comment but their son and daughters had very little to say except that it was all before their time and anyway was just "a piddling little affair that got turned into one of them myths and legend things. Just a tale, isn't it? I mean, basically, how could it possibly be true? It's just a laugh, isn't it?"*

*A laugh? We shall never know!*

*Juliet Mason*

I awoke resolved to visit Sarah, our intriguing next door
neighbour. I wanted to know how she was managing the new
and wildly enthusiastic puppy. It was, however, nearly mid-
day before I eventually rang her doorbell, having spent the
morning obtaining my grandmother's approval of the story I
had polished the night before and then sending it not only to
the local paper, the Woolcot Gazette, but also (in a state of
blind and almost certainly misplaced optimism), to my own
London daily. I was expecting nothing except possibly a
mild interest from the Gazette.

So I sat in Sarah's spacious and beautifully equipped
kitchen with nothing on my mind save Sarah herself and the
exploits and possible future of the dog Jake who was
nowhere to be seen. I wondered where he was and how Neil
proposed to solve his wife's situation. The dog's future must
surely be uncertain. It must have become apparent, even to a
possibly self-absorbed Neil that Sarah in her wheelchair was
in no position to care for a    puppy as young and as strong as
this one. There was also the matter of size. In a short enough
time the puppy would grow into a full-sized dog.    The
prospect was more than a bit alarming.

Neil was, in his usual fashion, "away somewhere" on
one of his business trips. I forbore to ask about these
because I was not sure the question would be easy to
answer. I had a feeling he talked very little about his job.
Sarah was obviously in love, which I suspected might be
obscuring her own sunny and forthright disposition, but
how I knew this was not easy to answer either. I just
knew, without knowing why or how.

Sunny she certainly was. She seemed to radiate
cheerfulness, a kind of happiness which was infectious. I
had asked my grandmother about her and had been told
that Sarah and I shared a grandfather. "Hers was Rupert,
Squire Williams' heir," she had said. "I merely married
Julian, 'the spare' whose sister Isabelle had been the
runaway daughter who had (predictably, if you read 'Lady
Chatterley's Lover') married the gamekeeper. Rupert

married into the wealthy Kent family and their son, Daniel, married Rachel and changed his name from Croft to Kent in order to join his father's firm. Sarah is their daughter. She has another brother, Jack, who is an I T wizard and runs his own branch. J K Kent Electronics," which I understand is beginning to make an astonishing amount of money." My grandmother had laughed. "Confused yet?"

"A bit but I'm working on it. So was it Sarah's father who bought Woolcot House and turned it into flats? Of course, his daughter would have first refusal, especially being handicapped."

"Not only that, but Neil was jailed briefly for possession and when he came out they had nowhere to live. On condition, of course, that he kept off the drugs and drink and accepted a job with the firm."

"And has he? Kept off the drugs and booze?"

"Nobody knows because Sarah isn't telling. Put it this way, whatever he's doing or not doing, her M S won't be helped by the presence of this particular husband."

I had had one last question before disappearing on my errand. "So what exactly does Neil do?"

"Well, there's the rub. Nobody knows for sure. All we know is that he's an Account Executive with J K Kent Electronics and he drives a nice, posh-looking car of which he takes the greatest care."

I nodded. A nice-sounding job for life for Sarah's beautiful ex-convict husband. "Can't be bad," I said.

Having been given these facts by the fount of all knowledge herself, I was able to enjoy a reasonably far-ranging conversation with Sarah without venturing into any Neil minefields.

Not yet anyway. Privately I resolved to delve a little deeper. Sarah was happy, though, to talk about her brothers, Michael and Jack, and especially about Michael's little son Peter who was, I was given to understand, utterly enchanting and perfect in every way. "I expect you'll meet him," she said happily. "You must. I shall insist upon it."

I agreed that I must and would, then rose to take my leave. "By the way, where is the dog? I was expecting a slobbery greeting."

"Neil took him to work. He should be back soon."

Sarah escorted me to the door to meet a surprised Neil climbing the curved steps two at a time, keys in hand. Sarah was delighted and myself disconcerted to find the recent subject of both my thoughts and questions materialising on the doorstep. Neil swiftly converted his expression into a brilliant smile of welcome, fully directed at me, while at the same time planting a kiss on his wife's cheek. Yet despite the brilliance of the smile, I felt rather than saw that Neil Chalmers was not altogether happy to see me. So I said goodbye to both and crossed the wide entrance hall to my grandmother's door. There I hesitated, drawn by the delectable garden smells drifting from the open main door. But the urgent need for fresh air and beauty was overtaken in the end by the equally seductive cooking smells issuing faintly but persuasively from my grandmother's kitchen.

Having discovered I was hungry, I forgot all about the Kent family, Little Billy and his feathers and proceeded to follow my nose. Life had more to offer than poignant little village mysteries and I was about to enjoy the rest of my holiday with untrammelled pleasure.

My grandmother met me at the door with a glass of sherry.

"Oh boy, something smells good," I sighed. It was, of course. I thus enjoyed my meal in blissful ignorance of a vital piece of information – one that I always knew to be possible but for which I was not prepared.

On that particular day there had been no bombs, no earthquakes, no droughts and no celebrity scandals.

My story had hit a slow news day.

# CHAPTER SEVEN

The first indication of it came when my phone played its usual musical riff and I picked it up. The female voice at the other end was unfamiliar but confident.

"Hi, I'm Ellen from the Gazette. I presume I'm talking to Juliet Mason otherwise known as Gemma Croft?"

Wondering how she had deduced my real name, I simply told her that whoever I was I was not prepared to discuss anything at all with anyone from the press.

"That's a shame. I like your piece about Billy Foley's Feathers and if you're available some time today I'd very much like to interview you. We are definitely running it, it's just that I'd like a bit more personal background information. Like how you got the story in the first place and why you're using a pen name. You know the sort of thing. You should do, you're in the same line of business after all. Anyway, I take it you were writing about the old Woolcot Hall and the Croft family. I'd like to see the place, get the feel of it, sort of thing. Given your experience I'm sure you know exactly what I mean.

I said yes I knew the sort of thing but that in this case no more information was necessary. The story was not about me. It stood on its own. And that is how it would stay. Besides, it would hold no deep interest for anyone but local people as it was a story from the past.

"But that's exactly what the readers want," said Ellen, pouncing on my words like a cat on a mouse. "A good, meaty local scandal in a familiar local setting – especially an old family mansion. I mean, how romantic is that?"

"Which is precisely why my answer remains the same. The story stands as it is, romantic enough without additions."

"In that case," said the indefatigable Ms Gazette, "I shall get the information from elsewhere. There must be quite a few people who'd be delighted to tell me about the

Croft family, including of course where you fit in. If your name is Croft then it must be your family scandal. So come on, Gemma or Juliet, be a sport."

I thought hard for the briefest of moments. Someone taking my poignant little story and turning it into a lurid one was very certainly not what I had had in mind.

"The Gazette only comes out weekly," I said at last, so your deadline must be passed by now. If you did write anything it would have been superseded by hotter news by the time your paper ran it. So as far as I am concerned, I repeat – no further information is required or wanted in any way.

"You're a reporter yourself and I know who you write for."

"This story is not about me so you don't need my personal details. If you want to try bigger papers, so be it. I'm on holiday anyway so, if you'll pardon the expression, it's no skin off my nose and you can naff off!"

Far from being dismayed, Ellen sounded amused. "Sorry dear but you've aroused my curiosity now so if I don't get the details from you I shall get them from somewhere else. "

"Besides the Gazette who do you write for?" I asked.

"Anyone who wants my stories. I'm freelance."

This changed my perspective a little. "Well go ahead, Ellen from the Gazette, I'm afraid you won't get any more answers than I did. Too long ago, and it's hardly headline stuff. I'm surprised even you were interested enough to bother following it up. So, like I said, if you want to waste time trying that's up to you. Meanwhile Bye Bye."

I closed down my phone and went thoughtfully down to breakfast before climbing into my car. It was now necessary to discuss the situation with my grandmother. I was not looking forward to it.

I found her finishing her breakfast coffee and even more pleased to see me than usual.

"Guess what?" she said. "I've just had a reporter on the phone asking if your story was about the Crofts. I didn't tell her anything but she wanted to contact you personally so I gave her your phone number. Did I do right? I've been a bit worried."

No, she had not done right but I smiled my reassurance. "That's fine darling, I've just had an interesting conversation with her myself. Grannie dearest, we need to talk."

My grandmother eyed me narrowly for a moment. Then nodded. "I think you might be right," she said. "But please can it be after lunch? I hate ruining my digestion with bad news."

I smiled but was obliged to agree.

The sitting room was bright with light streaming from the large window overlooking the drive and the front garden. Everything out there was burgeoning, flaming into colour and variety, late wallflowers giving way to banks of border plants with early roses and riotous pansies and geraniums giving promise of glories to come. The room itself was large but, in a way impossible to define, cosy and welcoming at the same time. Everything in it was in harmony with everything else despite the fact that nothing really matched. The occasional antique jostled with the new and the not so new, most of which I guessed came from local charity shops. My grandmother bought what she liked regardless of fashion and, with clever placing, it all sipped seamlessly into the whole. Envying her skill would have been pointless since I doubt if she realised she possessed it.

We had enjoyed a pre-lunch sherry followed by a meal full of taste and warm freshness cooked by our genie of the kitchen, and now we were sitting opposite each other in our own comfortable chairs, nursing cups of coffee.

"Right," said my grandmother, "'the time has come, the walrus said.........,'

"You remember that a woman rang you this morning asking for my number?"

"I do."

"Well she rang it and I answered. Her name is Ellen and she writes for the Gazette and whoever else takes her stuff, and she wants to interview me personally. Not just me. She wants all the sordid details of Croft scandals from the past, and has come to the correct conclusion that because she has now identified me as a Croft, I am or was part of the scandal– or at least knew everything about it. She's right about the family name, but not right about my wanting to add anything, so she is promising to research the background herself, interviewing everyone in sight, I imagine, to unearth all the juice gossipy bits that please the public. She's right about gossipy bits selling papers, but as this is a family matter I am not prepared to give her what she wants. In any case," I added, "after the research we both did among the locals, she isn't likely to get any more out of them than we did. Except of course that some of them may well be tempted to embroider their own facts once they realise that's what Ellen of the Gazette is after. In fact, the juicier she can make the story the happier she's going to be. So how do you feel about it? After all, I did promise you I would keep it local and simple. The chances are," I added, frowning, "her story won't get anywhere since it has already been run, and that was only because mine happened to hit a slow day. So although I don't imagine she will follow through on her threat – because that's what it was – I still feel very guilty and don't want to make it worse."

My grandmother smiled, quite cheerfully, I thought, considering that I had expected a rebuke. "Don't worry, darling, whatever she writes isn't going to affect me or the Crofts, since the scandal is such an old one. And if the Kents object, then we can cross that bridge if and when we come to it. On thinking about it, I've come to the conclusion that that sort of child abuse – for that's what it was after all – is not only part of history but can happen now just as easily. And should be highlighted," she added, with a small nod and a frown. "I've been wondering too how the Foleys are taking it. You did ask to interview them so it's a bit late for objecting."

I was relieved. "So the answer is 'Publish and be damned' then. Good, I like a fight – provided my nearest and dearest don't get hurt in the process."

We spent an enjoyable afternoon in the side garden, where seats and a table with summer umbrellas to give shade were arranged on a large area of decking close to the trees. There were long deck lounges, and more comfortable padded deckchairs in bright stripes of red and green and we had provided ourselves with cool drinks and a thermos, in case the sun disappeared behind the small banks of dark clouds creeping slowly from the East. The air was still and the sunshine warm enough for lounging, so we were happy simply to sit in the midst of beauty and the vivid colours of the mid-May border.

It was not until late in the afternoon that my phone rang. I sighed. The idyll was over. Ellen from the Gazette was asking if I had thought any more about being interviewed. She added that she would be happy with a telephone interview, if I had the time to answer a few questions. I agreed, with the proviso that I may not answer some or any of them, and that she would be given facts only – no personal opinions. (I am only too aware of how easily words can be twisted). With that assurance, she went ahead, and as most of the questions were innocuous I had no hesitation in replying to them.

I told her I lived in London but gave her no address or contact number. Yes. I lived alone and no, I had no 'partner' of any kind – male, female, spouse or 'live-in'. She wanted to know why so I told her the truth. "Plenty of offers," I said cheerfully, "and plenty of company of all kinds, but so far no-one whom I wished to take seriously. Certainly not for a lifetime."

"Oh, come on Gemma," she laughed, "I don't believe that for a minute. A girl like you?"

"How do you know what sort of girl I am? Or what I look like for that matter? So far as I know we have never met."

"No but I've seen your photograph in the paper. You are not unknown in journalistic circles, you know, so no good hiding your light under a bush!"

I smiled. "And the word is *bushel*, or perhaps you're not bothered about misquoting the Bible."

"All right, be pedantic, but the meaning remains the same. I know what you look like, and I don't believe you are boy-or-girlfriend-less."

I told her she would be well advised to do so but was of course free to believe what she liked, and that in any case I was refusing to answer more questions of an intimate nature."

"So you're not in Little Woolcot to escape from some lover's pursuit?"

This time I laughed. "I am in Little Woolcot to visit my grandmother, which I do at least twice a year because I am fond of her. And since she was the person who told me the story of Little Billy, I don't think I need say any more than I already have."

"Okay, then how about the Kent family? The big electronics firm whose cash saved Woolcot Hall so your much-loved grandmother could live in one of the flats?"

"The Kents? What about them? They have nothing to do with the story and were not involved in it in any way. And of course we are grateful they took over the hall before it fell down but as an investment it was a good idea and seems to be paying off nicely, so no nepotism there."

"Yes, unfortunately we all know that 'money makes money' Nice to have enough for such investments and even nicer if we could all enjoy it. For example why haven't the Foleys been offered a Grace and Favour flat?"

"I fear you must take up those questions with the owners, or with the Foley family, not with me. I am only an insignificant little cog in this matter."

It was Ellen's turn to laugh. "The insignificant cog that lives in a very nice flat in Notting Hill and writes stories for a well known daily newspaper. Come clean, Gemma. And you haven't answered my question about the Foleys, which has intrigued me."

I closed my eyes. I had known what the result of this interview would be for me. I was mentally kicking myself for having fallen into a trap any experienced journalist would have avoided at all costs. Why hadn't I been 'out' when she rang?

"Since you seem to know all about me anyway," I said, "I see no point in continuing this interview, so I shall say Goodnight and Goodbye." I replaced the handset quietly and thoughtfully, overcoming a strong urge to bang my head on the table. Then I returned to my grandmother, who had retired once more to her sitting room, and helped myself to a large glass of her sherry. Had there been anything stronger to hand I would have helped myself to that too.

"Not good?" Obviously my chagrin was obvious.

"No."

"Care to talk about it?"

"No. Not yet. Tomorrow. I think I should go and bury my head in Little Woollie's nice pub and come back fresh and ready in the morning."

"That sounds like an excellent idea to me, so off you go before you drink any more of my sherry and fail a breath test." And apart from the breath test this was precisely what I had in mind.

Unfortunately fate once more stepped into the picture and changed my design. I had just collected my bag and was making for the front door when my phone rang again. I considered ignoring it, but as it was a late call I felt it might be an urgent one, so I dug the phone from my pocket and answered it.

Sarah's voice was strong but anxious. "Oh Gemma, I'm so glad I caught you. Could you please come in? Now if possible?"

I took a deep breath. "Yes of course," I said.

# CHAPTER EIGHT

Sarah answered the doorbell herself, wielding her chair deftly through two doors before leading me through to a conservatory where flowers bloomed in tubs and along what I could see of a border filed with roses and foxgloves. Through the wide picture windows with their trailing greenery, a dusky but obviously graceful garden was still visible. Although the light was fading, it seemed clear that the grass had recently been immaculately shaved in perfectly aligned stripes. It seemed to call clearly for croquet hoops. Borders were showing signs of plentiful life and colour and the whole picture was enchanting. I wondered who did the spade and weed work. Now, however, was not the time for small talk.

Having made sure I was in fact my own non-threatening self, she opened the door wide and motioned me inside. In the light of her wide entrance hall I surveyed her, before she turned suddenly, obviously embarrassed, "Tea? Coffee? Nightcap? "

"Forget the niceties," I said firmly. "Liquid refreshment later, please. Just sit still and tell me why you wanted to see me so urgently. What's happened?"

Her reply was slow in coming . "I'm afraid you are not going to believe me," she said at last.

"Try me".

Sarah smiled suddenly and shook her head. "I don't know why I'm afraid, since it was you who got me wondering in the first place. Or rather, your article did. Of all people, you should understand."

My first thought was: "Please not another embarrassment." I was beginning to wish I hadn't written the story at all. Instead, I nodded and said "Okay, tell me. What have I done now?"

Sarah shook her head and smiled apologetically. "You haven't done anything, except open my eyes to something. Something that started weeks before you came here."

I frowned fiercely and pointed a peremptory finger at her. "Sarah?"

For answer she turned her wheelchair and led me into the immaculate and fully appointed kitchen. There she pointed to the corner where a long-handled dustpan was leaning against the wall.

"Look," she pointed and scooped up a handful from the dustpan. In her hand were three very white feathers, small and smooth and slightly curled, and tipped at wing point with a delicate sheen. "These have been appearing in ones and twos for weeks, but now they are coming in twos and threes. I pick them up from all over the flat, but next day they appear again." Then she turned bright but puzzled eyes towards me and touched the feathers. "And now they've started landing on me. I found these in my hair this morning."

"Have you told anyone else this?"

"No I haven't, but Neil has seen them. He told me to sew up the pillows so the feathers couldn't keep escaping. He doesn't like it because he read your article too. I think he's afraid I might be trying to get in on the act,"

"So you've only told Neil."

For the first time she looked embarrassed. Until now, only puzzled and enquiring.

"Well, one other person has seen them and I wish to God she hadn't."

"Who?"

She sighed and lifted up her shoulders and hands in a despairing gesture. "The reporter from the Gazette. I wasn't going to let her in, but she said she just wanted to get my reaction from your story because I am a Kent by birth. She was more or less inside before I'd had a chance to tell her I was too tired to talk. She's very persistent. And the first thing she saw was the dustpan full of feathers. She didn't say anything but I know she'd seen them and was obviously storing them away in her mind. In fact I think she pinched a couple. For what purpose I dread to think. The question is, Gemma, what can I do?"

By this time she was shaking. Until then she had been a little disturbed but seemed in control. Now she wasn't. I went to kneel beside her chair and took her hand.

"Well as of this minute you can't do anything and neither can I, except maybe you can consult your family. They will certainly have opinions and I'm willing to bet will come down hard on anyone who treads on the Kent family toes. Can you do that?"

Sarah frowned but nodded. "They won't be best pleased."

I laughed. "No, they won't, in fact they'll probably be hopping mad, but at least they won't be cross with *you*, which is all you need to worry about. Once you've told them you can leave it all to your highly efficient family team. They've got the power and the nous, after all. "

"Well, no I'm afraid it isn't as straightforward as that. They don't know about the feathers. No-one does, except you and this reporter. And Neil, of course, who thinks I'm making it all up. The rest of the family won't like it because they'll think it's a load of nonsense and raking up a past they've all been very happy to ignore as none of their business."

"Quite right too. It's a Croft story, not a Kent story."

"Anyone digging will find out that your grandmother Croft's brother Rupert married my grandmother Kent, and it was Rupert's brother Billy who was the "Little Billy" of your story. And now it's a Kent who's getting the feathers." Sarah sighed again. "I feel guilty and angry at the same time, even though the feathers started coming weeks and weeks before you wrote your article so it can't be cause and effect. So why I should feel guilty I can't imagine."

"Then you can stop because if it's anyone's fault it's mine. So let's have that coffee and talk about something else. Where's Jake? Has Neil taken him to work?"

For the second time Sarah looked upset. She moved away to place two mugs on the kitchen worktop, spoon coffee into them and stand them, one after the other, under a tap on a highly streamlined gadget which poured boiling water directly into the mugs. Finding placemats in a drawer, she put them carefully on the kitchen table.

She invited me to sit down, before asking politely if I would prefer to have my coffee by the window in the conservatory. She had already dismissed any offers of help from me, so I seated myself firmly at the table and accepted my mug of coffee with a smile of thanks.

Sarah placed her wheelchair within reach of the table and sat opposite me, at last looking directly into my eyes. We said nothing for a few heartbeats, then I raised my eyebrows in enquiry.

"Jake has gone." Sarah said.

"Gone? Gone where?"

"Neil said he was too strong for me and he took him away. Poor Jake was just beginning to settle in and he did so enjoy chasing the feathers. The trouble is I don't know where Neil took him and he himself won't be back for two days. I sent him a text but all I got was a reply text saying he'd explain properly when he got home but not to worry. Jake was being looked after and seemed very happy."

I held her hand but said nothing while I thought about this. Neil was, of course, quite right in that the puppy had been too young and boisterous for Sarah to control from a wheelchair, but to remove him without explanation was, I thought, not only insensitive but mightily high handed.

"Had he given you any reason for thinking he might do something like that? – earlier, I mean, before he took him away?"

"No. It was very sudden, and I miss that little dog. I got really fond of him and he made me laugh." Sarah removed her hand to brush away the tear or two that had suddenly made their appearance. I rose to my feet to fetch the box of tissues from the worktop and pulled out a handful. She accepted them with a nod of thanks and blew her nose.

"Actually," she admitted "I don't think Neil approves of all these feathers. He was cross with Jake for chasing them, which of course he did. What puppy wouldn't?"

My thoughts on the matter of Neil Chalmers were legion but I knew putting them into words would not help but hinder. Sarah was so obviously so under her charming husband's spell that any hint of disapproval from me would certainly hurl her into defending him. Whether she was also under his thumb was another matter. I was beginning to sense that in normal circumstances, independent and fully mobile, she was more than capable holding her own. I leapt happily upon the slight change of focus.

"This reporter has caught you at a bad moment, hasn't she? Bad enough to lose a pet without having family dramas suddenly thrust on you. When do you think of telling them, your family, about the feathers? I suppose if they keep on coming you will have to explain."

"I think I'll keep quiet about them for a day or two, just to see whether or not they carry on appearing. If not, all well and good, but otherwise they will need explaining somehow, and just now I can't think of a single explanation, can you?"

I admitted that for the time being I couldn't explain them either, but she had had a trying sort of day and needed her sleep. "How do you manage at night?" I asked, knowing that for too many nights Neil was not there to help her into bed. "Is there anything I can do right now? I can be quite handy, you know."

Sarah smiled, but said that so far she had managed to stow herself safely away unaided, except for undressing her lower half, which had by now become a routine challenge, one so far successfully overcome. "There's a knack to it, although I have to admit it won't always be possible. At the moment I'm in remission but eventually we have to be prepared for worse to come. Carers twice a day, maybe? Not a nice thought but it would be better for Neil. Being a burden is hateful. You have no idea."

"No, but I can imagine. Meanwhile what can I do for you now?"

"Nothing, Gemma, except perhaps turn the bedclothes down so I can hoick myself in."

I smiled and departed to the bedroom, where the crisp white sheets smelt of calm and soothing freshness. I would like to have studied the room more closely, but had no intention of seeming to pry, so I returned to Sarah and bent to kiss her cheek. She had already rinsed our coffee mugs and was waiting for me by the kitchen door.

"Gemma, thank you for coming. Just telling someone has helped enormously and I'll keep you updated. Shall I count the overnight feathers, if there are any?"

I laughed, said yes please, and opened the main entrance door to the fragrant night.

Tomorrow was another day and I too needed my sleep.

Early next morning before breakfast I stood In the old churchyard beside a fifty-seven-year old grave and read the inscription.

*"WILLIAM FOLEY, 1930 – 1938. Known affectionately everywhere as Little Billy, he leaves behind him his grieving foster patents and the sorrowing villagers of Little Woolcot."*

The grave was small, gravelled and unpretentious with one small flower holder embedded in it just beneath the headstone. Its simplicity spoke for itself.

I was there because I had woken early, to find myself a prey to long hard thoughts about what was happening here in Little Woolcot– not just what had happened, which was obviously important in itself, but what was happening in the here and now, and how much of it was attributable to my lust for writing things down. I had always written things down.

My early childhood was littered with scraps of paper on which the impeccably innocent romances of a seven-year-old were recorded, in pencil and probably in an untidy scrawl.

The habit had caused me embarrassment and (often) retribution in the form of laughter by my aunts and uncles. Not, however, by my parents. They never laughed at my scribbling. In fact they had encouraged me to write more, for which I never fail to be grateful.

If they too had laughed at my childish dreams that in itself would not have stopped me from writing them down. The dreams would simply have been sent underground, secrets to be squirrelled away in lockable diaries. I know this because I already had one of those but used it not for stories but for my deep and personal thoughts and feelings. Not even my closest friends had been privy to those.

So while I stood by Little Billy's grave and considered its possible ramifications now, in today's culture of cynical scientific 'facts', I was thinking too about the feathers in Sarah's flat. Where had they come from? What did they portend? How were we to treat this new phenomenon? I had spent my entire adult life as an observing agnostic-cum-atheist. Like most people in the 21st century I had an unswerving trust in 'Science' – in quotes of course and with a capital S. Who could argue against the great men who proclaimed its absolute truth? Who indeed? And who was I, little Gemma Croft who considered herself invincible and right about more or less everything, to rock such a sturdy boat? It was going to take more than a few feathers to do that.

# CHAPTER NINE

I didn't recognise, at that moment standing beside a small boy's grave, that a tiny, hardly detectable ripple had disturbed my peace. All I knew was that there had to be a reason for Billy's feather story and that I was going to find it. Magic was all very well in its place, but that place was not in present-day Little Woolcot in its new and different culture, not to mention a reasonably new century. And it was in that frame of mind that I betook myself to Croft Court for a late breakfast with my grandmother.

She was surprised to see me, and even more surprised that I had forgone my usual hotel bacon and egg. I told her where I had been and expressed an urgent longing for something savoury on toast followed by more toast with marmalade thickly spread.

"It's all this getting up early," I explained. "But please will you go and sit down while I cook my own breakfast in your lovely, swanky kitchen. It will be a pleasure. And if you saw the kitchen in my flat you would understand why."

My grandmother laughed but refused point-blank to go and sit down and followed me into what looked to me more like a hallowed emporium dedicated to the worship of food and chef-dom. There were gadgets on all sides, on gleaming worktops, with smooth cupboards containing who knew what – probably even more gadgets. I drew a deep breath and prepared to enjoy myself. This was not the first time I had cooked there, but in a strange sort of way that couldn't be put into words, it felt like it!

Sitting comfortably at the island work station which also served as a breakfast bar, I tucked into my poached egg on toast while my grandmother sat opposite nursing her own mug of tea.

"One thing I don't understand about Billy's grave," I began between mouthfuls, "is that it mentions his grieving foster patents. But they weren't grieving, were they? Did they have a change of heart, or were the words a sop to their guilt or something? I can't imagine they were popular in the village"

"No, they weren't. They didn't court popularity and there were too many stories about them anyway, but I suppose they had to put something on the grave, and of course it had to be flattering to themselves. After all they were responsible for the grave stone. That was something they definitely couldn't get out of. But they did pave the whole grave over with stones to avoid having to look after it. There were too many people watching them. With hindsight one can't help feeling sorry for them. How frustrating to be shown up by a snowstorm of white feathers which they couldn't explain. They did make light of it, but the snowstorm was just too big. It would have taken a thousand pillowcases if not more, by the time it all ended."

I chewed thoughtfully. Having mentally digested the delightful image of a gigantic swirl of white feathers., upturned faces gaping in bewilderment, my mind took a new turn, from the past unexplainable to a present situation which may or may not have an explanation. I decided to tell her about Sarah and what I had seen and heard the night before.

Grannie's eyes grew large, as I knew they must. "How very odd," she frowned, "but it's early days yet. Anything can happen. They could stop coming ."

"They could. But what we definitely don't want is for the reporter to pick it up and run with it. She is more than capable, from what I've seen of her so far, and as a phenomenon it could be a worry for Sarah, and for you, too The problem here is that the Gazette woman has already seen a handful of them and probably pocketed a couple.. It would be much, much better if she didn't see any more."

My grandmother nodded, then smiled at me from across the table and shook her head. "I agree with you about Sarah, but she has an influential family so she's not without support if she needs it. As for me, I'm quite capable of holding my own, so please don't worry. In fact I don't think you should be worrying at all. You are on holiday, darling, so what the Kents do about their daughter's feathers is not your concern."

I did not agree, but gave a token, smiling nod, said "thanks" and spread marmalade on my second slice of toast. There was, after all, more to life than feathers.

We had planned, my grandmother and I, to spend a peaceful morning in the sunshine talking about...well, about anything at all except feathers, and I had just made myself comfortable in one of the recliner deckchairs on the patio around the corner of the house when my phone rang. Reluctantly I wrinkled my nose and picked up the handset.

"You should have switched that off," Grannie spoke with closed eyes, but since I am incapable of ignoring phones of any description I announced myself to my caller in what I hoped was a polite but dismissive tone. This did not, of course, work. The caller was Sarah.

"I did as we said and rang my brother this morning. He wants to see you. He'll be here in about an hour. Do you want him to come straight to you or will you to come to me?"

I asked her to hold on while I relayed her message to my grandmother, who insisted on being present. "If he has come to talk about your story," she said firmly, "I am the instigator and I was there at the time, so really it's me he should be talking to." Since her presence would certainly diffuse what might well turn out to be a sparky interview, I turned back to the phone and explained to Sarah that we were at that moment sitting on the patio enjoying the Spring sunshine, so if her brother would care to join us he would be welcome.

Normally I would have preferred not to disturb Grannie's peaceful morning. That, I considered, would be most unfair, given that despite her protestations the whole thing was really my fault.

"Is this good or bad news, your brother's visit?" I asked. "Is he going to hang me from the nearest bough for involving his sister – although, to be fair, it wasn't me who involved you but a nosy reporter who couldn't keep her nosy nose out of your kitchen". Even as I said this I smiled, knowing I was indeed calling the kettle black. It was, in fact, Ellen's job, as I was in a very good position to know, only this time it was my family and possibly the Foleys, who would be the victims – and it was my head that was destined for whatever chopping block was coming our way.

Sarah sounded amused. "He's very nice, my brother," she said, "He's always been my favourite," which didn't answer my question.

"I'm sure he is," I murmured, hoping rather than believing this was true. If he were not, I would need both patience and tact – plus a control over my temper which could rather too easily rise to a bait. The last thing I desired was to spoil what felt to be a growing friendship with Sarah. She would certainly take her brother's part in any falling out. I sighed and, not for the first time and certainly not for the last, wished I had never heard of Little Billy or his feathers.

But I had, and my bones were now telling me there was a reckoning to come.

Nemesis arrived in the form of a very angry young man without a shadow of a doubt prepared for battle. Sarah's brother was tall, dark and, at that particular moment, wearing a forbidding smile. It was a token smile, a lot of teeth but not a single eye crinkle as of one who knew he was interrupting a private *tete a tete* but didn't care. He was obviously determined to continue doing it anyway and in none too friendly a manner   He nodded, with a brief attempt at politeness, towards my grandmother then he turned the full force of his light brown searchlights upon myself. I felt rather as though he were trying to pin me to a board like a butterfly and would, if provoked, tear off a wing or two for good measure. He had reckoned, however, without the Croft red-headed genes, tempered though they were by a judiciously applied dark auburn hair rinse. If anyone in this contest (for that is what this interview promised to be) was to be pinned to boards, that person would not be me.

"Good morning," I smiled up at him in polite but lukewarm welcome. "You must be Sarah's brother, but I'm not sure which one. She didn't say. But please sit down and help yourself to some freshly squeezed orange juice. It's a speciality of Mrs Simmons' who should be calling us to lunch fairly shortly. Meanwhile how can we help you?"

Out of the corner of my eye I thought I saw my grandmother's lips twitch, but the impression was gone in an instant. Instead it was the brother who smiled. His smile was frosty. "You don't need to ask me that" he said, "since you know perfectly well why I've come and I'm interested to hear what you have to say."

In reply I filled a glass with 'freshly squeezed' and presented him with it. "The trouble is," I told him, "I'm not sure what I'm being accused of. Perhaps you would enlighten me."

"You have written a story for publication involving my family which is having a disturbing effect on my disabled sister. Furthermore," he went on grimly, "you have now involved the local press in some sort of cock-and-bull story which will certainly have a deleterious effect not only on her health but on the whole Kent family."

I raised my eyebrows. "Excuse me," I said, with frostiness quite equal to his own, "but in what way am I to blame for whatever cock-and-bull story an outside reporter is dreaming up? And, while I am about it, have you had the full truth of this story from your sister?" I turned to look enquiringly at my Grandmother and asked her she had any comment to make.

"Only that before casting accusations around," she said calmly, "perhaps one should ascertain the full facts, which I suspect Mr Kent has failed to do."

"Precisely," I said quickly. "So maybe Mr Kent would like to explain," and I turned my own searchlights upon what appeared to be a young man in the throes of deep emotion. "Oh yes, and before we go any further, you didn't answer my earlier question.

Which brother are you? The elder or the younger? Sarah didn't tell me."

"My name is Jack," he replied tersely, "but I assure you my elder brother is as angry as I am and would like a full explanation from you."

"Not until I know what it is you are both accusing me of? A pity he didn't come with you."

"Okay! Did you or did you not acquaint this reporter person that Sarah was now being plagued with feathers after reading your story in the paper? Since Sarah assures me you are the only person she has told about these mystery feathers, plus Mrs Croft," he added with a token nod of apology in her direction, "whom you now seem to have blabbed the story to, it can only have been you. The reporter woman had the nerve to ring me this morning to ask for my comments."

If anyone could be described as breathing fire from his nostrils, that person would certainly be the man standing before us like a tall, dark dragon. If I hadn't been so angry myself I might have laughed. Certainly I wasn't scared.

"In that case, I think you should have another talk with your sister. She will tell you that this 'Reporter woman', whose name by the way is Ellen, worried Sarah so much by finding a handful of feathers in a long-handled dustpan that she sent for me in a panic. It was only then that your sister told me about the feathers and asked my advice about the reporter."

Jack was about to interrupt but I kept going. "And my advice was to ring you with the full story, which I assume she did."

"She didn't need to. I had heard it already from your Ellen."

"*My* Ellen? In what way is she My Ellen?"

"You know her by name and you wrote the original story, so don't pretend you don't know the woman personally. Reporters presumably help their own."

By this time I was so astonished that for a second or two I could only stare. "I am very much afraid, Mr Jack Kent, that you know nothing whatever about journalists, who would willingly kill for a good story. Besides which, I recommend that you leave us in peace and go back to Sarah forthwith, and to get the chronology straight before you burst into flames." We stared eye to eye. "Luckily for all of us, I can see Mrs Simmons coming to tell us our lunch is ready. So unless you would care to join us I shall say goodbye."

If Jack's expression were anything to go by, he would have felled me on the spot. He did, however, manage to retain good enough manners to say thank you but he must reluctantly tear himself away.

"But don't imagine you will get away with this." he finished, through teeth so obviously gritted I had an almost irresistible urge to recommend a hasty visit to his dentist. With another polite bow to my Grandmother he turned to walk away, giving me a shaft from the light brown searchlights as he went and passing a smiling Mrs Simmons without pausing in his long-legged stride. There was so much fury and frustration in every line of him that he stomped his feet with every step like a small boy deprived of his longed-for ice-cream. In silence watched him go. I could have felt sorry for him but I didn't. Battle had been joined.

# CHAPTER TEN

Immediately after our excellent lunch of rich beef stew and dumplings, followed by fresh fruit salad with cream, I left Grandmother nursing her post-prandial coffee and walked across the wide entrance hall to ring Sarah's doorbell. With unwonted speed she called "Come in, it's not locked."

She was in the conservatory, enjoying the sunshine still brightening the afternoon. In response to the sun's warmth the flowers were bathing the garden in glowing reds and pinks and blues. Sarah, too, was dressed in fresh, green shades, bright and clean in a flowered blouse and a long green skirt. I wondered, not for the first time, how she managed the business of showering, dressing and keeping herself so immaculately presented to the world.

"You're looking extremely pretty, Mrs Chalmers," I smiled, lowering myself briskly into a convenient basket chair. "How do you do it?"

Sarah's acceptance of this was perfunctory., "Thank you, but I do have help, you know. Someone's going to be coming in now for half an hour night and morning to make sure I wash behind my ears. My father arranged it this morning. And Neil does what he can, of course," she added.

"Excellent," I said. "Perhaps if I had someone to make sure I do all the things little girls are taught to do, I might conceivably look as good as you do this morning, but I somehow doubt it. A couple of hours may just do it, but then I don't have your head start."

Sarah frowned. "Come on, Gemma." she said. "Stop dithering. Tell me what's happening. I have had a very angry brother here, grilling me about my own story. I ask you...! What happened to filial loyalty?"

"What indeed? Don't think he believed me, either. Comes to something if he'd rather believe a reporter. Did he lay into you?"

Sarah had the grace to smile. "Not really. He was cross, though, especially when I gave him the true order of things and proved you weren't to blame. As a matter of fact," she added, a trifle mischievously, I thought, "That didn't make him any less cross. More, in fact. What he actually said was 'Now I suppose I shall have to apologise to the bloody woman'."

We both laughed outright. "Oh dear!" I said, "I obviously didn't endear myself to him. Was it something I said?"

We laughed some more, then Sarah said, "Very likely, and quite right, too. I'd hazard a guess he was even ruder to you, so he should jolly well apologise. And I shall tell him so."

"Don't bother. That will only make it worse. If he does he does, if he doesn't I won't break my heart. Not," I added quickly, "that your brother isn't, as you say, a nice person. Just that he wasn't being especially nice this morning so my opinion could be jaundiced."

"To say the least."

"Precisely. So now tell me, have you had any more feathers? And did you tell Jack about them?"

"Yes and yes, and he still doesn't believe I'm not playing tricks, or not subconsciously influenced by your article."

"A sort of copy-cat instinct."

"More or less, but in a disturbed way. Maybe he's blaming the M.S."

"Much more likely to be blaming me. How many more feathers have there been then? Can I see them?"

"Of course." Sarah wheeled herself over to a corner cupboard where she pulled out a cardboard shoe box. "I'm almost afraid to open this," she said, "in case they fly out in the draught and then I won't know how many more have come since then. There were about 20 last time I looked, but they're so hard to count. They sort of fly about."

As she spoke she was studying the still closed box when a feather landed softly on her arm. She carefully lifted it off and handed it to me. There was another in her hair. I said nothing. There was nothing appropriate to say. We looked at each other, then slowly and with great care she removed the lid from the box. It was filled to the top with small, soft, white, slightly curling wing-like feathers. They were well beyond counting. I regarded the one in my hand with a kind of awe, then reached out to place it with the others As I did so, the entire boxful rose in the air and began swirling around Sarah's head.

By this time I was holding my breath. Then I whispered "It looks like we've just opened Pandora's box," and was filled with foreboding.

Between us and, in almost total silence, we gathered up as many feathers as we could, although by this time they had multiplied and would no longer fit inside the shoebox. So we found a much larger container and attempted to persuade them into it. Mostly they behaved quietly, but several escaped and could not be caught, so we left those to do what they would and finally sat down at the kitchen table, each with a mug of tea which we clung to in a desperate desire for warmth and inspiration.

We stared at each other, Sarah and I, bemused, confused and out of our depth. Eventually she broke the silence.

"What's happening?"

"I don't know. Whatever it is, what are we going to do about it?"

"I - have – absolutely – no – idea," Sarah said, slowly , shaking her head and closing her eyes.

"I suppose you have to tell your husband, but what about your parents? I imagine one of the boys will mention it to them at some point."

"Unless they agree to keep it quiet. None of them will believe us anyway." Sarah smiled and gave a little huffing gasp. "Nice to think one's husband and two brothers think I'm cuckoo. I'll have to tell Neil, although I'm afraid they'll all send me away to be psychoanalised or something. Funny farm here I come."

I laughed briefly. "I that case they'll have to take me too. I don't know what's happening, either. I just know something is and it's nothing to do with your imagination or I wouldn't be a witness to it myself. But poor Jack. He's angry enough with me anyway. He's bound to blame me for everything." Then I frowned. "One thing is absolutely certain, though. The Gazette must not get wind of this. Not a breath. Not a jot. Once the press get hold of it you will have no peace, so we have to tell your family to keep shtumm - or else."

"Or else....what? We have no bargaining power."

"Yes we do. I know what the press can do even if they don't, and believe me they wouldn't like it."

"Yes they do know about the press. Having such a large family firm leaves all of us Kents open to newshounds from all sorts of directions. But how about your grandmother?"

"She'll be fine. She won't let us down. She might like to see the feathers though, so perhaps we can invite her in. And in case she's a wily old bird and has tricks up her sleeve that we wot not of."

Sarah nodded and had begun to move towards her phone when it rang. She announced herself, then waited, said "No, don't bother. There's nothing new to tell you. Goodbye," and replaced the handset,

I raised my eyebrows? "Ellen the Gazette?"

"Yep!"

The phone rang again. This time Sarah picked it up without giving her name. Then she sighed. "Yes Michael.

And no, I have said nothing but if you like to come round I might have something to show you. Have you by any chance mentioned any of this to either Mum or Pop or both?" There was a pause while she listened. "Only Jack, Gemma and her grandmother. Neil knows up to a point, but he's at work, but Gemma's here now if you'd like to speak to her yourself?" Sarah nodded, said "Okay see you soon" and replaced the handset again.

"He's coming round?

"They both are. And he wants to know where Neil is. I told him he's at work but it didn't satisfy him. He particularly wants to see you, though."

"I bet he does. Shall I fetch my bullet-proof vest?"

"Perhaps if your grandmother was here as well?"

"Excellent idea. I shall ask her at once," I said, moving towards the door.

"Please don't leave me Gemma. I never know what's going to happen next. Can you ring her instead?"

I nodded and picked up the handset and speed-dialled my Grandmother's number. She answered at once. "Yes of course, darling" she said. "I wouldn't miss this for the world so don't you dare keep me out of it. And don't worry about fetching me, it's only across the hall. See you very soon."

I smiled at Sarah. "She's on her way."

Within minutes my grandmother was ringing Sarah's doorbell with a small flurry of white feathers swirling about her feet. She joined us in the kitchen, brushing her sleeves.

"I've had an idea," I said to both of them. "But we'd better be quick." I found the emptied original shoebox, picked up four stray feathers and placed them carefully inside. Then I closed the lid, sealed it with some sticky tape I found in a drawer and signed my initial across the seal. At my request the others did the same. We wrote that the box contained four feathers and added the date and time. Then I replaced the box on its shelf. There were now two of them side by side, the original shoebox now sealed and the larger one we had found as an overflow. .

We were only just in time. The doorbell pinged again, but this time I opened it cautiously to find Ellen from the Gazette smiling at me from the threshold. She put her foot firmly onto the carpet, closely followed by a stern-looking Michael, Jack and a small boy of about four years old.

We all stared at each other, each nonplussed by the presence of the others. It was Ellen who recovered first. "What a happy coincidence," she said, smiling triumphantly at me.

"Indeed," I agreed, "but I seem to remember Sarah telling you not to come, so perhaps you should go away again, as this is obviously a family party," and I pointed to the small boy, who gazed up at me with fixed absorption. "I'm Peter," he announced firmly, holding out his hand. "Are you the reporter lady because I think you should go away now."

I smiled. "No, I'm not the reporter lady, I'm your Auntie Gemma, and Ellen here is the reporter lady. And you are absolutely right. . She is gatecrashing a party, and you know you mustn't do that. It's not nice."

Peter nodded. "Yes, Daddy said." He agreed. "He said it's not ...." Peter screwed up his face. "Not sochally septable."

By this time the family had entered the flat and had congregated with Sarah in the kitchen, which she had had no time to leave. I knew she would be anxious to draw all visitors away from such close proximity to the little snowstorm of loose feathers, one of which now adorned her head. "I *was* going to say," I began with heavy irony, looking with raised eyebrow at Sarah, captive in her chair "that everyone had better come in, but since they've all done so I suggest we move to the conservatory. There's a nicer view  Except of course for you," I added, pointing at Ellen. "I know you're only doing your job but please do it elsewhere. This is a family party."

Sarah began to move her wheelchair, but before she could do so a flurry of feathers danced at her feet and rose to land indiscriminately on everyone in the room. I raised my eyes to heaven.

The damage had been done but no-one said a word.

# CHAPTER ELEVEN

It was Jack who broke the silence. He looked sternly at Ellen, who seemed determined to be present. "I presume you are not deaf," he said firmly, "which is the only excuse I can think of for not leaving when asked politely to do so. So I am telling you again. Please leave *now.* If you don't go at once and if you breathe one word of anything you have seen or heard, I shall sue your paper and I shall personally sue *you*I" And with that he pointed to the door and stood with his arm outstretched. "**Go**" To my surprise the gesture was not melodramatic but oddly authoritative. The girl smiled sweetly at him, said goodbye very nicely to the room in general, made a comic face at little Peter, who delightedly pulled one of his own, and departed. Peter, who suddenly seemed spellbound, accompanied her to the front door, whether to continue his face-pulling or to see her safely off the premises was open to doubt.

I had been surprised at Jack's gesture but even more so at the air of authority he had assumed. It had seemed entirely natural, and was so far from the furious small-boy image of the morning that I would have found it hard to recognise this one had I not seen both. But I had and the change was, to me, extraordinary. He turned back to us all, as we trooped into the conservatory and seated ourselves in comfortable chairs. He was studiously avoiding my eye. Apologetic he might be pressumed to feel, but he was showing none of it here and now.

Michael was the first to break the bemused silence which had fallen on everyone else. He spoke easily and with the charm of someone accustomed to addressing important meetings or delinquent employees. The perfect Personal Relations person. If anyone were to smooth ruffled spirits, that person, I felt, would certainly be Sarah's brother Michael.

"Okay so now tell us what's going on. Jack seemed to suggest at first that you were playing games with your duvets and pillows, but I think he might have changed his mind somewhat." He looked directly at Jack. "Am I right?"

Jack nodded. "More things have come to light since then," he said, "but perhaps Sarah can give us a demonstration."

Sarah turned to me. "I'm not sure I like the word my brother has just used," she said, "making it sound like a magic trick, but do you think, Gemma, that we should show them our container?"

"If they don't mind being suffocated by the contents," I smiled, "although there are enough specimens floating about the place already." I went through to the kitchen to fetch the larger container and handed it to her. The smaller box I was keeping in case further evidence was called for later. "Here you are and best of luck. I'm afraid it has to be you doing the honours."

We smiled at each other, then Sarah very gently began to raise the lid. "Here goes," she murmured and took it off altogether. For a moment nothing happened and I was half expecting a moment of complete bathos, when suddenly, with a rush and a swirl, what seemed like a host of pure white feathers rose into the air and flew in a circle around the room. The response was, as usual, total silence. Then Michael whispered "Good God" and Jack put both hands to his head and gave a short, gasping laugh. He turned to his sister. "I owe you an apology," he said quietly. Then he threw his head back and gave another gasping laugh. "Rather more than one pillow and one duvet. Good grief, look at them."

We all stood still and looked. The only movement in the room was Peter's, chasing the feathers, grabbing a handful where he could. I was so relieved that Jack had rid us of the press presence that I leaned back against the door, unconsciously barring it from invasion, whether now or in the future I hardly knew.

As I did so someone pushed it from the other side, first gently then more roughly, forcing me to step aside. Neil edged himself into the room and saw the feathers coming now to rest on Sarah, her wheelchair and on most of the furniture. Even the floor had its white, fluttering coverlet and we all had some of our own. Peter was now shouting with joy. But at the sight of his Uncle Neil he became suddenly quiet again. So did everyone else, for a few seconds, then Michael and Sarah spoke together. And we all suddenly came to life. It was as though Neil, with his blonde beauty, had cast his own spell.

Michael said, and his voice no longer held the suave charm of the Personal Relations Executive "Hello Neil, where the blazes have you been all day?" And Sarah said: "Oh Neil, I'm so glad you've come."

Neil replied to neither. Instead he frowned angrily at his wife and pointed to the feathers. "Is this your next trick? What the hell are you playing at, you stupid girl?"

We all stared. Then Sarah dissolved into angry, frustrated and bewildered tears. My grandmother and I went immediately to the wheelchair, myself to squat beside it holding Sarah's hand to my cheek while Gran held her other one and stood making gentle shushing noises. Her brothers came too, to stand around her in a protective phalanx. Neil, disconcerted by what was clearly the family mood, stayed where he was, rooted to the carpet and waving away any feathers that came near.

This time it was Michael who took the stand. . His face was stern. "You may be her husband, Neil, but her family doesn't allow anyone – anyone – to belittle our sister with misconceived and ill informed rudeness. Do I make myself clear? Now come in, for heaven's sake, and behave yourself. We are about to fetch our parents here so perhaps you should revert to whatever good manners you may have left."

Since Jack's father was his boss, this had an instant effect on Neil, who was now looking bewildered, nervous and truculent all at the same time. If I hadn't been so furious with him I would have been tempted to laugh, but as Sarah's tears had subsided, I stood up. Grandmother remained where she was, but lifted up her head in dignified disapproval.

The Crofts had joined the Kents in their protective shield.

Michael found his smartphone, pressed a speed dial and spoke to his parents. He asked them to come to Sarah's flat as soon as possible since a crisis had arisen which needed the whole family to be present. We all watched him nod, say "Good, thanks." and replace the phone. He turned to us. "They are on their way."

"I think this calls for sustenance," I murmured, spoke briefly to Sarah and passed through to the kitchen, where I set out what I hoped was the correct number of cups and saucers and a large plate of assorted biscuits and small cakes from a tin. I carried them all back on a tray and placed them carefully on the mosaic-topped coffee table. Then I approached Michael and said: "As this is a Kent matter, I think perhaps my grandmother and I should leave you to it."

Sarah, who was now keeping a watchful, if bewildered, eye on everyone, including her husband, cried out: "Don't you dare leave us, Gemma Croft. You are more involved than anyone, and so is Mrs Croft. After all," she added, turning to my Grandmother, "You were alive the first time. You know more than anyone. So please don't anyone go. I need you all. I'm confused. I don't know what's happening or why it's happening to me. I mean, why me in particular? So please stay and help."

Grandmother stood beside the wheelchair and shook her head. "I'm very sorry, Sarah, but no-one understood it the first time so I am as much in the dark as you, only I feel guilty because telling Billy's story seems to have opened a stange sort of box of tricks."

I shook my head.. "But if it's anyone's fault it's mine."

Sarah frowned at me.. "No it isn't. It can't be. The feathers began even before you got here only I didn't tell anyone because I thought one of the neighbours' cats had been catching birds. "

"Well, whatever or whoever, the question is; what are we going to find at the bottom of it this Pandora's box? And what are we going to do about it?" Then I laughed in amazement. "Good heavens! Was that only this morning? It seems years ago."

"Gemma's right," Jack said, unexpectedly coming to my rescue. "Whatever and whoever started it is beside the point, at the moment anyway. We need to decide what we're going to do." He turned to my grandmother, "Mrs Croft, You are not only the oldest and wisest here, you were, as Sarah said, the only one who was around the first time. We would like your opinion."

"Hang on a minute," Michael interposed with a raised finger. "I think we should wait till Mother and Pops get here. They shouldn't be long now. They said they were on their way which means," and he glanced at his watch, "five more minutes at most."

"In that case," I said, firmly moving towards the teapot. "I suggest we take a break until they come. That's if the tea is still hot. If not I can make some more." I lifted the lid and peered into the pot. Then I poured some into a cup for myself and tasted it. "It'll do for now. I'll put the kettle on again for when your parents get here," and departed once more for the kitchen. I was still there when sounds of arrival at the front door sent me back to the conservatory to meet The Boss himself, who was busy laughing down into Peter's small face as it peered up into his own, and detaching two small arms from their hearty clutch around  as much of his grandfather's waist as he could reach.  Then he threw Peter up in the air and caught him again.  He didn't see me.  Suddenly shy, I hung back and watched Mrs Kent kneel smilingly beside her daughter's chair, to take her in a gentle hug.

Over her mother's shoulder Sarah saw me standing motionless and silent.

"Gemma," she cried, "come and meet my mother."

With that, both parents turned and I was held transfixed by the intense scrutiny not only of their two pairs of eyes but of everyone else's too.  It was as though no-one had seen me before.  And for the first time in many years, I blushed.  Then suddenly a voice broke what had been a spellbound silence.

"Where's Peter?"

# CHAPTER TWELVE

At once the eyes that had been turned on me were redirected. Everyone looked at everyone else.

"Look in the kitchen," I suggested. My grandmother said she would check her flat and we all dispersed. I went with Grannie into the hall. The main front door was open and a small trail of feathers littered the entrance and the curved steps into the drive. Without pausing, I followed the trail. No small boy was to be seen chasing the wonderful fluttering things that had entranced him earlier and nothing lay obligingly on the drive itself. I smiled wryly. This was no game of fox and hounds. Somewhere out here, I knew as if by some osmosis that Peter was in this very large garden and free to roam, either enticed or following his own native curiosity. With photographers to be expected everywhere ready to pounce, he must be found, quickly found, and whisked away from harm. He would be easy prey.

I tried to call his name, but realised that by doing so I was alerting any possible watchers to the fact that a vulnerable victim was loose and waiting to be caught. So I kept quiet and started a circuit of the garden close to the house. For once there was no-one to pounce on me with unwanted and time consuming questions. I hadn't gone far before it dawned n me properly how big this place was and how well kept. I had, in fact, been walking for at least five minutes before nearly completing the circuit and had arrived at the spot where my grandmother and I had enjoyed our peaceful morning in the sun. I recalled with some sense of injustice the arrival of Jack Kent with his accusing air and badly disguised anger.

It was then that I spotted a forlorn small figure sitting disconsolately on a swing that hung from one of the tall trees on the other side of the lawn. He was sitting, head down, perfectly still. I heard a small sob and went across the grass to kneel by the swing.

"Oh dear!" I said sympathetically, producing a tissue from my pocket and handing it to him. "Did you get lost?"

With his head buried in the tissue he sniffed a tiny "Yes" and wiped his nose.

"Well you're not lost now because I've found you, so you can tell me all about it while we walk back to Auntie Sarah's. Where is everybody anyway? Did you meet any strange people with cameras?"

There was a small nod. Peter finished wiping his eyes and nose and solemnly handed back a very wet tissue. "That's better. Are you ready now?"

Unexpectedly, he leaned forward and clasped me around the waist, burying his face in my jacket. I picked him up and he legs closed about me, a wet face burying itself in my neck. The face snuffled again. I felt an unfamiliar surge of emotion and hugged him tightly before putting him back on his feet. "Well, whatever it was it's gone now, so let's go and find that cake."

Peter sniffed, nodded and pointed to one small knee where a graze was red and showed signs of bleeding. "I hurt my knee," he announced.

"Oh my goodness, you are a wounded investigator aren't you? I expect Auntie Sarah will find a plaster as well as cake."

Peter was showing signs of life and renewed interest. "What's 'vesti – vesti – ?"

"An investigator," I replied solemnly, taking his hand firmly in mine, "An investigator is someone who's good at looking for things."

Peter looked up at me with suddenly bright eyes. "Yes," he said, "that's what I am. I was looking for feathers but there aren't any out here, not any, and while I was looking all these people came up and started asking me questions. One of them was the reporter lady that gate-crashed. She told me her name but I forgot it. *She* was nice."

"I'm glad she was nice. Did she ask a lot of questions too?"

"Not new interesting ones. Not ones she hadn't asked before. She told the others to follow her and they did. I didn't see which way they went. Should I have followed them to see?"

I told him he had done absolutely the right thing. "Was that why you didn't come home, or perhaps you were still looking for the feathers?"

He told me the story as we crossed the grass to the front door, his hand comfortably in mine without pulling away in a bid for freedom. He had been badly frightened.

"I tried to run away from these people with cameras but they wouldn't let me and then the reporter lady came and told them to stop. Her and me we sat on a bench and she asked me if there'd been any more feathers and I told her about the box full of them and how they all floated up and went swishing about. Like this - Swish, swish!" He pulled his hand from mine while he demonstrated how huge the swishing had been and how high they had flown. "Way, way, way, up taller than anybody," he grinned happily, graze and fears forgotten. "She was fass-nated and we laughed a lot. Then she took me to the house and left me outside the front door 'cause she didn't want to go in and be shouted at."

"Quite right, too. I wouldn't want to be shouted at either."

"And that's when I grazed my knee." Peter stopped grinning and frowned. He held up the offending, not very clean limb, pointing to it and hopping on one leg.

"How did you do it then?"

"The door was shut and I couldn't reach the handle or the bell. It was very 'zasperating and I got cross and tried and tried knocking but nobody heard me, so I climbed on a big stone to reach it and fell off and that's when I hurt myself. I tried and tried and *tried* but nobody heard me so I went back to the swing."

"Very sensible," I nodded. "But here we are already. If we're both good there may be a piece of cake for both of us as well as a plaster."

Peter giggled. "You can't eat plaster."

I agreed that plaster wouldn't make very good sandwiches and turned the round, heavy handle to open the door.

"Look what I've found," I announced in triumph. "Here is one intrepid, wounded adventurer in need of a plaster and a large piece of cake."

I realised then how easy it is to make a four-year-old boy happy.

Almost at once, Jack appeared behind me and Peter was whisked away to be ministered to by three adoring women. Meanwhile Jack produced his phone to send texts to the rest of the party. The search was called off. Michael and Neil had eventually migrated to the grounds in their extended search and they arrived within minutes of each other. When everyone had gathered, my grandmother returning to us after exploring her own flat from room to room, I gave them the bad news. The fat was now in the fire, the damage was done, and Sarah's feathers would from now on be public property.

In the sudden shocked silence, I relayed what Peter had told me about "the reporter lady" and the family asked me a great many questions which by now I was almost too tired to answer. So after a decent interval while they discussed the matter between themselves, and while Mr Kent senior phoned the police to report the finding of his son, I slipped out of the front door, to beauty, peace and silence. It would not, I knew for sure, be for long.

It wasn't. After only a few minutes Jack was sent to find me. We stood together on the grass, staring at the garden but seeing nothing. "You're needed." His tone was abrupt

"Always nice to be needed," I replied, not moving.

"I'm serious. They need you in there."

"I know. They are probably blaming me for everything. Well, they should have taken me seriously in the first place. You all should," I said, still not moving. Then I turned my head to look at him. "And what about your apology, rather grudgingly offered not long ago? Are you reneging on that too?"

Jack sighed and clutched his hair. "Oh for God's sake, Gemma, stop being scratchy and help us out here."

I smiled. He had reminded me once more of Peter. "Perhaps if you stopped being rude to me.....? Incidentally, why are you rude to me? What have I done except write a story with not one reference to a Kent anywhere? It's Sarah the feathers are following, not me and I didn't even mention her. If you notice, I didn't even write it under my own name, so no Crofts are mentioned either. So do you just not like me for reasons of your own?"

Jack shook his head. He turned to face me and grabbed me by the arms. "I suppose it hasn't occurred to you," he said, suddenly loosening his hands with another head shake. "to ask why I *should* I like you? You've made me angry and lose my temper and you've put me in the wrong. The last thing I want is to like you. The reason I'm behaving badly is not because I don't like you. It's because I'm trying damned hard *not* to. You've made me look small, dammit!"

I gave a gasping laugh. "Well if you put it like that...! But that's no reason for bad behaviour and if that's all you can come up with as an excuse then I'm afraid that doesn't cut it. It would help if it made sense. We are speaking English, right?"

He turned away and took a few slow steps on the grass, returning even more slowly until he was facing me. "Okay, Gemma Croft, but it works both ways. If I stop

being rude to you, then you must stop being rude to me."
He held out his hand. "Deal?"

I sighed and shook his hand. "The trouble is, when you
get angry you remind me of Peter." This time it was his
turn to gasp. "I suppose that's fair enough." He admitted.
"Better than nothing anyway."

We turned to retrace our steps to the front door. I was
determined to show nothing in my face, but the memory of
a tall man stomping like a four-year-old held a unique kind
of appeal. Something so barmy and so at odds with the
dignity and authority he had shown earlier simply had to
be genuine. I was saved from smiling when a bright
yellow Mini Cooper swept up the drive and stopped beside
us. A young woman wearing a neat navy business suit
with immaculately white shirt collar and cuffs climbed out
and said: "Hi Jack, I've come to collect Peter. Straight
from work, as you can see, but Michael told me it was
urgent so here I am. Where is everybody?"

I shut my eyes. I had been saved by a yellow Mini but
was not precisely sure why the thought annoyed me. I
simply knew that it did. The conversation, however, could
not have continued in any case because Michael appeared,
running down the steps in a hurry. He looked vastly
relieved to see his wife. Within seconds he had joined us.
"Ruth my sweet, thanks for coming. Peter is on his way.
We saw the car. He'll bring you up to date but we have to
talk anyway. Urgent family pow wow taking place here."
He turned to Jack, "And you've been a hell of a long time
fetching Gemma. What kept you?"

Neither Jack nor I replied, but greeted a wildly
enthusiastic Peter as he did his best to throw himself down
the steps to be picked up by his mother and hurled around,
giggling with delight. "Mummy, I've been having *such* a
time. You'll never guess. And I grazed my knee – look –
and I've collected more feathers." He displayed them in
his hand, turning confidently to me to explain that the
reporter lady had been so interested in them that he'd
given his precious four feathers to her. "I told her she

86

could keep them 'cos there's lots more in there. She did thank me," he added, as if in mitigation. "'fact she was very nice and *intrested.* I like her. Daddy can she come to tea? She wouldn't be gate-what-you-said 'cos she be 'vited wouldn't she?"

Michael looked non-plussed, as well he might. There was so much information in Peter's ingenuous speech that it would take minutes for us to entangle it all. But he smiled and gave the usual evasively parental reply "We'll see," with which Peter had to be content. Instead, he turned to me and said "Aunty Gemma, the reporter lady was everso nice, really *really.*"

"That's good," I smiled down at him. "But you'd better go home for tea with mummy now. That's if you've got room for it."

Peter screwed up his face and put his finger to his lips, from which I gathered that the cake was now to be forgotten. Then he added in an urgent whisper "And I didn't cry, did I?"

I shook my head and pursed my lips. "Of course not. The very idea!" I whispered back. We said goodbye to him and his mother and followed Michael back into the house. On the way Jack touched my hand very briefly and said: "We must talk."

I nodded, equally briefly. No other reply was needed, or possible. The Kent family awaited us in various states of anxiety and frustration and from their combined expressions I understood that all the support I could muster was going to be required.

# CHAPTER THIRTEEN

I entered to find a room pregnant with questions ready to be hurled in my direction. Then everyone spoke at once. I shook my head. "Sorry I didn't hear any of you. Please can we start again?"

It was Mr Kent senior who took the floor first. "How did you know Peter was outside? Did you let him out? And I want to know about the box you had just opened. This box," he added, thrusting it towards me.

I sighed. I knew I would be blamed, but not in so direct a manner. "Which shall I answer first?" I enquired.

Jack's answering voice was quiet but firm. "Pop, how could Gemma possibly know where Peter was? I think she showed more sense than any of us." His father made the sort of huffing noise which means that someone is reserving judgment. Jack had moved a little closer to me and now stood behind my right shoulder.

"I guessed," I said shortly. "Someone must have left the front door open and there was a small trail of feathers. I found him sitting on the swing. As for the box...."

Mr Kent interrupted me, "Just a minute young lady." There it was again! If he addressed me as 'young lady' once more I would be tempted to reply in kind as 'old man.' As it was, he continued what was turning into an inquisition. "If the door was open why didn't he come back in?"

The question made me smile. "He's a four-year-old boy. Perhaps he was enjoying himself, especially when he was being entertained by the reporter lady, which is what we need to discuss – urgently! And in any case, when he did try someone had closed the door again and he couldn't get in. It's the reporter that's bothering me.""

"Not so fast," he frowned. "What have you to say about your box?"

I stopped smiling and sighed. "It isn't my box, it's Sarah's, and she opened it, not me. We do have another, though, sealed and signed by all three of us. You may inspect that one if you like, or if Sarah likes. It is her choice after all. "

"Of course I've inspected the box and I've seen who signed it, but as for the number of feathers that remains to be seen, but if you think I'm going to swallow a story about only four feathers going in...."

Jack spoke from behind me. "Pop," he said firmly. "Be careful. Gemma's grandmother could accuse you of calling her a liar and you've known Mrs Croft for a long time."

Stumped for the moment, his father looked crosser than ever. "Yes, well...." Then he drew in his breath. "Of course I'm not calling any of them liars, but you have to admit the whole thing is suspicious. There's a mystery here somewhere and I want to get to the bottom of it."

"Exactly!" I exclaimed. "That is precisely what it is, and every one of us here wants to unravel it – which we won't do by calling each other names. Is it your wish to open the sealed box now, at once, or would you rather work out our campaign plans first? Now that the Gazette woman has seen the feathers and talked to Peter, we need to act fast. The story is still newsworthy so she won't be dragging her heels over it. "

My grandmother, who had been sitting quietly but in some obvious tension, now spoke. Her voice was gentle but firm and brooked no opposition. She was afraid of no Kents, senior or junior. "I suggest we open the taped box now so we'll know what we're planning for. After that, we can calm down, have a glass of something and finish up whatever Peter left us of the cake. Then, since I will then have no more to say for myself except that I remember this very clearly from fifty-odd years ago and I was as mystified then as I am now, I can leave you to work out your campaign and retire to my own home for some peace and quiet."

"Of course," we all said at once, uneasily conscious that our wrangling had, without our intending it, included an 85-year-old lady who was also an innocent bystander.

All this time Sarah had taken no part in the conversation and I realised for the first time how very tired she was looking. How could we forget that this young woman was not in her wheelchair for fun but because she was suffering from an aggressive form of a terminal disease. And once again I was filled with a sense of foreboding.

I asked her if would like to open our box there and then and she nodded. I walked through the kitchen where I picked up the sealed box with its signatures and brought it to her. She picked up the scissors, with, I felt, a certain amount of difficulty, showed the signatures to her father then cut the tape.

What happened then left everyone speechless. Cloud after cloud of feathers swirled above us, flowing from the box in what looked like gleeful, blissful freedom.

No-one said a word, except for Mr Kent's muttered "My God!"

After that, we swept feathers from the chairs and table and sat, in silence, to solve an impossible puzzle. Once begun though, it took barely an hour to decide on our plan of action. After his call to the Almighty, Mr Kent senior calmed down sufficiently to drop his pejorative manner – for the time being only, I felt sure. I was to write my own version of events for my own paper, to obviate the lies and suppositions that could now be expected from the media in general – for of course Ellen and the Gazette would now leave no time before broadcasting their own version, to be followed by the papers in general and possibly the television, not to mention Facebook and Twitter and the rest of the social media. I had no illusions. The rest of the family would refuse either to be interviewed or even to comment. Sarah was not to be left alone at all, day or night, for which reason Neil was to be given as much time off work as required. The feathers were to be researched by everyone, from swans to ducks to pigeons to seagulls, and all questions relating to the Kent family were to be referred to Mr Kent himself as spokesperson.

Michael as Chief Executive of the general engineering firm would field enquiries and research possible psychological, human aspects. Jack as physicist and CE of the Electronics firm, would focus on the scientific angle.

Finally, I asked the question that had been on my mind from the beginning. "Who did leave the door open? Who was last in?"

No-one replied for a heartbeat, then Mrs Kent spoke in her gentle voice. "I'm afraid it was me," she said. "We were in a hurry to find out what all this was about and I didn't think of the main door. I assumed it belonged to all the apartments, not just this one."

"It does, and it needn't be locked – just closed. So someone from upstairs must have come in after you and closed it. Poor Peter. He must have been scared to death."

After that there seemed to be nothing more anyone could say, so Mr Kent offered me a grudging apology for apparent rudeness (which I was given to understand stemmed from anxiety only), I left the room, said a brief goodbye to my grandmother, promising to be back later since I was resolved now to sleep in her flat rather than leave her isolated, and finally took myself out into the late, fragrant evening, to restore some order to my chaotic thoughts.

I was joined after a few minutes by Jack, who stood beside me but, thankfully, said nothing.

I was first to speak. To him I confided my fear. Little Billy had been happily pursued by similarly beautiful and unidentifiable feathers, and Little Billy had died.

He murmured "Yes," put his arm around my shoulders and I turned into him, putting my face against his collar. Then I wept.

Without speaking, Jack led me to his car and drove us both directly to the Lamb, where I must pay my bill and collect the few belongings I had left there. He came in with me, seated me firmly at a table and asked what I would like to drink. Almost bereft of speech myself, I murmured something unintelligible and watched him depart to the bar. I wondered in a vague sort of way what he would bring but really didn't care much. He brought a glass of Chardonnay. "The safest" he said. Glasses in hand, we sat opposite each other and, for the first time, stared eye to eye. His were of a singular shade of light brown which I had never seen before. The light colour gave them a piercing quality which, at that moment, was belied by a gentleness of expression.

Jack began. "So?"

"Thank you," I said at last. "For some reason all this has got to me. Guilt, I suppose, and fear for Sarah. I don't think I could have driven myself here safely, but it does mean you have to drive me back again. Sorry."

"Don't be. And don't think of taking anything back to Croft Court tonight. You're too tired and anyway I intend to get you nicely drunk. Stay here for another night. I'll pick you up first thing to take you back. And please don't argue; my mind is made up."

I explained that my grandmother was expecting my return, but he cut me short. He had suddenly and very obviously placed himself in charge. "Ring her and tell her you'll be back in the morning. I take it you have a key?"

I nodded. "That sounds pretty good to me," I said at last. "And please can we not talk about feathers any more tonight? I am up to here with feathers," and I put my hand to the top of my head. "In fact I think they've taken over my brain."

"No feathers. Agreed. Does that mean we can continue our interrupted conversation?"

"I suppose it does," I sighed. "Although I'm not sure I shall make much sense of that either."

Jack smiled and shook his head. "I don't believe you, but since I intend to do the talking it doesn't really matter."

I considered both him and his words. Being told what to do or think was a novel experience, one that I would normally either fight or ignore. This evening, however, I felt as though the stuffing had been siphoned from me in a whirlwind of small white wings,, rather as if I were the pillowcases and duvets from which they should have come but hadn't.

I was emptied of rational thought. Studying his face I decided, for no good reason that I could explain, to trust him. "Okay, you talk, I listen," I said. "Fire away."

"I told you earlier...."

"You told me a lot of things earlier," i murmured.

"Maybe so, but right now I am talking and you are listening, remember? Or have you forgotten already?"

I shook my head.

"Good. Where was I?"

"About to tell me what you tried to tell me before, I think. You're as bad as I am."

We both smiled. "Right. So the truth was – still is – I've been doing my best to dislike you ever since we met...."

"Just this morning? Or was it yesterday?" I frowned. "If it was this morning you've had a long, hard fight then - all of ten hours at a guess."

Jack frowned, then laughed. "Bizarre, isn't it? Less than ten hours and I'm trying hard not to admit to liking you. Actually, I'm finding it difficult to believe myself only I know it's true. And," he continued hastily, "I wouldn't have been saying anything at all if you hadn't decided that I disliked you. I just couldn't let you go on thinking...."

I shook my head. "Don't apologise, I didn't like you much either. I thought you were arrogant, bombastic and ill mannered and you might have been Peter in a temper. I half expected you to stamp your foot. There was steam coming out of your ears." I laughed suddenly; the memory was vivid and somehow ludicrous.

Jack was not so amused. "Well, as a character assassination I'd say you'd done a pretty good job. I was hoping you might have changed your mind since. After all, I changed mine."

For a long moment I said nothing, then I touched the back of his hand with a tentative forefinger. "As someone who has just cried on your shoulder, I rather think I rest my case. Its' difficult to think badly about a person when you've just blown your nose on his hanky."

Looking amused, Jack said: "We'll drink to that," and lifted his glass to touch mine. We drained them. Picking up both, he took them to the bar and returned with two freshly filled ones. "Which brings us to a new question. What happens now?"

What indeed, I thought. Instead I replied that I wasn't in any state for decisions, big or little, so '*que sera sera*' and all that, and let's just enjoy being friends rather than meeting with pistols at dawn. "Besides," I added, "I need you on my side."

"Meanwhile," he smiled, "you are going to phone your grandmother and go straight to bed. Now! Agreed? Meanwhile I shall finish this drink and say goodnight, see you at 8.30 prompt."

I sighed. Bed and sleep and release from cares were all that filled my mind just then. Responsibilities and decision-making, fights, researches and mystery feathers would be back to trouble me tomorrow.

But not tonight, please not tonight.

# CHAPTER FOURTEEN

I awoke next morning to enjoy a last 'cooked-by-someone-else' breakfast before paying my bill and waiting outside for my lift back to Croft Court. The morning was cool and I hoped Jack would confirm my guess that he would arrive in time. My backpack was at my feet. I sat on the bench outside the hotel entrance, considering my feelings not only about him but about returning to feathers and conflict and a terminally sick new friend. A large part of me would like to go back several days to a trouble-free start to my three-week holiday. I was not ready yet to give up the solitude and independence of my quiet room at the Lamb Inn. Yet I knew very positively that I must. The situation had embroiled me, whether I liked it or not, and curiosity alone would now drive me on.

"Come into my parlour, said the spider to the fly..." I quoted, wondering how many more webs of curiosity were to entrap me before I gave in. "But cats have nine lives," I continued, happily mixing metaphors and cheering myself up in the process, "I should have some left, surely."

I had just come to the conclusion that I may even survive, even though I was no cat, and that I was going to be very, very busy, cats, spiders and all, when Jack's car appeared at the entrance and parked. He jumped out, picked up the backpack, said "Good morning" in a cheerful voice and installed me in the front seat of a very shiny and official-looking Mercedes. I wondered if he cleaned it himself, but dismissed the idea as not only unlikely but almost blasphemous. All the same, I asked him.

"Do you have two cars, then, and do you wash them with your own hands or do you have minions to do it for you?"

"Neither. I put them through the carwash. And now to business – did you sleep?"

"Fits and starts. You know how it is, your body wants to stop but your mind doesn't so you just go round and round. I slept in the end, though. Did you?"

"Same as you, only my mind was running in slightly different directions."

I didn't ask what the directions were because I was not sure that I wanted to know them. Instead, I said: "I have a problem. Well, a lot more than one, but this is a biggie. I only have three weeks holiday and one has gone already. How long will this business take to unravel? And if it hasn't unravelled in three weeks how can I bear to leave it? I won't want to go back to London." In fact, the thought came to me with a small jolt that I didn't want to go back to London anyway, unfinished business notwithstanding.

"Then if it hasn't cleared up, don't go. Tell them you have a scoop. Better still, tell them to boil their heads.""

I pulled a face. "But it's my job. It pays the rent."

There was silence for a moment. Eventually, Jack broke it. "It's too early to say what I was thinking of saying," he said, "but there may be other options."

I was saved from replying by the sight of the Croft Court gates and the circular drive which Jack negotiated with the ease of much practice. The car came to a stop neatly beside the front steps.

"I'll take your case up, then I must go and earn my own money or we'll all be in the suds." He accompanied me to the entrance, handed me the backpack then turned and kissed me briefly but meaningfully, before climbing back into his gleaming chariot and departing with a wave.

"Now for it!" I murmured, turning the key in the front door. My brief idyll was over and Reality was about to take its place.

The first sign of events to come was when my grandmother met me at her own front door. "Thank God!" she said, "I've been watching the drive."

I studied her carefully. "What's happened?"

"Nothing really, only Mrs Simmons isn't coming today. She rang earlier to say something had cropped up - and we all know what that means - but that she would do her best to look in later today to explain. Oh yes, and Sarah is anxious to see you."

I screwed up my eyes and considered Mrs Simmons. We had all left her out of our calculations and I wondered why. Was it that unobtrusive house helpers were to some extent invisible, like postmen and delivery vans? Surely not. She was Mrs Simmons, a person in her own right. But she was more, wasn't she?

"She is Ted Foley's daughter, right?" I mused. "Her father was a bully to his foster son, so let's hope he isn't being a bully to Mrs S.. I'll just dump my backpack in your spare bedroom then I'll nip round to Sarah's. Did she say it was urgent?"

"Just a.s.a.p. But have you had any breakfast? At least have a cup of something."

I explained that I had eaten not wisely but too well, threw my case onto the spare bed, told my grandmother to go back and sit down and crossed the hall to ring Sarah's bell.

Neil opened the door. "Good," he said, "Things are hotting up here and I want to go and stock up on the daily papers."

"Okay. Fine. Off you go then. I'll look after Sarah till you're back."

I received the full blast of his brilliant smile as he shrugged himself into an anorak and vanished through the door and down the steps. I watched him go with a certain wry amusement. He certainly knew how to show a clean pair of heels.

Sarah was on her way to meet me from the kitchen. I bent to kiss her cheek but had no time for anything more because the phone in my pocket vibrated against my hip.

Jack's voice said: "Gemma! Good. I was hoping to catch you. The whole thing seems to have blown wide open. I'll be with you as soon as I can get away. Anything new happened your end?"

"Haven't had much time to find out. In fact I haven't even exchanged more than a hello with Sarah, who looks as if she might try and grab this phone so I'd better be quick. It's just that my grandmother says Mrs Simmons isn't coming today, so lunch is debatable."

"Okay, I'll bring takeaways. Fish or Chinese?"

"Wonderful. Whichever you choose, but enough for five, I should think."

"Did Mrs Simmons say why she wasn't coming?"

"No, but it isn't hard to guess. Why did we all forget she was a Foley? Have we all got blinkers on or something?"

Jack laughed, said he'd see us soon and broke the link. I sighed and turned at last to Sarah who was looking very fetching with three feathers in her hair. I picked them off. "Sorry I didn't hand him over but he'll be here as soon as he can get away. Feathers still coming, I see."

"Yep! The only problem is that Shelagh, my new morning carer, came in when they were all over the floor and wanted to know what was going on, and was what the papers were saying true? So now we have two more witnesses and it won't stop there, will it?"

I shook my head. "Neil's gone for all the papers. We'll have more idea when we see those. Is this the carer your father arranged for you?"

"She came early this morning to suss out the situation – what I need and when, sort of thing, but she'll be coming twice a day. Or someone will. More if and when I need it. It means Neil doesn't have to help wash and dress me. Not that I can't do a lot of it myself, but there are things - you know."

I agreed there certainly were things, and asked if she had had any breakfast and would she like a coffee now this minute? She replied 'yes she had' to the breakfast, courtesy of Neil who was a fair cook when he put his mind to it, and that she, Sarah, was quite capable of producing coffee all by herself thank you Gemma.

We were both laughing when the phone rang again. This time it was my own mother, calling from her home in London. "Gemma, sweetie, what in heaven's name have you been up to? You're supposed to be on holiday. It sounds as if you'd have a more peaceful time here. Your dad agrees we wouldn't mind being dumped on if you need a bolt hole, but we would rather like an explanation, if you don't mind."

"Sorry, mama, but the explanation would confuse you even more than you are already so I'm not going to try. As it is, I'm confused enough myself. All I can say is that it's probably going to get worse before it gets better and I can't leave Gran to face it alone, but thanks all the same. I can't pass you over to her because I'm in the next door flat, but we can ring from hers when I go back."

"Yes please, Gemma. I think I may get rather more sense from her than from you. Of course I could always come down to see you both and get the story first hand."

I closed my eyes. I loved both my parents dearly but two more people on the scene – two more witnesses to be plagued and protected – would only add to the complications we were already juggling.

"That sounds lovely," I said, "but I'm afraid it wouldn't help right now this minute. Better I put it all in an email and you come when we know a bit more what's happening. I'll ask Gran to ring you as soon as poss. Meanwhile I have an urgent phone call to make so I'll dash off and speak to you later. Love to Dad."

"No coffee for me," I called to Sarah, "I have to go back to Gran's to give her a message and to ring my editor. I should have done that an hour ago but too much has happened. I'll be as quick as I can."

Sarah wheeled herself back to me, nodding with wide eyes and an air of expectancy. I stood at the open door, one foot in the hall. "Please Sarah, don't answer the phone unless the display tells you who it is. And don't open the door to anyone except me, Neil, Jack, Michael or your parents. Everyone else has to identify themselves. Okay? Promise?"

With her small nod, which I took to hold a promise of sorts, I had to be content.

I delivered my mother's message, then spoke to the editor of my paper, explaining the situation and asking what he would like me to do with it. I was told he had already read the latest story in the other papers, alerted no doubt by the Gazette but mainly by freelance Ellen, who had written in great detail about the state of things as she knew them but with alarming exaggeration. A case of "a little going a long way", I thought ruefully. He, the editor, had been about to contact me but I had saved him the trouble. Now he wanted the full – and this time correct – story of events so far and, and he wanted it immediately. Ellen may have grabbed her scoop, but she would not be allowed to keep it.

"Am I not too close to it all?" I asked him.

"Normally I would say yes, but you're both a family member and our 'man on the spot'"

I liked the 'man on the spot' and smiled. From an editor fully informed of what was politically correct and what wasn't, he was being far from correct himself, but to put him right was not on my job specification, so I merely pointed out that in this case 'on the spot' was dead right.

I was warned to expect a photographer later in the day and told firmly to "go and get on with it. I want it filed within the hour. "

The story was easy to write. He had asked for facts, so facts were what he was given, but those held quite enough drama on their own without further adornment from me. The only additions were that research was being done to identify the source of the feathers, if possible their composition and their quantity, insofar as it were possible to guess things that flew around at the lightest puff. He had warned that I would no doubt be contacted before long by other interested parties, some of them legitimate, but I should let him know as soon as that happened.

I had just finished the last sentence and sent the report on its way with a farewell kiss when Jack arrived, loaded with savoury rolls of stiff white paper and a large box containing five generous pieces of crisp, puffy battered fish. The smell was intoxicating. Sarah had laid knives and forks on the kitchen table and produced dishes warm from the oven, with a colourful collection of vinegar, slices of lemon and what looked to me like mayonnaise in little Chinese lacquer bowls.

Jack greeted me with a quick nod but no indication of our past conversation, except for a brief press on my shoulder. Since romantic dalliance was not on my agenda, at least for now, I was more than happy to concentrate on the fish and chips, which was just as well because within minutes our kitchen picnic was interrupted by the doorbell.. Neil had arrived, quickly followed by Michael with an eager, bouncing Peter in one hand and a sheaf of newspapers in the other. Both men immediately asked the same question.

Neil said: "What's a man with a camera doing by our gate?" And Michael asked why men with cameras and recording gear were wandering around the gardens.

Sarah and I looked at each other.

"This is what you were expecting, isn't it?"

I nodded. "It's the beginning," I frowned, one fingernail tapping my teeth. "It's surely too early for my lot, and anyway they would come to the door and identify themselves, but don't any of go us out until we're sure, or If we have to, don't talk to anybody."

"But that's nonsense", Michael argued. "Ridiculous. They're trespassing. We have every right to order them off our property."

I sighed.

It really was beginning.

# CHAPTER FIFTEEN

Since Neil too had come armed with newspapers, we laid them all down on the kitchen table, to be thoroughly perused once the sticky plates and boxes had been mopped up and removed.

Then began the ransacking. Headlines, every page and every column had to be investigated, most of which yielded astonishing results. The Gazette had excelled itself, thanks to Ellen's inspired imagination. Nothing had been left out and every detail had been exaggerated until the result was barely recognisable, even to me. The other papers had been later picking it up, but had made the most of whatever they could scramble together.

"You have to hand it her," I remarked at last. "She hasn't actually told any downright lies, just embroidered the truth to make it read better, and who can blame her? I've done much the same myself in the past."

"In that case I wonder you haven't been sued over and over by this time," Michael frowned accusingly, "as you certainly should have been."

There was a small chuckle from behind me. "Be careful, Mike," Sarah grinned, "Gemma's on our side, don't forget. Don't upset her. She's quite capable of turning you into mincemeat."

Jack, too, thought this was funny. "It's this Croft hair," he said, tugging a small handful from the back of my head. "But let's not be distracted. What is our plan of campaign?"

I told them about the email only just submitted to my paper, written as "their reporter on the spot," I said, with a nod to correctness. I told them I had written only the true story so far, and would wait to see what the editor, or sub-editors, did with it. "I was told not to embroider, so I didn't, but the truth is so odd anyway that I didn't need to."

Michael however, threw his own weight into the discussion, giving me one bleak, frowning glance. "But whatever happens, I refuse to be imprisoned," he announced firmly. "I shall come and go whenever I please."

"Of course," I nodded. "I have no authority to tell anyone to do anything – least of all bunk down for the night on Sarah's floor. I can only offer advice, which is to say as little as possible – in fact *nothing at all* if possible. And that's all I can tell you.. Would anyone like coffee?"

Sarah glanced at her husband who was leaning against the fridge-freezer with his arms folded. "Could you do us all some coffee, please Neil? He's a very good cook, did you know?"

From behind me I heard a sound from Jack that could have been either a huff or a smothered laugh. His whisper was only just audible, spoken into my right ear. "How to become a *cordon bleu* chef with one instant coffee!"

I refused to reply, merely tapping a rebuke on the hand now resting on my shoulder. As I did so, the flat doorbell claimed our frowning attention. Michael flew to open it, disclosing my grandmother, her hand raised for a further press on the bell. She was apologetic but the expression on her face brooked no argument. She was coming in - or else! As she stepped into the room a small flurry of feathers fluttered up from the floor beside her.

"Good morning everyone," she began, smiling down at Peter who was sitting on the floor scrutinising and pocketing feathers. On seeing the new ones, he was on his feet instantly to collect them and would have vanished through the door in search of more had Michael not grabbed him firmly by the tail of his bright red pullover.

"What did I just tell you not to do?" he asked him, "You are a menace, young Peter, and I want you under my eye at all times."

"Where's his nanny?" Jack asked. "Isn't she supposed to do that?"

Michael shrugged. "Hasn't turned up, and if she had I wouldn't have trusted her not to blab to the nearest nosey reporter. Especially," he added," if there were photographs involved. She's vain enough in all conscience,"

"I'm afraid they mostly are at that age," said my grandmother. "I know I was. Would you like me to take Peter away to my flat? Keep him safely amused?"

Peter shook his head. "Can't. I'm counting feathers."

I laughed. As a tension diffuser, there was surely nothing to equal a four-year-old boy.

The main entrance doorbell rang. I went to the conservatory window to see the curved steps. Standing confidently upon them were a photographer and what was plainly an interviewer-cum-presenter. She saw me and held up a placard with the name of my own paper written in large firm capitals.

I opened the door to let them in.

"Hello, I'm Mags, you must be Gemma and this is Sarah? Your gateway and garden are full of lurking photographers. There's a tv van lurking somewhere too, but the others followed me in. I told them this was an exclusive interview and we sailed in unmolested. That is, so far. We have to get out again. I hope you have spare beds here?" Mags spotted Peter sitting on the floor surrounded by a small hillock of feathers. She squatted beside him. "Hello? Are you helping to clear up or do you just like this feathery stuff? There's plenty of it isn't there?"

Peter was running out of hands so he offered some to Mags, who took them graciously and began counting them for herself. "There's loads and loads and *loads* more," he confided. "Aunty Sarah used to keep them in a box but she said there are too many now so they have to be swept up. I wish we could keep them all. I like them, but Daddy won't let me take them home."

"I'm not surprised," she laughed, "it would be like living in a snow storm only with warm snow."

"Wouldn't. They only come to Aunty Sarah."

Mags stood up. "Oh well, in that case I have to agree with Daddy." She looked around at us, all seemingly transfixed with wide eyes and nothing to say. "And which one is Daddy?"

At that we all came to life, suddenly, as if someone had flicked a switch. Michael came closer, told Peter to be quiet and play with his feathers, and held out his hand to Mags. "That's me," he said. "I have the dubious honour, and this is my brother Jack and this," putting his hand on Neil's shoulder, "is Sarah's husband, Neil. The tall, wise-looking lady is the original Mrs Croft of the Little Billy story, and you must already know our cousin Gemma, Mrs Croft's granddaughter. My parents are ready to join us if necessary."

The young woman sized us all up, then said "Thank you. Right, shall we get on with it? I'd like to start with Sarah please." She placed a tiny microphone to the neck of Sarah's dress, then placed herself a knee-length away with her own microphone in one hand. The photographer stood immediately to her right. "Please just relax and ignore us."

I smothered a giggle. The situation was familiar to me but even so the exhortation to relax with cameras and microphones mere inches from one's nose never failed to amuse me. How optimistic can one be? However, I also knew that after the first few minutes – sometimes only seconds – the strangeness of it melted and everyone was caught up in the story they were about to tell. Both in the giving and receiving of it all the phenomenon always felt to me like a small psychological miracle.

"Shall the rest of us disappear?" we asked.

"That's up to Sarah."

We all looked towards the wheelchair, but Sarah seemed more than happy to have us around her, merely suggesting that someone take Peter into the kitchen to ply him with milk and biscuits.

The next hour slid by so quickly that it was all over, with Mags packing away her notebooks and microphones, before we fully realised it. Throughout all the interviews feathers were slowly and gently landing on our heads and by now covered Sarah's shoulders and knees. I wondered how well they would be photographed, or even if they would be visible on film at all. Mags had made no comment of her own, just asked pertinent questions of everyone present. Finally, she said she would like to talk to their parents, but would prefer to see them in their own home if possible. "Save them being harassed on their way in and out of here." She explained.

"Of course," Jack reached for his own phone and pressed a speed number. His mother answered, apparently agreeing to the visit and, armed with the Kent home address, the news crew opened the front door.

A sizeable phalanx of men and women with cameras and microphones was grouped around the steps. We swiftly closed the door again. Sarah explained about her own side entrance with its wheelchair access and ramp, and we all hurried towards it, ushering Mags and the photographer through it and down the slope into the side garden, where they promptly disappeared.

in the kitchen a returned  Peter sat happily on the worktop kicking his legs and nibbling biscuits, we all heaved a sigh and sat around the table with cups of coffee and, at last, plenty to say.

Michael was first. "Where's Mrs Simmons?"

We told him.

"Where's the dog? I imagined he'd be having a fun time in his own little heaven with all these feathers to chase."

We all looked at Neil. "He was too strong for Sarah, strong enough to overturn the wheelchair and definitely too strong for the lead. He was taking us for walks, not the other way round. It's a shame, but I simply daren't leave her alone with him."

An unspoken but certainly palpable comment about why a puppy as strong as Jake had been chosen in the first place, hung in the air. It was Jack who asked where the dog had been taken. Neil had his answer ready and prepared. "My friend has taken him. He fell in love with Jake so the dog's gone to a good home."

I glanced at Sarah, who had said nothing. The morning's events had left its mark on her face which was now pale. I knew what the others, I hope, didn't – that she had not been consulted either in the choosing or the taking away of a puppy she was rapidly growing to love.

"Personally," I said at last, "I think we've all had enough, especially Sarah, so do you think perhaps we could leave her in peace for a while?"

Since this obviously found favour everywhere, my grandmother returned to her own flat and the Kent brothers bundled an unwilling Peter down the ramp into Michael's car - presumably to take him home before going in search of a handy pub. On his way out, Jack placed his hand briefly on the back of my neck and murmured "Well done," and "See you later perhaps?" before following his brother and a struggling Peter out of the side entrance (which by now had its own small phalanx of waiting press) to their cars.

I sighed and turned to Sarah. "Are you hungry or just tired?" She shook her head and replied in one simple word. "Tired," she said. "After all those fish and chips. I think I'll go to the conservatory and sleep."

I kissed her cheek, patted a feather away from her eyebrows and, smiling hopefully at Neil, went back to sit in welcome peace in my grandmother's comfortable armchair.

One hurdle had been surmounted. All I had to do now was wait in patience for the next. But there was the rub. How much patience did I have?

# CHAPTER SIXTEEN

In silence I collapsed into my grandmother's chair, legs out straight before me and eyes closed. In silence she placed a glass of sherry into my hand and left me in peace. Finally she spoke. Her voice was calm and comforting.

"None of this is your fault, you know" she said. "So stop beating yourself up. You are supposed to be on holiday."

"Some hopes," I murmured, almost to myself.

"I'm sorry for Sarah and her family, but you came here to escape from a stressful job and what happens? You land yourself in an equally stressful situation. No, not equally, considerably more stressful because you feel involved. Well, however sorry I may feel for the others, you are my granddaughter and I'm not having your holiday wrecked while you're with me. So please switch off your phone, drink your nice sherry and relax while you have the chance."

"Yes Grannie," I said, "but...."

"But nothing. If you're hungry I'll make us both a sandwich, otherwise please shut up or I'll tell your mother."

That made me smile, as she knew of course that it would. The last thing I needed at that moment was my over-anxious parent clucking around this up-to-now inviolable place, talking with no commas or full stops, feeling my head and offering unwanted cushions for various parts of my person. "Don't you dare," I said. I was rewarded with a chuckle, followed by a silence so blissful that I longed for it to continue unhindered for eternity – and beyond, if necessary.

It didn't, of course. After only ten minutes the spell was broken once again by my phone. I wrinkled my nose in distaste and reached for it. My grandmother exclaimed: "What did I just tell you to do?

I glanced at the display. Jack had only just left with Michael, so why was he ringing me now? "Hello Jack," I sighed into the phone.

"Oh whoah!" his voice registered dismay. "That doesn't sound too good. Were you busy or would you like something to eat?"

"No I'm not busy – trying not to be, ever again, and I'm not at all hungry either but I suppose we ought to eat or drink something eventually." I raised my eyebrows and looked at my grandmother, who shrugged and opened her hands. "Why are you ringing me now? You're supposed to be in a pub with Michael. What's happened?"

"That was the plan, but we had a call from Pop. He wanted us back there as of NOW, so Mike went and I'm coming to you and Sarah. "

"Tell me," I demanded, now thoroughly awake.

"I'll be with you in ten minutes and can explain then."

"Okay. See you in ten."

I replaced the phone and made a face at Grannie, who shrugged again and looked disgusted. "Your mother always did as she was told, so what went wrong with you?"

"Cause and effect. You know what they say about teenage rebellion."

"In your case lifelong rebellion would be nearer the truth. So what's happening now?"

I explained and went across to Sarah's flat, where I found her door on the latch.

"You know you're supposed to lock yourself in," I remonstrated. "Do you really want people with cameras wandering in at all hours?"

"No, just you."

"Well you're soon going to have Jack as well. I think he has news of some kind, whether that's good or bad your guess is as good as mine."

Sarah nodded. "He rang me too but I'm not hungry."

"Pity we can't boil some feathers up for soup. There'd be enough for a fullscale National banquet."

Sarah smiled and picked one up. "Yes but they're so beautiful. I couldn't possibly boil them, let alone eat them." She produced a large paper bag with an air of triumph. "Look what I've been doing," she said, "This was as an aid for thought," and she opened the bag with a flourish.

There, in her hands, was the most exquisite fan I had ever seen. I took it carefully to study it in detail, and was astonished. Layer upon layer of white, soft, faintly curling little wings, caught together at the back in rows by a piece of netting, each layer overlapping the one before and seemingly splayed out on wafer-thin sticks. Unfurled, the fan had become a wing of its own, something fragile, burnished and heart-wrenchingly beautiful. I found I was holding my breath.

"Did you just make this?" I whispered, provoked at last into a semblance of speech.

"All last night. Didn't sleep until it was finished."

"But it's..." I shook my head, unable to say any more.

Sarah gave a joyful little laugh. The whole thing was a delightful game. "And I found something interesting about them. They all seem to be the same shape, very gently curved, but some are big and some are a bit smaller, almost as if they are graded, like the sort you see on a bird's wings – the bigger ones on top and the smaller fluffy ones tucked underneath."

I picked up a few to examine them in more detail. "So it's a question of finding the right birds, then, but I've been looking out for white birds and there don't seem to be any, except the occasional white pigeon. The swans on the village pond are still there, both of them, and they certainly haven't lost any feathers. There haven't been any cygnets lately either, as far as I know. Not recently anyway, and I'm sure they were carefully counted when they were there. Besides, cygnets are grey. The village is proud of its resident swans, so any plucking would have been noticed and anyway they can be vicious so it'd be a question of 'first catch your swan'. Besides,, are any of their feathers the right size for swans?"

We were still studying the fan when Sarah's doorbell chimed. I opened it to admit Jack bearing several folded papers. "Was this door locked?" he asked.

"No. Sarah has cabin fever and she likes us to come and go without having to let us in every time."

Jack frowned, then he smiled and once again his total demeanour changed. "I've brought a selection of sandwiches for when anyone wants them. It's a choice of egg mayo, ham and salad or cheese and pickle – courtesy of Foleys bakery, which brings me to my next question. Has Mrs Simmons shown up yet?"

"Nope. They've probably locked her in her room with crusts and water."

We were both laughing when we joined Sarah in the kitchen. I thought again how very predictable we were, always congregating there when the apartment was filled with comfort and elegance everywhere else. Was it an English habit, I wondered, or was it world-wide? No, I decided, not exclusively English since according to reports the French apparently lived most of their home lives lingering over meals and conversation, a habit which was decidedly not our own most of the time. It seemed to me that a great many families, a huge percentage perhaps, now ate their meals on their knees, often at different times from each other with conversation probably limited to "Where's the salt?" or, "Throw the remote over, will you?"

Jack handed me the packages. "Right, can you stick these in the fridge? Business first, I'm afraid."

I did as requested and seated myself at the table, "So what's the news? It must be urgent."

"Sarah's new carer has blabbed. Practically everywhere, apparently. Pop is about to sack her."

I was aghast. "*No!* He mustn't. The damage is done and sacking her will only make it worse."

"Well, you know Pops. He's made his mind up."

"I don't care. If he has any wits he'll unmake it. How far has he gone?"

"Don't know, but we're probably too late to stop him anyway."

"Can we try, at least? Could you get him on the phone? Like *now?*"

Jack stared at me. Obviously I didn't 'know Pop'. He was right, but Pop didn't know me either and he was about to find out. "Please can you ring him Jack? Please, please? I'm serious."

Frowning, he pressed a speed-dial number. "Jack Kent," he said, "Will you get my father for me? Now please ......and I don't care if he is a meeting or even 200 meetings, just get him, will you?"

All three of us waited in silence. Sarah waved her fan to and fro, savouring the softness in her hands. "Pop? Jack here. Have you sacked the carer yet?" He glanced at me and shook his head. I held out my hand for the receiver. "Gemma needs to talk to you. I'll hand her over."

Without listening to his father's reply, which sounded at second hand rather forthright and none too complimentary, Jack passed the telephone to me and I spoke into it.

"Good morning Mr Kent, please may I advise you very, very strongly not to sack the carer, if you haven't already."

"What if I have, and why should I take your advice?" Mr Kent's voice was peremptory, coldly questioning my right to dictate terms – any terms at all, it seemed. I was not surprised. I was challenging The Boss,. I supposed this didn't happen very often, and certainly not twice. Gratefully, I remembered that he was not *my* boss and that his jurisdiction over me was firmly family based, and not even on his own family but mine. I was not one of his own. I felt that any respect for my opinion would be due entirely to his respect for my grandmother and I was duly grateful. She had never yet let me down.

"Of course you are completely free to ignore anything I say, but I hope you won't because sacking her carer will only open your daughter to more harassment. The girl will be angry, mostly because nobody told her specifically to keep her mouth shut, so your name will be mud."

Mr Kent huffed into the phone and said "Well, that wouldn't be the first time and we've always survived. More importantly, she has broken a cardinal rule in caring and deserves to be fired on the spot. Confidentiality is basic."

I sighed. He was making politeness difficult. "Mr Kent, I'm sorry to say this, but it's a bit late for legalisms and it's Sarah who will pay the price as well as your firm's good name. Do you really want to..."

I was interrupted. "And whose fault is that?"

"Sorry again, but we're talking about damage limitation here, not my past mistakes. Keep the girl on as Sarah's personal carer and fill her in with the whole situation. Enlist her support and *then* assume her complete discretion. Sarah's the sort of person who gathers friends and supporters so I'd put money on her charming any carer whoever she is. I don't need to tell *you* that, naturally. I've only known her two weeks and she's totally charmed me. The carer's name is Shelagh, by the way. Please Mr Kent. A lot depends on it."

I held my breath, then he said: "Well, I suppose it is your area of expertise, so I won't sack the girl, but on your own head be it. And," he added, "don't try to bamboozle me because it won't work. Now please hand me back to my son."

I pulled a face into the phone. His "please" had held no politeness; It was simply a command based on the assumption of being obeyed at once – please or no please.

I didn't listen to the rest of Jack's brief conversation with his father, contenting myself with refilling the kettle.

"Sarah said "Well done Gemma."

Jack said nothing.

# CHAPTER SEVENTEEN

I was turning to ask whether it was too soon for anyone to need coffee, or tea, or in fact anything at all, when the front door opened again to reveal the jubilant face of my grandmother. "Guess who's here?" I half expected her to do a "Ta-Daaah!" but she resisted what was obviously a strong urge. Dignity at all costs, Mrs Croft? Mrs Simmons followed her, a trace hesitantly, I thought, and stood before us looking apologetic.

"I'm so sorry about earlier but they didn't want me to come. I've only just sneaked out. There was no way I going to let Mrs Croft down after she's been so good to me, and it's got nothing to do with her anyway."

We all greeted her with cries of thanks for turning up at all. I told her it was very brave of her and Jack asked who exactly was it who had tried to stop her coming.

"Mostly my daughter and her husband but mainly my dad. He's furious about all this – this publicity. He said it was all a lot of trumped up nonsense and ought to be ignored. He said it was the only way of dealing with these people." She glanced apologetically at me. "Sorry Gemma, but those were his words."

I laughed. "Don't worry about it," I assured her. "I'm quite sure he meant me anyway, and I've been called worse things, believe me. And now I think we all deserve some refreshment." I looked around. "Where's Neil?" I asked.

"Gone to get the papers, I think." Sarah's voice was calm. She was playing with her feather fan and not quite with us in the room. "He said he'd only be a tick."

I wondered how many minutes or hours constituted one tick, and how one measured them. So many ticks to the hour, maybe? I decided that Neil's ticks were probably made of elastic but, however long or short they might be, he should not be leaving his wife alone in the flat with the front door unlocked.

Jack was frowning. "Well, Mrs Simmons," he said, ignoring for the time being my reference to his brother-in-law. "Since you came after all, we're going to have to trust you."

There was a hasty nod from Mrs Simmons and an eager "Yes, yes of course."

"How much do you know already?"

"Only that these – feathers I suppose they are, well they look like feathers don't they? – they keep coming to Sarah but nobody else and we don't know what they are or where they're coming from. Only," she continued, "they're just like the ones in the Little Billy story, so my dad is angry because he got the blame for Billy dying the way he did. But like I told him, I work for Mrs Croft, and all this has nothing to do with her so he can't stop me coming, and anyway who's going to cook her lunches and keep the place nice? So that's what I'm going to tell them when they ask me – which they will, seeing as I got out without them knowing" She suddenly grinned. An impish-looking dimple appeared in one rounded cheek, somehow making her look even more like the amiable pin cushion she so closely resembled. "They'll be crosser than ever, but they don't own me. I'm just a sort of piggy-in-the-middle to them. Well, I'll piggy *them*."

We all clapped. "So long as they don't lock you in," I said, "in which case use your mobile and Jack'll climb a ladder and rescue you, won't you Jack?"

A grinning Jack was saved from replying by the door opening once more. This time a cross-looking Michael strode into the kitchen, followed closely by a chastened-looking Neil. .

"What's going on here?" Michael stared at each of us and, if the stare wasn't accusatory it looked remarkably close to being one. My grandmother replied for all of us. She alone had not been included in what was obviously an otherwise general disapproval.

"Mrs Simmons has come after all, as you can see. We've just been hearing about it."

"Very good of her, I'm sure. Better late than never, I suppose."

I frowned back at him. "Hey!" I said, shedding my tea towel and putting my arms around Mrs Simmons' comfortable shoulders. "That's no way to thank a very brave lady. She is to be applauded."

Appeasement was obviously not on Michael's personal agenda. "Oh? Applauded for turning up to do her job?"

"Exactly." By this time I could feel my temper rising, but realised I was not alone in this since everyone started talking at once. He threw up his hands and turned his attention to Neil.

"As for you," he began, but my grandmother intervened yet again.

"Mr Kent," she said, "We were just about to have some coffee while we worked on our plan of campaign. You've arrived just in time."

I of course followed her lead. "Coffee coming up," I said, "perhaps we should all sit round the table. Not quite up to conference standard but if we sit in the conservatory we may not keep to the point. It's far too comfortable. Don't you agree, Michael?"

Michael said nothing but pulled a chair nearer to the table and produced a notebook and biro. Jack was refusing to meet my eye. He simply sat down opposite his brother. The rest disposed themselves wherever they wished, leaving an empty chair for me next to Sarah's wheelchair. Throughout what had so nearly become an altercation, she had remained lost in a dreamy silence. I returned to the kitchen and added two more mugs to the growing collection on the worktop. After a brief pause Neil joined me, fetching milk and sugar and switching on the coffee machine.

"Thanks," I murmured, adding, very softly so that only he could hear me, "Where *did* you get to? Were you held up by photographers?"

He smiled his thanks. "Of course. The blasted press are all over the place. And then the bloody paper shop was full of people asking me questions. There's even a tv van parked in the road. I don't think they caught me but I was glad to escape with my life. I only got through because Mike scooped me up at the gate and I'm not sure how he got that far, to be honest."

I was suddenly struck. This was the first time I had ever heard Michael's name being shortened to such an everyday kind of syllable. It didn't suit him but I liked it.

I laughed. "Executive manners? Company car? Or did he just plough through them scattering bodies on the way?"

Neil began to look more cheerful. He managed a quiet chuckle. "Wouldn't put it past him."

"Is he often like this? "

"Like a pompous prig, you mean?"

I spluttered. "Neil, we are speaking of your beloved brother-in-law."

"Yes. A pompous prig. And yes, he is often like this. More often than not, in fact."

The coffee machine burbled its readiness and he poured coffee into waiting mugs while I found the biscuit tin and the remains of the cake.. "Ok, chaps, here we go. Crofts and Kents forever undefeated."

"And Chalmers. Don't forget the Chalmers."

"Impossible," I said and together we sailed back into seemingly insoluble problems.

Michael and Jack were seated, but Mrs Simmons and my grandmother were hovering. "Mrs Simmons feels she should be getting on with her work, now she's come, and I don't feel qualified to make decisions on what is a really a Kent family problem."

I frowned at her and vigorously shook my head. "Well I need you, and I'm quite sure everyone else does too, so do at least sit down and drink this coffee. Mrs Simmons," I added, pointing to a vacant chair, "please accept it as a token of our gratitude for braving all opposition like the heroine you are."

Looking slightly more pink than usual, Mrs Simmons did as she was bid and chose a chair nearest to Sarah's wheelchair, where she was welcomed with an encouraging smile and the re-emergence of Sarah to everyday life. Until then she had been totally engrossed with her fan and her thoughts.

"And don't worry too much about housework today," I added. "We've got sandwiches if we're hungry and this is more important anyway."

Michael began tapping his biro. "Now that's settled," he said, "I propose getting on with this – this business. Has anyone anything to report? Jack, have you been researching the feathers? Gemma, have you contacted your editor?"

I told him all contacting had been done first thing that morning and I was in the process of updating a factual report to be sent in as soon as possible. Jack had sent off a selection of feathers to his lab for testing and awaited results. Michael was just about to launch into other research aspects, including the psychological one, ("Was it all in Sarah's mind?") when fortunately we were interrupted once more. Had we not been, Michael's suggestion would have sent the whole table, cakes, biscuits and all, into uproar and he would have had severe difficulty as self-imposed chairman in holding his meeting together.

The door, however, had opened on his wife Ruth, looking anxiously at her watch, and ushering before her a wildly excited small boy carrying a handful of bright new feathers.

"Sorry Mike," Ruth said, "but Peter's nanny hasn't turned up and I haven't time to drop him off at playschool, so I'll leave him with you and pick him up later. I'm late already, so no time to chat. Sorry. Hello everybody. " She gave a general wave around the room and left us..

"Don't forget to shut the outer door," Michael shouted, half rising from his chair to pick up his son and place him firmly on his knee. "And as for you, young man, you will behave nicely or I shall donate you to the zoo. No running off this time, okay?"

Peter, who was obviously delighted at the prospect of being donated, wriggled with pleasure. "Please daddy, can we go to the zoo? Please, please? And can I be a giraffe - or a meerkat like the ones on telly?"

"Certainly not. I shall put you in with the spiders. And if you're good and quiet I won't leave you there for a whole year. Maybe until your birthday. Now shut up and sit still."

We all watched with interest and curiosity as Michael's whole personality changed with the presence of this small child. I remembered how his father had played with Peter the first time he and I had met, throwing him up and catching him and allowing him to spread his small arms around his grandfather's large body.

We tried to continue with our meeting but the spell had been broken. Our attention now was on Peter, not on his father. To no-one's surprise, the suggestion of a Sarah-inspired psychosomatic feather storm was not to be raised again today, although I rather expected it to be raised again by someone else at some future meeting.

For Sarah's sake I hoped not, but would be ready with contrary evidence all the same should it be needed.

Neil produced the sandwiches brought by Jack, at which point my grandmother, Mrs Simmons and I made our excuses and left – they to appease Mrs Simmons' conscience and myself to finish writing my report.

The Kent brothers and sister, with a happy, wriggling Peter picking up and studying new feathers as they

121

alighted on Sarah's head and arms, were now alone together to sort themselves and their problems into some sort of cohesion. And I was happy to let them do so. The Kent family could, I found, be a little overwhelming.

As for Jack, after his brief, totally unexpected and apparently highly reluctant declaration of love,, his behaviour to me since then had been a puzzle that I had no energy to solve. Instead I addressed myself to emails and decided to forget him.

I was, however, reckoning without yet another turn of a screw in what was becoming a bewildering series of them. A knock of our door revealed a disconcerted Mrs Simmons.

The police had arrived.

# CHAPTER EIGHTEEN

An embarrassed Mrs Simmons was so apologetic that I smiled, closed down my laptop and told her to send them in. I took a deep breath. What now, I thought, what now?

A young and smartly uniformed male constable accompanied by an efficient-looking and equally smart female one entered the room and asked if I was Mrs Sarah Chalmers. I explained that my name was Gemma Croft, but that Mrs Chalmers lived in the next apartment. "Immediately across the entrance hall," I explained, "but I will take you to her myself. The poor girl is having enough shocks, I might as well soften the blow a bit. And anyway I think at least one of her brothers may still be there. If you would like to follow me?"

"Just a moment. May I ask how you and Mrs Croft are involved?"

"You may, but it's a long story." I forbore to comment on the fact that he evidently knew my grandmother's name. He obviously knew her quite well because he was looking distinctly uncomfortable at having to question her at all. .

"Hello Stephen," she said, rising from her chair and holding out her hand. "How's your mother after her accident?"

Stephen had the grace to look abashed. "She's recovering nicely, thank you Mrs Croft. It was a nasty fall but she's game. I'm sorry to be a nuisance, but we do need to see Mrs Chalmers on account of there's a horde of people outside the door and we've had complaints from your neighbours who say it's all to do with a story you wrote for the papers." He turned to me. "Is that true Miss?"

"Not really, I said, "but it will do to be going on with. And who are these neighbours?"

By this time, with a polite smile and nod to my grandmother, the two constables were following me across the hall, where an irate lady wearing a long enveloping cardigan and trainers was breathing fire at the bottom of the stairs.

"You!" she cried, pointing at me. "It's all your fault. Now will you please call off your bloodhounds and let me get to my car?"

"I'm really sorry," I began.

"So you should be."

"Excuse me," I began again, "but I don't know who you are. If you are a resident here, your car park is on the other side of the building."

Constable Stephen coughed. "This is the lady who called us." He explained. "The front steps and the drive are full of people with cameras and mikes."

"Yes, and the car park. They wouldn't let me through."

I hesitated for a brief moment, bottom lip between my teeth. "I think maybe you should come with us," I said at last. "You might like to hear the full story"

"Not if it's going to take all day."

I told her it would take whatever length of time she chose to stay and listen to it, and we all trooped through Sarah's door which this time was thankfully unlocked. Sarah was in the conservatory, looking bright-eyed and expectant.

"I've been watching," she told us. "And you, poor soul," looking at a trifle less irate but no less assertive lady who stood among us, hands on hips, ready to give battle if given the smallest provocation. "How quick you were to shut the door on them. I was cheering you on."

"Sarah," I touched her arm. "This lady called the police and they've come to find out what's happening."

Sarah clapped and said "Oh, well done!" She turned to smile at the constables, who by this time seemed not too sure which feet to stand on. "I'm so glad you've come. Now perhaps we can get rid of them and we can get back to normal."

I stared at her. I had been prepared for a shocked and bewildered girl and was finding a happily confident one apparently without a problem to her name. I asked her if she knew the lady we had brought with us. "Oh yes," she smiled, "this is Mrs Carmichael from Suite 4, immediately above this one. We don't see you very often, do we? You usually use the side door into the car park." Sarah turned back to her (by now) stunned audience. "Although it looks as if you've have had just as much trouble getting out that way as well."

Constable Stephen's efficient cohort moved towards her, flashing her police identity badge. "Sorry," she said, "We don't want to upset you, but could we get some facts straight please. If you don't mind, we need to know what's going on."

"Perhaps if we all sit down," I suggested, pointing to the array of comfortable cushioned bamboo chairs surrounding us. I turned to Sarah. "Have both your brothers gone? And where is Neil?"

This was beginning to be a recurring theme. Sarah shrugged, not looking one whit troubled or in need of solace. "Nipped out," she said, "I expect gone for today's papers, but he'll be back."

We all sat down. We all looked at each other. No-one else coming forward with suggestions, I started this particular ball rolling. "Like I said, it's a long story so how about if you ask us questions?"

Constable Stephen, who had by this time flashed his own badge, was evidently not happy with the assembled audience, especially as my grandmother had chosen that moment to join us. A lady who, I suspected, had known him from childhood was about to be put on the spot. "I've decided to join you," she said, addressing the room in general. "since this is mostly my fault."

Notebooks were produced and the questions began. An hour later, it seemed we had not only given the police all we had in the way of explanation – such as it was – but had also mollified the upstairs neighbour. She even agreed to help us outwit the press. Boxes of feathers were produced and opened, to the usual stunned silence, and the flat was once again buried under a soft white snowstorm. "These came in the last few hours," Sarah declared, brushing a handful from her skirt and flicking another from her forehead.

Suitably bewildered and having filled their notebooks, the police prepared to leave. Unfortunately the front door burst open as if someone had kicked it, and a harassed-looking Michael appeared before us, shutting the door behind him and proceeding to lock it. "*Now* what's happening? For God's sake are we to have no peace?"

Apparently not, I thought, as he caught sight of the two police officers and fixed them with a glare. "And what do *you* want?"

"Information, Mr Kent" said Stephen peacefully enough, "which we now have. He introduced himself, flashing his warrant card for Michael's benefit. "And this is Police Constable Murray. So now please may we deal with his crowd and get rid of them as fast as we can. Unless, of course, you have anything you'd like to add?"

"No, Gemma knows my views. I have nothing further to say, except that it's about time you did something about this – this – this *siege*. And who called you anyway? Certainly not us."

Mrs Carmichael identified herself and stood back, leaving the police to deal with any further members of the embattled Kent family.

The constables opened the door and closed it firmly behind them. The door was thick enough to muffle what they said, but whatever it was the effect was, if not immediate, at least fast enough to clear the drive of press. Any of us who desired to leave could now do so in relative safety. Nobody did.

I sighed and turned back to where Mrs Carmichael stood in the conservatory doorway, obviously watching it all with interest.

"I'm really sorry you've had all this trouble," I began. "Are the other residents complaining too?"

"Of course they are, but they don't want publicity any more than I do so they won't do anything positive for themselves."

"In that case, please may I have some names and addresses so we can call on them personally? I think they deserve to know what all this is about. And I'm sorry but although you gave your full name to the police I didn't catch it, so may I have it please? "

"Of course. My full name is Evelyn Carmichael."

I gasped. "Evelyn Carmichael? The novelist? You won a Crime fiction award quite recently. I know it's a daft question but why don't you want publicity?" Privately I was beginning to consider her own motives and feeling a little at a loss about my own 'writer' status. On occasion there can be quite a gulf between so-called 'serious' writers and journalists in general.

Our own resident fiction writer gave a small smile. "I came to live here in order to be unmolested, to give myself peace and quiet, but there are one or two people living here who wouldn't be averse to getting in on the act. It might be a good idea to have them on our side, don't you think?"

Since by this time Michael had disappeared into the conservatory and was presumably getting himself up to date with police and press and the latest feather count, I grinned at Mrs Carmichael and suggested she approach the Kent family, who were after all her landlords - or at least the vendors of the property she herself had either bought or was renting. Together she and I went back to the conservatory to find a happily unrepentant Sarah showing off her feather fan and gleefully describing how the police had gone through the press "like a knife through butter" she said. "And then he herded them all out through the gates. It was gorgeous."

This was a new Sarah, mesmerising in her glee.

Michael seemed less impressed. More to the point he was enquiring into the whereabouts of Sarah's husband, who should have been there but wasn't. Again Sarah shrugged, confident that Neil would return when he'd done whatever he'd gone out to do. Gone was the besotted wife hanging onto his every word.

"Michael," I began, "Mrs Carmichael..."

"Please call me Evelyn,"

"This is Evelyn Carmichael who lives in Suite 4 and she tells me the other residents are angry and upset at what they think of as "being imprisoned' in their own homes. So we are suggesting that they are all contacted and visited personally with the true explanation and hoping they'll join us in the fight. In which case," I added, "could we have a list of names and suites so we can get on with it? Evelyn says she will help.

Michael was at least mollified by this new initiative and frowningly agreed to furnish us with the list.

"As soon as possible, please?" I begged, trying not to sound bossy but probably failing.

Michael took the hint, albeit reluctantly as it came from me, but with an acknowledging nod to Evelyn. He was even ready to give us the names now, this minute, by using his smartphone which, apparently, could do everything except print the copies. He then retired to Sarah's quiet, computer room to use her own printer. "I need peace in which to concentrate," he told us. The four of us, my grandmother, Mrs Carmichael, Sarah and myself, were left alone to do our own concentrating.

"Please sit down," Sarah told us. "We might as well be comfortable while we wait. Meanwhile, I would love to hear about you, Mrs Carmichael. I have read your books and thoroughly enjoyed them, but hadn't the faintest idea you were sitting writing them in the room right over my head. You've kept it very dark."

"Everyone here needs a place to hide – an escape, I suppose, but I need it so I can write my books in peace. No callers, no phones, just music if I want it and a pleasant garden to walk in if I feel so inclined. It's not quite the case for everyone. We have an ageing film star who refuses to be seen without her makeup, and an also ageing 70s pop group called the 'Starlights' who like to wander around in a an odd assortment of weird garments.. I think they play their guitars to each other while they sing along to their old favourites. They don't appear in public any more., I'm happy to say. Nice women but...!"

I laughed. "Evelyn Carmichael, you are a wicked woman and just what we need. Welcome to Croft Court."

She had no time in which to reply because Michael reappeared holding two A4 sheets of listed names and addresses which he handed to her, rather than to me. Then he turned to kiss his sister on the top of her head, asked her to tell her husband to contact him *at once* the minute he returned, and exited with some dignity towards the entrance.

Having fulfilled his current obligations, Michael frowned and said he had to get back to work, so would we mind Peter and see he didn't get out again. Then he too left, closing the main door firmly behind him.

I began to laugh. It was a weak laugh involving as it did a modicum of despair. "Oh well," I said. "That's today taken care of. Roll on, the rest of life, roll on!"

# CHAPTER NINETEEN

Mrs Carmichael and I looked at each other. So much had happened in such a short space of time that neither of us seemed to have the words to cover it. Then she handed me the list of names. "Would you like this or shall I keep it?" she asked, looking as nonplussed as I felt.

"Got a better idea," I said, goaded out of inactivity into sudden resolution. "Come with me and we'll do some more copies on Sarah's printer."

Three minutes later we re-emerged, each armed with duplicate lists and plans to visit as many residents as were available to be visited. We divided the house into subdivisions, then she moved towards the lift while I returned to Sarah and my grandmother, both of whom were watching Peter with amusement as he chased more feathers around the room.

I asked them if they needed me for the moment, was told that no they didn't, and made my way yet again to the door. Not, however, before stopping, hit by a new thought that flashed across my mental vision. I went back to Sarah in her wheelchair and stared directly into her eyes.

"Now listen, you," I began firmly. "I want to know exactly how you are and when you next see your doctor. Someone somewhere is going to start asking questions."

"How am I?" Sarah seemed surprised. "I'm fine, and I have an appointment at my doctor's next Tuesday. Why?"

"Is it possible to bring it forward?"

"Yes if I ask him. Do you want me to?"

This was a difficult question in that yes, I did want the appointment brought forward but I personally had no authority to insist on it. Until Neil came home all I could do was make suggestions. I turned to my grandmother for support. She was looking grave.

"Yes, I do," I said in the end. "A check up is always a good idea and if you're due for one anyway..." I paused. "Have you contacted Neil to see where he is?"

"I've tried, but he's not answering his phone. I expect he's in a meeting or something."

"Quite possibly," said my grandmother, quietly removing a feather from Sarah's collar. "Please may I have another look at your fan? It is exquisite, did you know that?"

Sarah found the fan and handed it first to Peter, who was told to treat it very carefully. It wasn't a toy but something very precious. I left them, the picture very clear in my eyes of a small rapt face gazing down at this 'very precious' thing he held in his hands, and with the assurance from Sarah that she would ring her doctor and ask for a home visit.

I was about to do some research into our neighbours. The puzzle was that nobody had thought of doing this before. I guessed it may possibly due to family privacy – or, as I chose to see it, Family Pride. If it were, then the situation had taken them far too far for any such hope. Both families were now firmly in the public domain and would remain there until a solution was found to the puzzle. Furthermore, so were our neighbours.

Going through to the hall and beginning to climb the curving staircase, I decided that ignoring them further was a grave mistake. They had presumably bought their suites for the sake of privacy and freedom from press intrusion, but the press had already intruded, whether we or they liked it or not, so their co-operation was now not only necessary but becoming urgent.

The first floor landing – if it could possibly be described by such a mundane word - was spacious and smoothly furnished with comfortable chairs arranged as conversation groups and a glass-topped coffee table on which lay a vase of pink and white roses that smelt delicious. Light streamed from a large window, throwing a pool of it across the grey-green carpet and giving it a silvery sheen.

The first door was Evelyn Carmichael's. It stood wide open. I poked my head tentatively through it and called her name. She appeared with a nod and an air of achievement. "I've done the suite opposite," she told me, pointing at a name on her list. "I've already met this lady. She is a retired soap actress, or perhaps I should say 'actor' now, and she appreciated my visited. She hadn't actually been outside for several days, being engaged in writing her autobiography and doesn't often read the newspapers, so was not really aware of what had been happening. She thanked us, though, and agreed to help us in any way she could. A nice lady." Mrs Carmichael consulted her list again, "Her name is Cecily Wells. I don't think she was one of the top stars, but since I hardly ever watch the soaps I wouldn't know anyway."

"Not a film star then?"

"Apparently not."

"Who is on the next floor, and how do we get to the suites facing the other way?

She pointed to a door on the wall facing the window. "I think it's that one. It's a sort of connecting door between suites on the same floor, I believe. I was about to try it."

I thanked her and told her to carry on please, if she would, while I went to the floor above. Once again giving myself the exercise of using the staircase - not so grand this time but grand all the same in its own way, to find myself on an equally comfortably disposed landing with two doors facing each other. The cosy armchairs were there and the coffee table, a marquetry one this time, but there was no vase of flowers. The window, however, was still large and shining down brightly on a carpet this time in a pleasing shade of pale terracotta.

I chose one and rang the bell. The name on the door merely said. "Pendersby. No callers, no advertising." I smiled and pulled a face at such an uncompromising notice. My expectations of welcome were not high.

The door opened suddenly and a very hairy moustache and beard revealed themselves in the aperture.

"Yes?" A thin, pale hand, much at odds with the hairy face, came round the corner of the door and pointed to the notice.

"I'm sorry to intrude," I began, "but we've all been rather bothered by the press here lately and we wanted to make sure you weren't having problems with them yourself – seeing that I understand you prefer to guard your privacy."

"Who are you? Are you the owner?"

"I'm Gemma Croft, and because the matter has become rather urgent, I am representing the owner, Mr Kent, who is not available at the moment. Maybe you've seen the newspapers recently?"

"Not if I can help it. Why should they interest me? I get what I want from the radio. Television and the internet are too bloodthirsty for me. Not happy until they see the blood and tears. Satisfied? Now please go away."

He made as if to shut the door, but I pursued him with more questions. "So you won't have read any reports on the press activity outside your home?. May I ask that if you are ever harassed in any way, you will please make no comment to them but let Mr and Mrs Chalmers know in Suite No 2. If you drive, your car may be under observation."

"We have CCTV."

"That's excellent. We are asking for your co-operation in this Mr Pendersby," I added, briefly consulting my list, "The person most under siege is a young lady with Multiple Sclerosis and she doesn't deserve to be hounded in this way."

The eyes pierced through the gloom of his abundant beard and bushy eyebrows. He frowned, said "Hpm" withdrew his hand from the door and closed it firmly.

I spoke quietly through the rapidly diminishing space. "I'll take that as a yes, then. Thank you so much," then grinned at the blankness of a door shut firmly in my face.

I drew a tick beside his name, added a question mark, and was about to turn away when the door opened abruptly once more. "Don't bother with next door", Mr Pendersby spoke through a slit. "They're away. Hawaii."

The door closed again and I grinned even more widely. He was at least showing good will and somehow I knew he would co-operate if ever called upon to do so. I gave his name another tick, one with a flourish this time, and walked towards the door leading to the upper floor.

The next flight of stairs was narrower, of course, since they had obviously been leading to the servants' quarters, but nevertheless they were just as gracefully furbished as the ones before. This time the stair and landing carpets were in a tasteful shade of creamy beige but instead of giving onto a landing with armchairs they revealed instead a formidable-looking mahogany door, on which was written "Ange and Luce."

"Oh well, here goes!" I told myself, and made use of a massive doorknocker in the shape of a lion's head. The response was instant. On the threshold stood a figure straight out of a 1970s fashion history book. Bright pink hair was cut short at the sides leaving a tall brush on top. A long tee shirt emblazoned with a circle of star signs led the eye down to opaque black tights and pink trainers. Above them all shone a face that should have matched the rest but didn't. This one was lined, wrinkled and beyond question ageing, even though covered by the thickest make-up I had ever seen. Mascara and eye-liner lay densely black around round, green eyes and rouge left circles of blush on skin encrusted with pale powder.

We stared at each other, this face and I, each as surprised as the other. And behind them, hovering uncertainly, stood a young male figure with one towel tied around his waist while another briskly rubbed a mop of damp blonde curls. A corner of the towel was lifted so he could see me and once again I found myself staring, only this time the eyes staring back at me showed horror and disbelief.

"Hello Neil," I said.

# CHAPTER TWENTY

The pink-haired vision opened the door widely, looked from a seemingly paralyzed Neil to myself and back, and said "You'd better come in." And as Neil showed every signs of trying for an immediate escape, she put a hand on his arm and smiled encouragingly.

Into this melee a third figure erupted out of nowhere, glared at me and said "I don't know who you are, but now you've seen him I expect we'll have to kill you. Would you like us to kill her, darlingest?"

Darlingest had the grace to smile. Instead he gently removed Pink Hair's hand from his arm and vanished towards an inner door. The newcomer shrugged and led the way to an enormous room with a bare but expensively laid wooden floor bright with scattered rugs and fitted comfortably with a few soft armchairs and deep floor cushions. She was as similar, yet as unlike as it was possible to be from her companion – rounded everywhere, yet still managing to mould her ample figure into generous curves. Her face, too, was round but totally innocent of cosmetics of any kind, leaving the sagging muscles and drooping skin to tell their own tale. She was every bit as old as the other.

"Excuse us," she said, pointing to the chairs and floor cushions. "We've not been very polite, have we? I am Luce and this," pointing to the sylphlike lady who was busy handing clothes through a half-open door to the hand stretched forth to receive them. "This is Ange. Proper name Angela. How did you know poor Neil was here?"

"Thank you," I murmured, slowly recovering from so many shocks at once, "I'm assuming your names are short for Angela and Lucy. Mine is Gemma Croft. We've all been worried about Neil, but that isn't why I've called. Nobody knew where he was and I think this is probably the last place I would thought of looking for him."

The two ladies, now together again and seated on adjacent cushions with their legs crossed before them wore an air of smug satisfaction.

"We know who you are and all about you, but we were right, weren't we Luce? This is the last place anyone would look. We thought he was so safe here. But if you didn't come looking for him, why did you come, then?"

I regarded them thoughtfully. They were raising new questions in my mind with every word they spoke. "If you know all about me, then you must know about the feathers and the press and you won't be surprised at my calling on all the residents here to warn them about photographers. They're all over the place and haunting the gardens and the gate. But first of all, before we say anything else, I think I need to know why Neil's in hiding. What is he escaping from?"

Ange and Luce looked at each other. Then they looked at the door, behind which their chief guest was probably dressing himself in more appropriate garments. For a brief moment I wondered whether they would be appropriate for myself, his hostesses or the outside world. I needn't have worried. Within seconds, it seemed, Neil had appeared soberly dressed in a dark navy suit with a crisp white shirt that had obviously been newly ironed.

"What shall we tell her, Light of Our Lives?"

The light of their lives was not brightly shining. He looked diminished. In point of fact he was terrified. "Are you going to take me back?" he asked. "Do I have to go?"

I sighed and stood up. "You're going to have to go back some time, you know, and the longer you leave it the more it's going to hurt – everyone, not just yourself What you tell them is your business, but you owe it to Sarah, if not to your employers, to come clean. You know perfectly well that Sarah adores you. Are you really going to leave her alone with everything?"

"She isn't alone, is she?" he mumbled. "She's got you, for a start, and all her family. I haven't got anyone."

Ange and Luce both cried out in anguish. "You've got us," they exclaimed together. Then Ange turned to me, anxious to explain. "He's upset about the feathers. He hates them. He thinks they're weird, spooky."

I nodded. "Well yes, they're certainly weird, but not really so spooky because they don't physically hurt anyone, they're just beautiful things that we can't explain. And if Sarah isn't spooked, I can't think why we should be. They come to her, not us."

"Yes, but..."

I bit my lip. There is no-one less likely to be comforted than a person who says "Yes, but..."

"Yes, but, "Neil began again, "it isn't just the feathers. It's – oh – everything."

To my dismay, Neil was beginning to cry. "Okay," I said, "There's so much you need to say, perhaps I should take you back to work via the coffee bar and we can sit in a nice neutral place while you explain. How about it? You can call at home first or go straight to work, whichever you choose, but please do something positive because otherwise we are all in a jam."

Luce wrinkled her chubby nose. "Don't you do anything you don't want, Neil Precious," she told him. "We should have killed her after all."

Neil frowned. "Wouldn't have helped," he said, "she's a reporter."

"Even better. She wouldn't be able to report, would she?"

I called the meeting to order. "Neil is right," I told her. "Nothing to be gained there. Everyone in this place knows where I am and what I'm doing, so can we be sensible please? Neil? Are you coming with me or not? I promise you, the sooner the better or it will all get worse. Honestly."

Neil hesitated. "I don't want to be recognised."

I regarded him from head to toe and decided that his one really identifiable feature would be his hair, shining now in newly brushed golden curls I pointed to it. "That is a bit of a give-away, I agree. Has anyone got a cap? Any kind of cap will do as long as it covers this up. Can't do much about his face though, unless someone has a cycling helmet with a mask."

Ange disappeared and returned almost at once, grinning with triumph. She held out a large man's flat cap of the kind one associated years ago with working men from Northern industrial towns. In my mind's eye was the stream of them coming through the factory gates going home for dinner, or off to the match for an afternoon of triumph or dismay.

I was delighted. "The very thing," I told them. Can we borrow this? And is there a nice everyday sort of anorak for the rest of him. A hood would be excellent."

"Neil can keep the hat," Ange replied, ruffling his curls before placing the cap squarely on top. She dropped a kiss on his shoulder. "Bring it back next time you need to escape. But all our anoraks are a bit vivid I'm afraid. Coats of many colours in fact, and the hoods would be more noticeable than anything."

Neil briefly kissed her cheek, sighed and picked up his jacket from the back of a chair. Thanks Ange. Just don't show me any mirrors."

I smiled. "Are we right, then? Okay, let's go. Goodbye, you two, and thanks for everything. I'll be in touch to let you know what's happening."

Together we walked to the door. I offered my hand to both. "Thank you for looking after him."I smiled, and stepped through to the landing. "Nice place you've got here," I added, glancing back. "When this is all over I could come for coffee or something one day."

The door closed before they had time to reply. "Right Mr Chalmers, which is it to be? Home first or coffee bar first? It's all the same to me."

Neil shook his head. "Not home," he said. "Not yet. I'll ring her from somewhere."

Together we went down the stairs to the door leading to the residents' car park and, no doubt due to the police presence, found it miraculously empty of cameras, notebooks and thrusting microphones. Maybe, I thought, they had found something more interesting to write about. Perhaps we had become Old News.

Perhaps.

Once inside the car I dialled Jack's number. He picked up at once. I told him Neil had been found, was with me and we were now on the way to a cafe in Woolcot where we could have a good long talk, and that his, Jack's, presence at the end of an hour would be greatly welcomed as the explanation promised to be very complicated. He agreed to meet us both and named a place where we would be left in peace. "See you in about an hour then," he said. "And good luck."

I sent a text to my grandmother, saying that Neil was with me and not to worry as Jack knew where we would be. I then dialled Sarah's number but was requested to leave a message. I handed the phone to Neil, who spoke very quietly but was heard to say he was with me, was about to meet Jack for coffee somewhere and would be home later with full explanation. He sent his love. Finally I added my own brief message saying Neil was safe and sound so she could stop worrying. Then I switched on the ignition and drove out of the car park towards the gate which was, as expected, manned by cameras and reporters ready and anxious to pounce. So much for my "old news" theory.

I told Neil to duck, hide his face, blow his nose, anything to hide a countenance so utterly recognisable to the press. I drove through at speed, with closed windows, heading towards Woolcot Raegis. A silver saloon appeared from nowhere and kept me company. Friend or foe, it was hard to tell. I kept a steady pace, keeping an eye on the saloon behind us.

"I don't like the look of that car" I said. Neil looked through his own rear mirror and said he thought it looked fairly harmless. This was, after all, a busy road. Not entirely convinced, with a twitchy feeling I found hard to explain, I decided to make a quick detour down a side street, taking a few left and right turns. The saloon continued to keep pace.

I arose to the sudden challenge. "No, we're being followed. I shall lose him," and found myself enjoying the game. "Hold on tight, Neil, we're going to have some fun."

I weaved and did U turns and investigated lanes and suburban streets I had never known existed until we re-emerged carefully onto the main road. There were no signs of a silver saloon, yet I hardly dared hope we had lost such a faithful tail.

The main road that we eventually joined went through a short stretch of trees and high bushes, with a few pull-in places. We were just about to approach one of them when the silver saloon reappeared, passed us and pulled in ahead, leaving me with no choice but to swing out to bypass it. The saloon stopped and the door opened. A middle-aged man in a leather jacket and chinos emerged and stood leanng again the driver's door. A folded newspaper was tucked under one arm. I tried again to pass him, but short of running him down there was no option but to pull up. I used the electronic switch to wind down my own window a fraction, but told Neil to keep his firmly locked. "Excuse me," I said politely, "Could you please move your car so we can get through."

The man carefully placed his folded his newspaper in a back pocket and approached the car, putting his fingers to the glass in an attempt to open it further. Then he bent his face to look at me. His was red with a spongey nose. "Oh, I don't think so." he said.

As suddenly as I could manage it, I reversed the car, leaving him nursing sore fingers. Turning the steering wheel I mounted the pavement to bypass him, but found my way blocked again, this time by a younger man in jeans and a black pullover, who stood with arms folded and feet straddled. Short of running him down too there was no room for manoeuvre, so I reversed again and this time hauled the steering wheel to the right, mounting the pavement on the other side. Once again my car was blocked. Another younger man stood there, grinning maliciously. He was armed. A small handgun was pointed directly at my head.

"Which would you like best?" he asked, "I can shoot your tyres out or shoot your eyes out."

"How about if I simply run over you?" I replied. "Would you prefer a front or back approach? I'm happy with either."

The older man with the red face man came back to the window. He nodded, and held out his hand for the gun. His henchmen stood back a little, to watch him use the butt to smash the glass, shards of which fell on my trousers and onto my right hand. It began to bleed. I could feel Neil beside me shaking with terror and realised I would receive no help from him.

"Stop being cheeky and listen," the older man told me. "As for you, bird-brain," he continued, pointing his gun at Neil, "get out of the car." With a mocked attempt at politeness he waved his free hand towards the large saloon, "Then you can get into mine and come with me so we can have a little chat."

I was now filled to the top of my head with a cold and bitter fury. It was as if the subdued autumn-rinsed hairs on my head had suddenly burst into life and into their true, natural fiery red. "Not without me he isn't" I said. "You touch him or me and you'll be plastered all over the national papers. There was a CCTV trained on the gate back there while you were wilfully damaging my car."

"So? I am merely issuing a polite invitation, and ooooops, sorry, my hand must have slipped"

"With a gun?"

"What gun?" The man did some sleight of hand and the gun disappeared. "So now get out, both of you. But only if you," he bowed to me, "insist upon coming along for the ride." He signed to his cohorts, said "Get them" and removed himself to a safer distance.

What seemed like many minutes but was probably only seconds later, Neil and I were none too gently hauled from my car to theirs and driven away, leaving Black Sweater to throw several lighted matches at my tyres and the bonnet until it burst into flames. I did not mourn the loss of my car but certainly mourned the loss of my handbag within which had lain my purse, driving licence and press card. Happily I had my smartphone in my pocket but had little hope of being allowed to keep it. That was, however, the least of my worries. I had no idea at all where they were taking us or what they had had in mind. Surely no feather storms, however spooky, could inspire such a drastic action as kidnapping two of the main players. More to the point I could expect no brilliant ideas to come from Neil, who now seemed paralyzed from shock. This, I thought, would be up to me, and the thought was not a happy one.

# CHAPTER TWENTY ONE

We arrived at a row of 1930s semi-detached houses, each one looking lived-in and more or less the same as its neighbour, apart from the occasional house that sported extra dormer windows or the addition of glassed-in porches and new, expensive front doors. Each had a separate garage to one side and one or two kept an extra overflow car in the drive. Not one of them looked the least bit sinister.

Neil and I were hauled again, this time out of the back seat and with the assistance of a flourished gun. Together we were escorted up the drive of the sort of house that might be inextinguishable to a casual visitor. One would need, I thought, a house number in order to be sure of the right place. The house we entered had Number 32 scrolled above the door frame and its entrance hall was probably identical to that of its next door neighbour – a small vestibule leading to a straight hall with stairs to one side leading directly to what I guessed would be a bathroom. The rather narrow hall ended at what was obviously the kitchen, as cabinets and a fridge-freezer took up the whole of the only visible wall. To the left would surely be a living room, or even a long living/dining room with, possibly a window at each end. We were not, however. allowed to peek into this holy of holies since we were being ushered up the stairs to a small room at the back, overlooking a long narrow garden with a lawn and a few optimistic border plants fighting for sunlight.

Once inside I had just time to notice the bars on the window, denoting a nursery or some kind of safe room. I guessed a nursery. This was confirmed by a half-opened door hiding the smallest toilet facilities it would be possible to fit into a cardboard box, plus a small child's bed in one corner and a cupboard or two dispersed around what little space was left. Apart from the bed there was a single child-sized chair. At any other time I would have smiled at the idea of Neil and myself squabbling over who had the bed and who would be left with a chair too small for either of us. I was, however, too busy and too worried to smile.

I was thinking. I was also studying our captors. If anything the two younger ones looked even younger in this setting. The older man seated himself on the bed and addressed us.

"Right now, you two, listen up. We haven't brought you here for nothing, and to be honest we only wanted one of you, but since you..." nodding at me, "...since you were stupid enough to insist on coming, we are having to deal with you both. And I don't like it."

"In that case," I replied coldly, "why not just let us go and start again? If you don't want me I'm quite happy to go away and forget you ever happened. Oh and by the way, I should warn you that my friend here has a black belt in Judo and I have one in Tai Kwon Do,"

The man looked as sceptical as he obviously felt. And since I was lying he was quite right. For all I knew Neil might well have a Judo black belt, but apart from knowing the basics I had no personal experience of martial arts of any kind. What was certainly true was that I had no intention of parting with Neil. I had gone to find him, had found him and was not about to lose him again.

"Yeah, yeah! And plaster us all over the national papers and television. Even if Mr Tomkins here wasn't newsworthy, you certainly are."

The man in the black sweater sniffed. "I told you we should have killed her but you wouldn't listen."

"Well, well, I expect we'll have to when we've finished interrogating the blonde beauty. No point in rushing things."

I turned to Neil. "He called you Mr Tomkins? Why the Tomkins? And do you realise this is the third time in the past hour that someone has promised to kill us. We're not having a very good day are we?"

The man in charge answered for him. "No, you're not, young lady." If anyone else calls me 'young lady,' I thought, my jaw beginning to thrust itself forward in fighting mode, I shall get really *really* mad. "And he's Mr Tomkins because that's who he is - Mr Tomkins. Not a good stage name, though is it, *Mr Tomkins*?"

"I've heard worse," I said, "How about Englebert? Or Shnozzle?"

"Shut up."

"I'm afraid I don't know your name," I continued. "I don't like calling you 'Old Man' but that's all we're left with at present."

"I said shut up and I meant shut up, so be quiet and *hold your tongue.* Or I shall be tempted to cut it out."

I sighed. "Oh well, 'Old Man' it is then."

He flicked his fingers at the young man with the gun, who came forward holding the butt end of it. As he did so I raised my foot and kicked him where I knew it would hurt the most. He hit my knee sharply at the same moment. We both doubled up. I fell against Neil, who held me up to stand on one leg against his arm. For the first time he appeared to be awake and angry. The older man looked disgusted.

"Can't you do one thing properly?" he exclaimed, leaving the bed and standing over his anguished gunman, "For God's sake tie them up, will you?"

The third man, looking extremely nervous, produced rope from his jacket pocket and pushed me backwards onto the newly vacated bed, trying to take off my shoes ready to tie my feet together. The faintest whisper in my left ear showed me that Neil was now fully awake and fully alive. "Let him" he breathed". I did so, biting my lips and biding my time as patiently as possible. My left wrist was tied to Neil's right wrist, making us conjoined twins, while his minion tied our own ankles to each other.

The Old man regarded us with a smug, satisfied smile. I longed to wipe it from his face and promised myself a pleasure to come.

"Now I'm going to leave you to think about your options. They're not good. We'll be back when it suits us. Meanwhile I have negotiations to finalise with your bossman so I shall have to take your mobiles. You are not trustworthy. And by the way, this room is bugged, so have a nice day." With that, he and his cohorts, one bent almost double and off-handedly supported by his unwilling colleague, moved towards the door.

I stopped him, hiding my fury behind what I hoped was a practical question couched in a politely questioning manner. "Terribly sorry," I said, "but I'm going to need the bathroom"

If a man could be rightly described as breathing fire and brimstone, it was Old Man himself. He glared. "Why in God's name didn't you say so before?"

"Fright," I lied. "It comes on when you're frightened. Everybody knows that."

"Well that's too bad. Your boyfriend here will have to carry you. A treat for him.

I gave a small gasp and pointed to Neil's feet which were now tied as tightly as mine. "Sorry again, but how is he going to carry me with his feet tied?"

"You can both crawl. Serve you right."

"But I haven't done anything to deserve this, and I'm afraid I can't answer for your furniture if I don't get to that bathroom in time – like now."

They all regarded me. I don't think any of them believed me, but they had no way of proving the lie. Old Man approached me, watching my feet carefully. He was obviously beginning to take my Tai Kwon Do threat seriously. He motioned the undamaged young man over to his side and told him to hold my right foot while he untied the left. Then he did the same for Neil, leaving his right ankle tied to my left.

"That's the best your getting so enjoy it. I'm sure your boyfriend will. That's if he wouldn't prefer one of these," he added nodding his head at the two younger men, "even though you've rather damaged one of them. But that's your problem, not ours. Now we really are going, so have fun." With that and a parting, malicious and slightly salacious grin, all three of them finally vanished through the door, locking it behind them and leaving us in peace to converse as we wished. We did wish. I was full of questions and plans and for once Neil looked as though he couldn't wait to answer them.

# CHAPTER TWENTY TWO

Any ideas?" I asked Neil, "apart from finding out whether we are bugged or not. They're not very efficient are they, so maybe it was an empty threat thinking we wouldn't know either way."

To my astonishment Neil gave me a broad smile and winked. "Don't worry about it," he said,

"Well, that's easy to say, but maybe you can tell me just *how* not to worry about it."

"Okay. I work for an electronics firm. I hate my job but I love their gadgets and I have quite a collection. Part of my job is showing my wealthy clients what's available. A lot of them are private eyes or work in some government departments. The ones that need the stealthy stuff. Now, put your free hand in my right pocket and empty it."

I did so. "A few tissues, a biro and a small bottle of medication and a few bits of crumpled paper. Oh, and an empty notebook. Well? Now what?"

With his left hand Neil reached over and picked up the biro. It was the fancy sort, silver-white in colour with the usual pointed , lidded top and clasp for hanging tightly to a top pocket. It was the kind which is for sale in any stationer's. This time Neil did something to the clasp and a sharp knife, about five inches long immediately sprang from the writing end.    He used the knife for cutting through the ropes around our wrists and ankles.

"One job done. Now we can have a bug hunt in peace."

"I think I'd like to kiss you," I told him.

"My pleasure, only maybe when we've got a bit more time."

For a few seconds I regarded him with fresh eyes. Then we got to work, searching under everything, over everything and along everything. All this time he was carrying his biro. Eventually I asked him why.

"It'll squeak if we find anything."

There were no squeaks, so Neil picked up the small bottle, obviously for a prescribed medication with a chemist's label and screw top. He handed it to me and I shook it. It rattled obligingly. Then I raised my eyebrows. "Ok Clever-dick? Now what?"

Neil said nothing but twisted the lid of the bottle. It appeared as normal as it could be. Then he twisted it a little more and spoke into it."

"Hi, this is Neil. Gemma and I have been kidnapped. I'll pass you over," and he handed me the bottle.

"If Jack is there, or if he can receive this, please tell him we are being held in a top floor nursery with bars on the window. The house is No 32 but I don't know the name of the road. It's through Woolcot Raegis and out the other side but not far because there's a kind of fairly upmarket housing estate. We are in a 1930's type semi detached which is like all the others except that this one has a dormer window and the front door is painted blue. I don't know who it belongs to but it is definitely occupied and fully furnished. I'm afraid I don't know the names of our captors but it's Neil they want, not me, so I don't think it's about the feathers. I'm just about to find out a bit more, but would appreciate urgent rescue and I don't know when they're coming back. Thanks everybody. We're using Neil's little phone gadget. God bless electronics. If you ring us back it will be in one of our pockets. Bye, hope to see you soon. The sooner the better. Gemma"

I gave Neil his medicine bottle back and looked hard at him. "There's more, isn't there? Please tell me, it might be important."

"Not with me, no, but I rather think this phone has a trace on it. Also it is on 'vibrate' so if you put it somewhere out of sight it won't be heard.""

"Let's ask." I held out my hand for the medicine bottle and spoke into it again. "Are you still there Jack? If so, can you trace our position from this phone call? Could be important. Thanks."

"Right," I began again. "Thank you Neil but there's lots I want to know."

"Go ahead. We seem to have plenty of time."

"To start with, who exactly are Ange and Luce and why were you hiding out in their flat?"

Neil grinned. He seemed to have recovered his *sang froid* remarkably swiftly. "They used to be a three girl singing band in the late 50s, early 60's. Called themselves The Starlights. You know the sort of thing – bouffant hair, back-combed like beehives. Short skirts up to, well as far up as anyone could go in the 60s. They were good too. They made a lot of records and most of them got into the top ten. Twice they were at Number One. So plenty of money."

"What happened to the third one? You said three."

"Yes. Kate. They were Angela, Lucy and Kate but Kate died some years ago and they lost heart so just gave up. They liked the look of this place a year or so ago, as soon as it was converted, as a matter of fact, and bought it. They just wanted to be left alone after years of being chased by the press and the screaming public. Being gay wasn't actually good news then, not like it is now. Anyway after the Beatles came in they never quite made it again. They were out of style. They did change their image , though, which netted them some more hits, but never like it was before. A pity. They were good in their own way."

"What about your hiding there? You must have known them quite well."

"We met in the entrance hall one day. They were friendly and I liked the look of them. They could see I was a bit miserable that day so they invited me up for coffee ad the rest, as they say, is history."

"Miserable? Are you still miserable?"

"Grimly. Or let's just say I'm desperate."

I regarded him quietly for a few minutes, to see if he would give some sort of explanation, then looked down at the medicine bottle I still held in my lap. "Desperate sounds – desperate. What's up?"

I hoped he would unburden his distressed self as quickly as possible from whatever was worrying him because I was extremely worried myself and felt our captors would not leave us alone for long. With a final sigh and a shrug, he said: "I hate my job, I'm spooked by the feathers, I'm upset by Sarah's illness and I'm being pursued by someone who has been blackmailing me for months. Get out of that one if you can."

What had begun as anxiety about my grandmother and Sarah, who had been left alone with Peter for the past hour and wouldn't yet be missing me had now turned itself into fear and anxiety for Neil and a deep, nagging fear for my own skin. I was torn between anger at myself for insisting on walking into this trap and the depressing realisation that I couldn't, in fact, have done anything else. Nor could I abandon Neil now. All that was left to us was to acquire as much information as we could and use whatever wits we possessed between us to escape from the net into which we had inadvertently dropped ourselves. I decided to lighten the tone a trifle, for my own sake as well as Neil's.

"The cap didn't disguise you very well, did it? We should have got you a spaceman outfit. Or even a crash helmet with a visor. Sorry, Neil, but having a face like yours is no help, is it? What is he or she blackmailing you for? What did you do – or perhaps what are you still doing? Is it drugs or betting or something worse?"

Neil sighed again. So I told him to please let me have it, straight and to the point – and briefly, please – because I needed to know what we were dealing with. "Is it our Old Man who's doing it? The one with the two inefficient boy friends?"

"Yep, but only because he thinks he can tap into the Kent cash. Unfortunately," he added, "someone seems to think my job is more important than it is. If only they knew, my rank is more or less lowest of the low. Nice job description, not much cash."

"So come on then? What have you been doing?"

Once begun, the story came tumbling out almost too fast for me take in and digest, but because the situation was not healthy I gave him all my attention. It seemed that at a fairly young age, when he was even more beautiful than he was now, and before he met Sarah, he answered an advert for male models. Some of it was legitimate, posing for men's clothing and outerwear, with the occasional plunge into lower and considerably more intimate garments, but then he was asked to make some commercial films. "Commercial as in under the counter" he explained. He knew, of course, what the films were likely to be, but at that age everything was fun and an adventure, so he agreed. And that was where his plan had, - quote - "come unstuck". The films were, of course, pornographic which was no surprise. The surprise lay in the dismal truth that he was unable to fulfil his part of the story. "They assumed, from having a face like mine, that I'd be gay or anyway a sexy guy. They tried me with women but that didn't work either. "You see..." he hesitated, then nodded and continued, looking down at his hands. "I'm neither. Not very sexy at all at the best of times. In front of a camera it turned out to be impossible. People like me do exist, you know. Asexual. Not enough testosterone." He gave a small gasping laugh, "they were reduced to using my face and then using a stunt man. A ***stunt man !*** Can you imagine? Anyway, they let me go, but never let me forget it. The tormenting didn't start straight away, not until I'd met Sarah and married her and got taken on by the family firm. What a gift! They obviously thought it was their birthday or something. And now I'm stuck because I haven't got any more money and Sarah and my bosses haven't a clue about any of it. So I imagine they're aiming to hold me for ransom or something. I'm really sorry, Gemma. I've dragged you into my mess."

"Think nothing of it!" I murmured, feeling none too pleased on my own behalf but anxious for him and his predicament. "So this has nothing to do with feathers?"

"Nope! Except, I suppose as an added incentive for me to find the cash."

I thought for a minute, then asked him why he hated his job so much. "Being nice and charming to wealthy smart-arses and keeping them sweet so they carry on ordering our pricey electronic must-haves. I hate the smart-arses but like the gadgets, and I only got the job because I'd been in prison for carrying drugs, so Sarah's dad took pity on me, or rather, took pity on Sarah, shackled to a jailbird. I came out to a brand new job and a brand new flat and a wife who seemed to adore me despite everything. Who could argue with that?"

"Okay. Granted. But what would you really like to do. I mean really, really?"

"Go back to modelling, only proper modelling this time. Something along those lines. Something with gadgets would be nice, like photography."

"Can you dance?" I asked suddenly. "Even dance and sing?"

"Yes. Both. I'm quite good actually."

"How about a job on a cruise liner as entertainment crew?"

For the first time, Neil smiled. "A pipe dream, but a pretty good one, if I wasn't married to an invalid."

I smiled back. He had certainly come to life again. I glanced at my watch. "How long have we been here? A good hour, wouldn't you say? By now Jack will start to wonder where we are, that's if he doesn't get my message. If he does he should be on our tail by this time. Shall I give him another ring?"

Without waiting for Neil's answer I picked up the medicine bottle, pointed the lid in the right direction and spoke into it. "Please will you get an urgent message to Jack. This is Gemma. Neil and I are still alone here, but

154

not for much longer unless they intend to starve us out. Please where are you?"

The reply came at once. "Gemma, Jack here. We're locating the road. Please leave that phone on so we can track it."

For the first time I actually laughed. "Jack you are wonderful. See you soon."

"One question? Where's your Grandmother? Can't trace either her or Sarah and they have Peter."

The laugh died within seconds. "I don't know. Please hurry."

Neil leaned towards the phone and gave the bottle cap one more tiny twist. "It's in vibrate. So won't give us away if it rings."

At that moment there were footsteps on the stairs and the key turned in the lock. "Well my little lovebirds, I hope you're ready to talk sense."

If I had been worried and fearful before, I was now trebly so. We had cut the rope tying us together and the Old Man was about to find out.

"Quite ready" I said, and quietly held Neil's hand. He gave mine a little squeeze. At least, I thought, I was no longer in this alone.

# CHAPTER TWENTY THREE

The light from the window had been growing dimmer and had reached the stage when very soon it would vanish altogether, except for a street lamp a few doors away. I felt the tiny pressure Neil's foot against mine and glanced down as briefly and as unobtrusively as I could. By some sleight of hand he had arranged the rope around our ankles in such a way that at first glance one would suppose them to be tied. I hoped my furtive glance hadn't attracted the notice of our host, but he was in the process of taking his gun out of his pocket and was not looking at me. I held my medicine bottle in my hand, hoping he would speak loudly enough to be heard by Jack. This our host did notice because he regarded it frowningly and held out his hand for it. I breathed a quick sigh.

"As you see," he said, bowing his head politely in my direction, "I have come prepared, so now we can get down to business."

"Where are your henchmen?" I asked, "Or should I say side-kicks? Personally I think they've been watching too many American films."

Old Man frowned. "I've told you before, Miss whatever your name is, to shut up and behave yourself. I have no wish to mark your pretty face, but I do have another line of defence, or should I say '*offence*'" He reached into the other pocket and brought out a vicious-looking knife. "And don't think I'm too soft to use it. This charming exterior hides a heart of stone. As for my henchmen, they are on their way and will be joining us shortly. We have decided to move you to a new abode as we consider this one too easily identifiable." He glanced down at the medicine bottle. "Drugs, I presume?"

"Certainly not. You are more than welcome to open the bottle and have a look."

"Ah, but not before finding out a bit more about them. I wasn't born yesterday."

"Of course not. Not even the day before yesterday. If you're any good with childproof lids you will find the bottle contains a herbal version of paracetamol, and I was about to take two when you so inconsiderately arrived to interrupt me."

"You open it," he frowned. "I don't trust you. If it blows up in your face all well and good. At least it won't be my face."

"This is true." I reached with my free hand, the other being supposedly tied to Neil's, and leaned sideways to offer the bottle for his help opening the small round lid. He took his time, looking at me with concern and sympathy. "You don't look well, Gemma. I think you should take them now as soon as you can. We don't want to you keeling over."

"Just get on with it, will you." The Old Man waved at us impatiently. "We have things to do."

With the heel of his hand Neil pushed down hard on the screw cap and twisted it off, but not before he had murmured into it, as if he were murmuring to me. "I hope they don't take long to move us. I'm getting tired of this bed. Pity the poor child who has to sleep in it. It's rock hard, and with bars on the window too. What kind of life does the poor kid have? I just hope they feed him proper food."

"Him or her" I murmured back. I wanted to give Jack as much time to find us as possible, but a forceful movement of the knife towards our faces obliged Neil to take off the screw top and flourish it.

"Okay. Now give it back."

With his free left hand Neil held out the bottle. The Old Man hung the gun by its finger guard over his thumb and transferred the knife to the gun hand. I watched with interest. How was he going to investigate the tablets without compromising either or both of his own weapons? He couldn't, of course. I was just preparing my feet for some urgent action when the door opened again, to reveal only one of the henchmen. I was pleased to note that he was not the one I had previously kicked, and sincerely hoped his absence was due to the injury I had had so much pleasure in inflicting. Old Man turned to look at him, then tossed him the bottle. "Take one." he said. I hoped it would choke him, since he had just ruined my plan. The boy, for that is all he was, frowned but obeyed, pulling a face but swallowing the perfectly innocent tablet, before handing back the bottle.

"Doesn't taste too good, but harmless I'd have said. I haven't died or blown myself up or anything."

Old Man looked disgusted. He threw the bottle in my direction, the screw cap only loosely attached. I caught both, replaced the cap and twisted it to the 'speak' position. Not that I was to be given a chance for further speech as Old Man said "Well, having got that over with, we can now talk business, and make it snappy because we'll be off to pastures new very shortly."

"Please may we know your name?"

"No. You know too much already."

"In that case, since you are obviously going to kill me, it won't matter if I know your name will it?

Old Man regarded me through slitty eyes, then he shook his head. "You're expendable, that's true, and I certainly intend to kill you, but whether here or in the new place is entirely up to you. First, though, I need to talk to Loverboy here, and you've wasted enough of my time already. So ready to talk, Mr Tomkins?"

Mr Tomkins signified readiness.

"Excuse me," I interjected politely, "but do you still want me to call you Old Man or may we have a proper name to call you by?"

The slitty eyes became steely ones. "I've told you to shut up. One more word from you and you're killed here and now in front of Loverboy and f...k the mess."

I made a zipping motion to my lips and nodded.

"Right, Tomkins Chalmers or whatever you're choosing to call yourself, you will now phone your bossman and tell him if he doesn't hand over the £2mllion he already knows about, his golden haired executive will be spread all over the national papers and thereafter, with no money forthcoming, all over the floor. And don't think he can track you by your mobile because I shall be leaving it here, so he will find an empty nest," and with a small flourish he placed Neil's smartphone beside us on the bed. "Now dial."

With his one free hand, Neil dialled. I sat in silence, my fingers tightly holding his and not daring to move them in case the loosely arranged rope should fall away from our wrists to give us away. "Good morning," Neil's voice was beautifully controlled. "This is Neil, may I speak to Mr Kent senior please? It is rather urgent, so I would appreciate..." After only a few seconds' pause, he continued. "Good morning Mr Kent, I am afraid I am being held to ransom. Gemma is with me and they are threatening to kill us both if we don't come up with some money. I believe you have already heard from our captor, but the latest figure seems to be two million. He glanced at Old Man. "...And rising, I think."

Old Man grabbed the phone. "Certainly 'And rising', so the sooner you oblige the better for Golden Boy and his nosey, gabby girl friend here." You will immediately transfer the money into the account I gave you in my recent note. Are you hearing me, Mr Kent?"

Mr Kent was apparently hearing him well and clearly. We couldn't decipher his reply but it caused Old Man's lips to be firmly pressed together as he closed the connection and slipped the phone into his pocket. "Right, then off we go to pastures new. The new accommodation isn't quite as comfortable as this, I fear, my lovebirds, and if your boss decides you are not worth the money, it will certainly be your last accommodation. So stand up and go ahead of me please." He signalled with his head, first to me then to Neil. "Lades first," he said, bowing in the proper courtly manner with one leg extended and the other arm sweeping across his ample chest. I was tempted to comment on people who watch too many costume dramas and out-of-date gangster movies, but this time held my tongue. Not that I had any choice, since he motioned his henchman to come forward. The young man appeared nervous, but in one hand he carried a roll of parcel tape which he proceeded to rip to the right size. The remnant he placed firmly, and uncomfortably, over my mouth. Had I not been faced with not only a gun but with what seemed to be a very sharp knife, I would have freed my leg and raised it to give the already wary young man a kick to match his colleague's. He was, I decided, very young indeed, no more than 17, I would have guessed - a leggy boy with acne scars and jeans so low in the waist that they threatened to slip off his narrow, youthful hips.

Just at that very moment, we were jerked to a standing position and revealed at last as unshackled. The ropes fell from our wrists and ankles. I was expecting an instant, unpleasant reaction but to my surprise there wasn't one. For some reason, the boy chose to say nothing, but went through a mimed slashing motion with his knife, freeing us to lead the procession down the stairs to the front door. This time, for future reference, I noted the blue tinted wallpaper, the open door to a living room painted in the same shade of blue, with one corner revealing a dining table, immaculately kept and polished, and one picture visible on the opposite wall. It was an unremarkable seascape with monster waves and thrashing sails battling a high wind.

We passed, unnoticed, into a quiet empty residential road where car-filled driveways signalled owners home from work. Even the tricycles and doggies on wheels were stowed neatly, suggesting children indoors having their supper. Only one face at the window appeared interested – that of a small boy with a companion West Highland Terrier. The dog didn't bark but glanced at his small master who simply stared without curiosity at our progress to the waiting car. There would be no-one to say if we turned left or right into the road, but I grasped my medicine bottle firmly and gave a tiny sigh when it suddenly vibrated in my hand. If Neil were right, it was alive and, I hoped, tracking us to our unknown destination. I dare not answer it. Should we lose it we would be very hard to find. And it would take too long. I had no idea how much grace we had, .

For the first time I was truly frightened. More than frightened, I was horrified for ourselves, for Sarah and my grandmother who might be anywhere, and for little Peter who was in the same real danger of kidnapping as we were.

I turned to Neil and found there were tears on his cheeks. "I'm so sorry, Gemma, this is all my fault. I'm so sorry."

I smiled, my own tears near the surface but not to be seen. They could come later, but not now – very definitely not now.

The medicine bottle in my pocket vibrated slightly but I could do little about it

"Jack," I whispered, "Where are you?"

Where indeed?

# CHAPTER TWENTY FOUR

The incipient tears resolutely blinked away, I tried to keep track of the route our captors were taking. It was only on glancing at me through his rearview mirror that Old Man was obviously struck with the same thought. He pulled over to the kerb, groped in his glove compartment and brought out the roll of parcel tape which he proceeded to tear into strips. He gave a flick of his head to the younger man, whom I had personally labelled Mickey Mouse, and electronically opened my rear window. He put both hands through the open window and I bit them. He swore, then slapped me very hard across the face. In silence he tore one of the parcel tape strips and placed it firmly across my mouth. Then he tried to place another over my eyes, but I shook my head so violently that he slapped me again, harder this time and reached to my face.

His hands were perilously close so I head-butted them. Neil, who was being mouth-taped, by Micky, released both his hands, grabbed both heads and pulled as much hair as he could reach. We were instantly rewarded. Old Man and Mickey let out simultaneous yells of pain, unclutched our fingers and withdrew their heads, to return at once with thick scarves which they tied, none too gently, over our eyes.

Rewarding and satisfactory this might be, but I was mortally afraid one of us would be shot or knifed as we sat in the back of the saloon. Reason suggested that it would be Old Man's car sporting the hard-to-remove blood stains and hoped he would delay his retaliation until we had reached a safer spot. Retaliation, however, was very much on his mind. With the rest of the sticky strips, he finally taped our wrists – not to one another this time but individually, and as tightly as he could and with deliberately vicious tugs. With a nod of satisfaction, he climbed back into the driver's seat, closed our rear windows and drove us all away.

I nudged Neil. Through a band of parcel tape and with closed lips, I did the best I could to whisper "Thanks. Brilliant move." Neil nodded. He had heard me. Reassured, I tried again. "How's your sense of direction?"

This time he frowned, so I pointed first at North, then over my shoulder, left and right. He continued frowning and looking puzzled, then I realised the stupidity of gesturing towards someone who couldn't see me. I whispered again. "Where's North?"

I was conscious that eyes would be upon us both, so turned my previous gestures into a sign of the cross. Under its cover, Neil whispered. "Ten o'clock"

Relieved, I understood. North was to our left and we were heading North East. From that point on, I counted the turns and tried to keep track of our route. We had been driving in a straight line for some minutes, which rather suggested a motorway, but the car turned suddenly down an incline to our left and paused at what was probably a roundabout.

It was at that moment that things started to happen which were hard to decipher, except that somewhere very near at hand a police siren was blaring. Old Man cursed and Mickey shouted "Look out." There was a bump, a scraping noise and sounds of hectic activity. My car door was opened suddenly and hands pulled me gently from my seat. On the other side, someone was doing the same for Neil. The scarves over our eyes were untied and I was looking at the extremely anxious face of the person I had most wanted to see in the whole world – my rescuer. A pair of scissors released my wrists and fingers touched my face, investigating what I assumed was the redness and bruising from the head slapping. Jack spoke quietly to the man standing next to him. "You can add assault to the kidnapping charges."

I found myself leaning against him. My legs were unsure and wobbly. He picked me up and placed me carefully on the grass bank beside the road, wrapping me in foil to stop the shivering.

"Sit still," he said, "I'll be back for you in 30 seconds, then we'll take you home"

Home? Was there ever a sweeter word?

I sat, wrapped in my foil cloak but still shivering, and watched with unresponsive eyes the headlights of vans, the twisting siren lights on the marked police cars and the ambulances, wondering in the vaguest way what was happening to everyone. Not that I cared much, except to chuckle a little at the stupidity of life – my life especially. The chuckle grew into a laugh and, before I fully realised it, into hefty, uncontrollable sobs that wracked my whole body. I put my head on my knees and howled into them. Then Jack found me and wrapped me firmly in his arms, lifting me onto my feet and holding me against him until I was weeping onto his shoulder. He rocked me gently and in silence until the tears had left me breathless and exhausted.

"Gemma, Gemma" he murmured. "I love you so much. I didn't realise how much until I thought I'd lost you." He picked me up bodily and carried me to his car, where he strapped me into the passenger seat and kissed the only part of me he could see. I felt the pressure on the top of my head and looked up. When he went to close my door I began to shake again, begging him not to leave me. "Please," I said, catching his hand. "Please don't leave me alone."

Thee was a small chuckle, a kind of gasping laugh, then a whispered; "Never again, Gemma Croft. Never. Just let me get into my car or you won't get home in time for supper," and with that I released his hand and let him walk around the car until he was in the driving seat, his left arm firmly around the very wet and bedraggled person I had become. I leaned back, beyond fear, knowing only that Jack loved me, that the nightmare of the past few hours was over. Relief and exhaustion overcame me. By the time we had arrived at Croft Court I was asleep.

I awoke to find myself being lowered carefully onto a sofa in a brightly lit room filled with flowers, which I only slowly recognised as Sarah's conservatory. Sarah sat watching me from her wheelchair, her eyes large and tear-filled. Beside her, in a comfortable armchair, sat my grandmother. She seemed as calm and restful as only she could. I was immensely glad she was there. In the background Neil sat alone. I was sorry for him and didn't intend him to be ignored. With one languid arm I beckoned him over and held his hand.

"Neil," I said, "Thank you for everything you did. I'm on your side."

Jack came to kneel beside me. "Explanations only when you're ready," he said firmly. "Sarah's carer will be coming back any minute. She's on her way and Mrs Simmons has been here all the time. She's making you a cup of tea. Are you hungry?"

I went to shake my head, then realised with some astonishment how long it had been since I had last eaten. Jack kissed my hand and released it, "I'll see to it," he said and left the room. He reappeared at once, giving me the thumb's up signal that says 'job done' to the world. He knelt beside me, holding my hand. Returning slowly to reality, I began to take in my surroundings and saw Mrs Carmichael's head appear round the door jamb. "Can we come in?" Jack said yes of course and rose to admit not only Evelyn herself but Ange and Luce and another rather noticeable lady whom I had never seen before. Even in my only-half-awake state I understood that had this lady ever entered my life I would certainly have known about it. She was stick thin, swathed in assorted but somehow harmonious drapery of bright colours, most of which clashed with its neighbour. Reds, orange, pinks of all shades and a sturdy mixture of bright yellows all fought each other around this straight, pillared person, topped by a head of bright silver hair and a pale, lined face whose slash of vivid red lipstick appeared like a wound. I smiled at her, feeling as though a rainbow had just entered not just the room but all of our lives.

Ange saw the smile and pushed the rainbow forward to be introduced. "Gemma, this is another of our neighbours, Eliza Redfield. She came to our aid yesterday, so we're grateful. Besides, she's fun."

The newcomer and I solemnly shook hands and regarded each other with curiosity, myself with dawning recognition. "But you're....."

"Afraid so,"

I had recognised a prestigious and world-renowned star of stage and screen from the Hollywood era some decades earlier. I beamed, and so did she. "I knew I knew you, but it's your voice that hit me. If you ever try going incognito, for heaven's sake don't speak."

By this time everyone was smiling and Neil had returned with a very appetising chicken sandwich with something spicy, crisp, fresh lettuce and small chunks of celery. Mrs Simmons followed him with a tray on which lay salt and pepper, a napkin, a knife and fork and a small bowl of vinaigrette. The smell, wafting before my only-too-ready nostrils, was like the first whiff of an ancient wine. I was instantly intoxicated.

I took a large bite, which everyone watched with intense interest, chewed for a second or two, swallowed and said "Right, now what's been happening here?"

"No, no, you first. We want to know *everything*." was the almost general reply, vetoed only by Jack who shook his head. My grandmother also smiled and shook her own head. "I think Gemma's story had better wait for Mr Kent and the police. They should be here soon. And perhaps it's better if Gemma only has to go through it once."

"Thank you," I told them, relieved for the time being of having to describe an indescribable experience with any sort of cogency. I had to work it out for myself before trying to relay it, least of all to the police and to the even more intimidating person of Jack's father.

Instead, I insisted on hearing about everyone else' adventures and was told that Mrs Carmichael had continued her apartment visits, winkling out our film star on the way and bringing her back to meet the others. Unfortunately when they returned to Sarah's flat, they found it, like the Marie Celeste, bewilderingly devoid of life. Peter and the ever attendant Mrs Simmons were missing from the kitchen and the back door was ajar. Without a second's hesitation everyone dived through it into the rear garden and the residents' car park. There they found Sarah in her wheelchair, Peter firmly on her lap, in the centre of a large group of people. These were all shouting at once, some of them shaking fists and others delightedly brandishing long, furry microphones. The noise and the seemingly non-stop flashing of cameras was, to privacy-loving Mrs Carmichael, not to be tolerated. Mrs Simmons was hovering near the wheelchair but unable to do anything except add her voice stridently to the uproar. That is" said Sarah, "until Eliza Redfield appeared, a bit like a firework before the bang."

At this point everyone in the room looked at Miss Redfield. Sarah laughed. "You should have seen the reporters change their tune," she said admiringly, "and you really should have seen our film star here. She just sailed in and took over. It was marvellous to behold."

I added my awe-filled thanks, then frowned. Someone was missing. "Wait a minute," I demanded, "Where's Peter now?"

I was assured that Peter had been collected by his mother, who was not pleased and obviously distrustful of the story she was being fed by this group of bizarre-looking residents. But Sarah was not to be deflected. She told how Eliza Redfield, who normally protected her anonymity with jealous care, sailed through forcibly with full rigging into the heat of the battle and faced them all, cameras, microphones, question-hurling reporters and family members indiscriminately. She had held up her hand and the noise stopped abruptly. The reporters had recognised her. Not for nothing had Miss Redfield commanded instant attention and life-long adoration from her public.

The scene had changed. The Kent family had been saved - but not excused, for they should not have been there. Why were they? What had led Sarah through the side door and into the certain bombardment of questions and flashing cameras? There had been no mention of feathers. Everyone was regarding Miss Redfield with admiration, even with awe.

"What happened then?" I asked, "Did the reporters vanish in puffs of smoke?"

It was Eliza Redfield who answered in the manner of one who is faintly surprised that anyone had felt the need to ask. "I told them to go, that I would talk to them later, and they went."

In the silence that followed my grandmother took over. "Now, if you don't mind, Gemma has had enough for the present. She needs rest, preferably bed, so I am taking her home and I'll finish the story myself. The police will be here very soon anyway and I think she should talk to them in peace and quiet. Meanwhile perhaps Neil will join us when he's ready."

Neil nodded, my grandmother held out her hand and I took it.

# CHAPTER TWENTY FIVE

The next few hours were spent in various interviews, first with the police and then with Mr Kent, senior, who had clearly been shaken by the myriad feathers rising from a supposedly empty box. Not that he was relaxing his suspicions of myself. These apparently were left, shaken but still obstinately present. However, he seemed more interested in Neil's part - none too kindly I thought - but at least I hoped to make a tiny dent in what appeared to be an automatic disapproval. Whether or not I succeeded in this I was in no position to judge. I merely made a private vow to engage Jack's support on Neil's behalf.

The police were another matter entirely. They didn't take much notice of Neil or his reasons for doing what he did. At least if they did they forbore to say so. I rather imagined they were keeping Neil's questioning to themselves, only asking me to comment from time to time on Neil's reactions. I did, however, learn that our Old Man was in reality a Mr Anthony J Creek, a small-time crook with big ideas. This did not surprise me. I felt quite capable of making a better job of kidnapping than he had done, a view the Inspector seemed to share.

"You were lucky" he said. "But then, a more efficient blackmailer would have chosen a better prospect than an electronics geek for a kidnapping spree. And he obviously didn't cotton on to the fact that, if anything, you are more ransom-worthy than Mr Chalmers. He simply didn't know what to do with you. You gummed up his works by just being there, and I hope your paper will appreciate it."

I doubted it, but said no more. Eventually I was left to my grandmother's ministrations and leaned back in one of her excellent chairs, feet on a footstool, eyes closed, sipping the glass of wine she had thrust into my unresisting hand. Not until I was securely reclined with my newly broached wine glass was I permitted to speak.

The warmth, the comfort of the chair and the smell and taste of Neil's sandwich all brought me back to a semblance of normality. I turned to my grandmother with raised eyebrows.

"Why was Sarah in the garden?"

"She'll have to explain that herself, but I personally think it was a sort of cabin fever. Probably other reasons but I haven't had time to find out yet."

I closed my eyes and had no way of telling how much time had passed before I heard the outer doorbell ring and voices in the hall. Almost at once our own doorbell gave its distinctive tinkle and my grandmother told whoever it was to come in. This time it was Neil, appearing subdued but not altogether displeased, quickly followed by an anxious-looking Jack.

"Come in," smiled my grandmother. "I've been hearing some very good things about you, Neil. Your quick thinking seems to have saved my grand-daughter's life."

Neil smiled back but shook his head. "Not so much quick thinking as my addiction to gadgets. It was Gemma's brains really, not mine, helped along by the toys."

I held out my hand to him and he came across to take it. "Toys or no toys," I smiled up at him, "I was very glad to have you there."

Jack seemed unimpressed. He shook his head. "That's all very well, but if he hadn't behaved like a prat in the first place you wouldn't have been there to be saved."

"True," I replied, frowning a little, "but let's not play the 'What If?' game. We all do prattish things, and if hadn't been there he would certainly have been held for ransom and possibly killed , so in this case I am thoroughly glad I was."

Jack came to stand on the other side of me, holding my free hand in what was patently a gesture of possession. Out of the corner of my eye I saw my grandmother's amused twinkle. I smiled at all three, gave Neil's hand a little shake, told him I was on his side and then let him go.

"You win." Jack smiled down at me, "When you're ready Sarah would love to see you. She says to tell you everyone else has gone so you won't be bothered again."

I closed my eyes. His hand was warm and reassuring. I could have asked whether the "everyone else" included himself, but I didn't.

"Tell her I'll be along in a minute", I said, taking a last sip of wine.

I found Sarah in her conservatory, sitting quietly in a darkness lit only by conveniently placed outdoor-indoor lamps and an unobtrusive heater filling the place with steady warmth. The garden itself was invisible, apart from the shadowy outline of the scented and flowering magnolia tree. Everywhere was peaceful, a little mysterious and permeated by wafts of fragrance from outside the great window. It was a watercolour evening. Beyond turning her head and motioning me to join her, Sarah said nothing. Neither did I. We sat together in companionable silence.

It was I who broke it. I was disturbed by her pallor which appeared to have nothing to do with the darkness and the lighting. Her eyes were large, larger than usual, I thought.

"How are you Sarah?"

"Thinking."

"There's a lot to think about. But apart from that, how are you?"

"I'm OK. Tell me about Neil," she said. "I've only got his version of things and I need to know the rest. I know you haven't known him long, but you seem to have had time together in your prison – time to spare for confidences." She smiled, "There's nothing like looking death in the face for spilling secrets, especially if the person you're spilling them to is a stranger."

I nodded. Secrets had certainly been uncovered in the little nursery bedroom, sitting side by side on a child's bed attached to each other as much by our situation as by the rope around our wrists. But although I understood her concern, I was loath to relay what had obviously been an intensely private conversation. I was sorry for Neil, but felt that what he had told me was for him to impart as he himself thought fit. He had been a surprise and I admired the new Neil and wished him well, but thought his future should be in his own hands – certainly where J K Kent was concerned.

On the other hand, of course, I had told him – twice – that I was on his side. He hated his job and longed to be an actor, or a model, and, If appealed to, I would help if I could, but had the right moment arrived?

"How much has he told you already?" I asked eventually.

"He hates his job, selling his precious gadgets to people who will use them in their own cold business battles. He wants to be a model, or even an actor or something in the creative line. I think he got bitten by the stage bug just doing the silly porn films and hankers after doing something more worth-while. But I don't understand why he was kidnapped, or why you tagged along putting yourself in danger. Perhaps you know."

I explained as succinctly as possible about the threat to reveal all his goings-on to her father but because Neil couldn't pay the blackmail money himself he thought the only way out was to disappear.

Sarah gave a sympathetic half laugh. "Poor lamb," she said. "His sexual preferences, or lack of them, don't bother me any more. M S can have funny effects. But my father and Michael are a bit – shall we say old-fashioned? They simply don't understand this equality bit when it comes to 'Being A Man,'"and she drew quotation marks in the air, "so he just thinks Neil is simply gay and, to him, bless his old-fashioned cotton socks, that is downright disgusting. I don't suppose he'll change now, and Michael is cut from the same cloth."

"Jack?"

Sarah chuckled and reached out a hand to me. "Don't worry, Jack's my favourite brother and he's as unlike the others as he can be. We take after mum, broad-minded but very definitely hetero. Live and let live and the choices you make are yours and nobody else's. I suppose you realise he's nuts about you?"

I blushed but did not reply. Instead I changed the subject.

"Sarah, please tell me why you went outside by yourself. So far no-one seems to be able to explain it. The nearest I've got is Gran's view that you had cabin fever."

She sighed. "It was complicated. I'm not alone here and I love my home, so no-one could truly call it cabin fever, but I was frustrated because you were all risking things to protect me and it wasn't fair. I didn't need protecting. Still don't. So I decided to go into the lions' den and tell them what they wanted to know. Unfortunately Peter saw me go and slipped out of the kitchen while Mrs S's back was turned. That did it, of course. All I could do was hold him firmly on my knee, tell him not to say a word, and then field the questions. I've never been under fire, but that's how it felt. Mikes, cameras, people hurling questions, shouting over everybody else. I told them the truth, as I saw it, but it was against heavy odds. Even Peter was overwhelmed, and that's saying something."

Sarah shook her head. "Aren't people odd?" she said, "Some of them seemed sympathetic but some accused me of fraud and kept asking how I did it. Where was I getting all the feathers? They were a bit disconcerted by the fact that there weren't any around at that moment. To be honest, so was I. I was thinking 'where are you when I need you?'. Then, right in the middle of it all Mrs Simmons came charging through the gaggle and picked

Peter up. Then she faced them head on. She told them straight. What a woman she is! She said if they harassed a child she would have the law on the lot of them – and she didn't mean their papers but them, individually. Then the others charged through the press, Ange and Luce, Evelyn Carmichael, the lot, and everyone was shouting at everyone else. If it hadn't been a chaotic nightmare it would have been funny. Finally, we were saved by our wonderfully colourful star, who sailed like a tall, exquisitely masted galleon into the thick of it and silenced the lot of them. You should have seen their faces. Now that *was* funny. Of course they all started again, only focussing on her, not me, but she simply raised her hand for silence, told them the fun was over and they must all *go - now!*

"And this is the really funny part. They all did go away, but as soon as they moved off a huge cloud of feathers dropped on them from the sky and followed them all to the gate. I'd love to know what they told their papers. Perhaps they think I have confederates up in the trees by the gate, waiting with quilts and bolsters to drop feathers on people they don't like. Will we get to see all the papers?"

My nod was grim and determined. "You certainly will," I told her. "What's more I shall be emailing my own version, with your permission. And I apologise here and now for the behaviour of the national press when they're let loose."

I meant it. Their behaviour was worthy of a front page story and I intended to give it one.

When the door opened to admit Neil, with the carer hot on his heels, I said goodnight, gave Sarah a searching glance, kissed her cheek and took my leave. My grandmother's door was not locked. I found her in bed, reading by the light of a tall, focussed beside lamp. She lowered her reading glasses and raised her eyebrows.

"Well?"

I stood in the doorway, by now longing for my own bed.

"I've been making discoveries," I told her. "And I think I'm in love."

My grandmother nodded. "Of course you are," she said. "Now go to bed."

I blew her a kiss, closed her door and did as I was told.

# CHAPTER TWENTY SIX

I awoke next morning, physically if not emotionally rested by an exhausted sleep. I was conscious that important, even life-changing, events had inserted themselves somewhere and somehow into my ordered world, and yet despite the shocks, I felt suddenly and ecstatically so happy that I simply had to get out of bed. Who needed sleep when whole new vistas were opening up before me like early mist lifting from a crazy but delicious new horizon.

What I did not expect, however, was the sudden eruption of my mother into this new, blissful dream. I love my mother but over the years have found that a little of her goes a very long way. If chalk and cheese were ever present in a relationship it was in this one. She fussed over me when I longed for peace. Her conversations were monologues and she seemed to talk on an indrawn breath, as if commas hadn't been invented. And she was never still for a moment, offering me un-needed extra cushions, footstools, more tea or coffee, chocolate biscuits and caramel creams when all I needed was to be left alone and there isn't a sweet tooth in my head anyway. Worst of all, she spoke to me as though I were six years old, asking about my "little friends" in an arch voice. To make matters even worse – for me at least - while still thinking of me as her baby girl, my mother is surrounded by an ever-present gathering of devoted admirers. Being treated like gold dust is always irresistible and gold dust was, and still is, a permanent feature of my mother's armoury. So when a familiar voice cried "Cooeee!" my little bubble dream was punctured like a balloon landing on a drawing pin.

There was nothing to be done, however, except go to meet whatever was coming. I arrived in the hall of my grandmother's apartment to find my mother, exquisite in a trim, pale blue suit with a faux fur collar and cuffs, followed by my serene-looking father, a sensible motorboat in the protective wake of a pretty, immaculately turned out yacht in full sail. My mother fell upon me with cries of delight. "Gemma *darling*, it's so wonderful to see you after the *awful* adventures you've been having. Whatever possessed you? You're supposed to be on holiday, for heaven's sake. But don't worry, Sweetie, we are here to rescue you. We're taking you back with us."

My father, safely behind her and out of sight, pulled a comic face, raised his eyebrows and shrugged. No words were required. He was intimating that it was nothing to do with him.

I smiled back. "It's lovely to see you Mama, and it will be nice having you here for a bit. Have you seen Gran yet? But I can't go with you I'm afraid. It's all happening here."

"I *know,* darling, that's why we've come. We read about this terrible kidnapping and we just had to come straight over to look after you. So after lunch we'll take off home and get you out of this chaos. You've been in such *danger*, darling, I couldn't bear to leave you here with no-one to look after you."

I laughed. "Darling Mama," I said, kissing her softly perfumed cheek, "I am most wonderfully looked after by a whole army of people, and don't leave Grannie out of this. She's been doing wonders here – the best support a girl could have, as you know quite well. She is your mother-in-law after all."

"I certainly am," said my grandmother, emerging from her sitting room with her usual undisturbable calm. "So what is all the noise about? Come in, Eileen, calm down and have some of Mrs Simmons' excellent coffee or tea, or even some hot chocolate – whatever you fancy." Then she kissed my father and gave him a quick hug.

"Thank you, Mother, and it's wonderful to see you again. It feels like ages, and I could *murder* a coffee, but I need to help Gemma pack. We want to be off again soon after lunch, don't we Bernard?"

Bernard rocked on his heels landing, as was his wont, on the sides of his feet. He was smiling at me and his eyebrows were still in their questioning position. I knew that, if necessary, he could use his authority to over-ride his gently forceful wife, but only if the situation required it. I decided that this situation very definitely required it, but followed the others meekly into my grandmother's sitting room, saying nothing until I saw which way the wind would take my mother's resolute little sailing boat.

"You are very early," my grandmother said, peering into the kitchen to switch on the coffee machine, left ready for our use by the always prepared Mrs Simmons. "You must have been up at the crack of dawn. Gemma and I haven't even had breakfast yet, so as soon as Mrs Simmons arrives we shall have breakfast comfortably together."

"Oh, I couldn't rest, you see," my mother smiled, holding out her hand to me. "I'd heard the news and Bernard had just looked at the paper and we were watching the early tv when this kidnapping business came up and I completely lost my appetite. I simply had to come and rescue poor Gemma."

I took her hand and squeezed it. "Poor Gemma is being very well looked after, thanks to Gran here, and a motley crew of the strangest and nicest people I've ever met. Most of them are retired celebrities who just want to be left in peace, but they've all come out of retirement to support me and Sarah."

"Who's Sarah? Is she the crippled girl who started all this feathers rubbish? "

For a moment I was too disconcerted to reply. Once I had recovered, I suggested that after breakfast we should all go next door to meet this Sarah person. "You'll like her," I added.

My mother made the usual humphing sound suggesting that there was no guarantee there. She was reserving judgment and meanwhile would continue to regard this 'crippled girl' as the villain in the plot, whatever that happened to be. The enticing smell of coffee rising to seduce our nostrils sent me into the kitchen to lay out cups and saucers and reach for the milk and sugar. I found myself urgently longing for the presence of the person with whom I had just dived headfirst into love.

Instead, Mrs Simmons came into view carrying a large shopping bag. "Breakfast?" she asked? "You haven't had yours yet, have you? You must be starving after all the goings-on yesterday."

I explained that my parents had arrived and had been invited to join us for breakfast and probably lunch, but intended to leave again in the early afternoon. "How lovely for you," Mrs Simmons smiled, "But if they want to stay, there's the spare room all ready, beds made up and everything."

Her words brought the whole situation to mind with brutal force and a tear dropped quietly and very unexpectedly onto my chin. "Yes, it's lovely, but you see they – they want to take me back with them. And I can't. I just can't. I'd hate it."

She put down her shopping bags and came towards me, reaching to give a warm, comforting hug. "Do you mean you can't or you don't want to?"

"I don't want to."

"Then don't."

"Yes, but..."

"Gemma Croft," Mrs Simmons interrupted me with a little shake of my armss, releasing me in order to look me firmly in the eye. "I have never, never, never seen you like this. Where is the strong, efficient, determined young woman we all know and love?"

I sniffed. "You see, perhaps Jack..."

The searching eyes narrowed. "Perhaps Jack...what?"

"He may agree with them." The thought of this sent more tears spilling down my face and onto the large jumper-encased bosom so close to me.

179

Suddenly I wailed. "I'm in love. I've never been in love before and I don't know how to deal with it or what to do."

The hugs were renewed with even more force. I could feel her shoulders shake and realised she was laughing. "Oh you poor lamb!" she murmured. "Of course he won't want you to go. He adores you, my pet. Just tell him you don't want to go – and I can think of two million reasons right now – and he'll be putty in your hands."

Her laughter dried my tears and I was beginning to laugh with her when my mother came to join us. "This is my mother, Mrs Simmons. Mama, Mrs S has come to cook our breakfast, but meanwhile here is the coffee," and I pointed to the loaded tray waiting to be carried through. My mother frowned. The tears hadn't yet dried and must have been distressingly visible, but my mother said nothing, merely gave me a firm 'I'll-speak-to-you-later' glance, picked up the tray and vanished with it through the door.

"I want to take her in to meet Sarah," I said, watching her stiffly retreating back, every line of which shrieked protest. "As soon as possible in fact. If I help you, can we hurry the breakfast up? I'm quite useful in the kitchen, believe it or not, and always feel spoilt when I'm here."

"So you should be. That's what you come for, to be spoilt. It's your holiday, though you don't seem to be having much of one so far. But you go back to it, my duck, go and be spoilt and I'll have the breakfast ready in 15 minutes max. Will that do?"

"Perfect," I smiled. "And you are perfect. An angel in fact."

She laughed. "As to that, we've had enough of those floating about here in the last few weeks. Everybody knows a white feather in your home means an angel has been, and I've lost track of how many we've had now. A whole heavenly host of them, judging by numbers which we couldn't count anyway, try as we might."

180

I laughed, please with the thought, then I too vanished through the door to give battle once again with my indomitable mother. It was, I decided, a clear case of 'the irresistible force meeting the immovable mass,"

This, however, was one battle I was going to win.

# CHAPTER TWENTY SEVEN

Despite picking daintily at her breakfast egg-on-toast, my mother seemed in no hurry to meet the 'crippled girl', her only request for haste being repeated suggestions that I go forthwith to pack for our journey home. So it was a reluctant lady who eventually crossed the entrance foyer to Sarah's front door – which was, as usual, ajar. I rang the bell briefly and stepped inside. My grandmother and my father were close on my heels but my mother hung back a little, only coming forward when I beckoned and led her towards the conservatory where I knew Sarah would be sitting in her wheelchair. She was, but she was not alone. Arranged on comfortable chairs around her were Mrs Carpenter, Ange and Luce and the carer. It was a peaceful scene which my mother proceeded to puncture, holding out a graceful little hand and behaving with the most charmingly understated condescension.

"Sarah, this is my mother," I said, trying desperately not to grit my teeth and probably not succeeding. "And hovering away in the background is my father. Mama, this is Sarah, who is one of the nicest people I've ever met and who has become a very close friend."

If Sarah were surprised at this hyperbole from me she didn't show it, merely twinkling at me and smiling broadly at my parents. She waved them to a softly cushioned sofa and I briefly introduced my mother to the rest of the party, though jibbing a little at 'Ange and Luce', referring to them as Angela and Lucy, late of the "Starlights".

My mother was charming to them too, but with reservations. She was obviously thinking "who are all these weird people", as well she might, since the Starlights were wearing an eclectic assortment of mismatching coloured top garments over what I suspected were deliberately torn knee-less jeans. I suddenly found the scene bizarre and longed to share the joyous entertainment it was so unexpectedly giving me..

At that moment, Neil added to the joy by making his own entrance accompanied by a large but obviously very young Labrador puppy. As I bent to welcome him, Jake knocked me down and proceeded to bestow big slobbery kisses on any part of me that he could reach. My mother was horrified. In her eyes dogs, all dogs, were dirty, insanitary and covered in fleas. I could sense, even without looking at her, that she was in the grip of a great many strong emotions at the same time – chief of which I guessed would be a command to get off my knees at once and go instantly to the bathroom to wash my face and hands.

In this she had no hope. By then everyone in the room, even including the careful Evelyn Carpenter, was dog-worshipping.

"Oh Jake, Jake, where have you sprung from?" Sarah was laughing with delight and grinning her thanks at a gratified Neil. "Have you brought him back for good?"

"Sorry, no , I'm afraid not. My friend will be coming to fetch him in about an hour, but I thought you'd like to see how he's grown, and look, he remembers you."

That Jake remembered Sarah had now become obvious in that his paws were on her lap and his slobbery attentions had been transferred from myself to her. The adoration was mutual. At the same time that Jake was doing his best to cover her face with a large tongue, she was wrapping her arms around this body of trembling doghood and trying to kiss the top of his head.

At the height of the noise and exuberance, the door opened once again and Jack stood over me, lifting me to my feet and brushing dog hairs from the clean jersey I had donned only an hour or so earlier. His first remark was prosaic. "I see Jake is back."

I smiled. "You've noticed."

Jack very gently tugged my hair. "I presume these are your parents."

Since my mother's eyes, now drawn from the horror of dog-watching, were looking questioningly at Jack, I sprang into action and introduced them. Jack I described as 'Sarah's brother'. My mother nodded. "So are you a victim of these feathers too, then?" she asked, with the slightly arch tone she normally uses when speaking to attractive young men. My father was rocking on his heels again, showing only a slight trace of the mixed discomfort and amusement I knew he would be feeling. He reached forward to offer his hand to this particular attractive young man and Jack took it firmly in his own.

I think that gave my mother her cue because she suddenly came to life, stood up and smiled at Sarah. "It's been lovely to meet you, dear," she began, "and I'm glad I haven't been covered in feathers myself although I can see there are a few around. They must be so hard so hard to brush off, don't you find? But now I must get Gemma packing so we can be off immediately after lunch. Come along, darling," she said to me, holding out her hand with the curling fingers and slightly beckoning gesture of one who would be obeyed – and obeyed *now.*

"Oh, are you going somewhere?" Sarah abruptly stopped kissing the dog and looked bewildered. "Gemma didn't say."

"Gemma didn't know," I told her. "I am as surprised as you are at the idea, but I'm not actually going anywhere."

My mother turned to Sarah, as one person to another who each has my interests at heart. "My dear, Gemma is supposed to be on holiday and she's been put in danger, so we are taking her home with us now so we can spoil her and keep her safe and give her the rest she needs."

There was a sudden silence. Everyone looked at my mother, than they looked at me. And I was desperate. If Sarah agreed with her I would be brought to a standstill. Under no circumstances could I fight them both. So I took the biggest risk of my life so far. I held my head up and spoke with absolute finality.

"I'm sorry, Mama but I can't possibly leave here now. I am going to marry Jack. We're engaged."

The silence had been hushed before. Now it was absolute. I had provided my mother – and everyone else – with the perfect *tour de force*.

I didn't look at Jack. He was probably as stunned as the rest of them and I had no idea whether his face would be registering delight or horror. Just at that moment I preferred not to know. Then, quite suddenly and after what seemed to me to last two hours but was probably only two seconds, there arose a hubbub of voices all talking at once. The result was very loud indeed. It even shocked the dog, who stopped trying hard to kiss every millimetre of Sarah's face and sat panting and looking bewildered. The only person not shouting was my mother, who seemed incapable of uttering anything at all. She merely stared at me in stupefaction.

Eventually, however, she regained the power of speech but what she said was lost in the delighted cries from everyone else. Ange and Luce were jumping up and down, clasping each other around the waist in a crazy dance. Evelyn was laughing and wiping her eyes and Mrs Simmons had captured the dog and was hugging and laughing into his furry, wriggling neck. As for Jake himself, he began to bark in sympathy which added greatly to the din. In the background as usual, my father was doing something rarely seen in my family. He was laughing gloriously aloud and, like Mrs Carpenter, wiping his eyes. My father didn't laugh as a rule. Normally, his shoulders shook and he twinkled, but this was something new and precious. From it I assumed he was pleased, but for the moment I wasn't sure of his reasons. His mouthed words, "Well done", mimed to me over Sarah's head when he had ceased wiping his eyes, made things no clearer and myself no wiser.

Jack placed an arm around my shoulders and whispered, "Seems a popular move with the onlookers. I think we should talk."

"Definitely, absolutely, unquestionably, without doubt," I murmured incoherently, still without looking at him. "Kitchen?"

At that moment Neil, who had absented himself from the general rejoicing as soon as it had begun, appeared among us carrying a tray loaded with champagne glasses and two bottles of Brut. The faceless man beside me gave a brief chuckle. "It seems not."

Neil's arrival calmed everyone sufficiently to stop shouting and start cheering, each reaching for a glass as it was handed to them. "I feel this calls for a real celebration," he said, busily popping the cork on one of the bottles. There was another cheer as the cork flew out and golden liquid foamed from the bottle neck. "I wish to propose a toast to Gemma and Jack, and to say 'Congratulations to Gemma for the best piece of histrionics I've seen for some time. Your timing, Gemma," he bowed towards me, "was perfect."

Everyone cheered again and I felt Jack's arm shake on my shoulders. "Absolutely, unquestionably, without a doubt," he murmured in my ear. I began to laugh, too, until I saw my mother's face and immediately felt sorry for her."

"So you see, Mama...."

"Darling, I don't understand. You didn't say anything about this before. Why didn't you tell me? I would have understood."

The answer was, of course, that until that moment I hadn't known myself, but I couldn't say that without implying that Jack hadn't known either.

Sarah was gazing at me with such delight that I reached forward to take her hand. "I'm so glad," she grinned.

"Glad you're marrying Jack and glad you're not going away today. You'll be my sister-in-law. Gosh, what fun!"

Released from her brother's grip on my shoulders, I knelt beside her chair and grinned back. "Of course, that's the only reason I'm marrying him," I said. "Didn't you know?"

"Perfectly obvious. But," she added, turning to Jack, "don't you think we should get our parents over here to share the celebration? I'm assuming they don't know already."

Jack waved a hand and nodded, flipping his phone and dialling a speed number. Everyone sipped and listened. "Hi Mops, is Dad there? I think you should both get over here as soon as possible, and will you tell Mike to come too, and Ruth if she can get away. Tell them they can bring Peter. We've got some news for them and we think the whole family should be here. Will you come? Don't take no for an answer from Pops or Mike. You know what they're like." He smiled down the phone, replaced the handset and turned back to me. "And now," he announced, "Gemma and I are going for a quick walk before the family get here. Have fun everyone and drink your champers."

With that, he took me firmly by the upper arm and steered me through the door to the foyer towards the sunny, perfumed morning.

My moment of reckoning had arrived.

# CHAPTER TWENTY EIGHT

"You'll need a coat," he told me. "It's colder than it looks."

I reached into my grandmother's doorway to grab the jacket that hung on the door and together we went out into a crisp, fresh Spring day. Across the front lawn, the silver birch stood gracefully within a circle of blossoming border plants, with the red, blue and gold of mid-May surrounding us. Everything was bright.

We stood on the grass facing the silver birch. When we spoke it was together, so we both stopped and faced each other without touching

"I need the truth..." Jack said.

"Please don't think..." I began.

He gave a small half laugh and nodded. "Okay, you start,"

Starting was good. The trouble was where to start the starting. "Please don't think you have to go through with this. It was a spur of the moment thing and..."

Jack shook his head as if to clear it and placed his hands on my upper arms. "But first I have to know. This spur of the moment thing, was it just a ruse to stop your mother...or... or...do you actually want to marry me? You seem to be giving me a reason to wriggle out of it."

I closed my eyes and hung my head. Then I looked up, straight into his eyes. When I spoke it was in desperation. "Of course I want to marry you. I'm as surprised as you are, and just afraid you might not want to marry me."

From that moment I had no way of saying anything at all because I was being enfolded in the most comprehensive hug I had ever received in my entire life. We were both laughing. Then, because my lips were close to his neck I kissed it. His response was instant and to be expected.

Breathlessly we regarded each other and the brightness of the day grew even more luminous.

"How long have you known?" I asked. "Until you rescued me I didn't know what to think. You were giving such funny mixed messages."

"I was trying very hard not to fall in love from the first minute but not succeeding very well. You were gorgeous and you'd made me lose my temper. In the end I decided I was a hopeless case and gave up. And you?"

"Absolutely the same, though I admit I fell for you when I saw you stomp away at that first meeting, when Gran and I were having coffee. You looked like a furious six year old."

"I *was* furious. You'd won the fight. Of course I was furious. I didn't know whether to kiss you or spank you."

We were just about to confirm our feelings in the only way possible when we heard the sound of car wheels. "Quick," Jack said, "Into the back door. Let's drop the bombshell surrounded by backup."

Laughing, we slipped around the corner of the house and into the side door and the kitchen, where Mrs Simmons was stirring something savoury in a large casserole dish. She winked at us as we dived through into the conservatory. Yes, I thought, it was good to have backup.

The door opened upon Mr and Mrs Kent, followed by Michael, Ruth and Peter, who fell upon the dog, joyously joining him in his feather chasing. The Kent family had arrived in force, complete to the last. My own parents were sitting on one of the squashy sofas, my mother in bemused silence. I was not sure she had even noticed that Jack and I had been anywhere. She was too busy gazing at the feathers that had seemed to appear from nowhere. The arrival of newcomers, however, awoke her to social responsibilities and she rose, a trifle shakily, from her seat. My father remained where he was, legs outstretched and hands folded on a stomach that was growing all too capacious. He would, I knew, stand up in his own good time. Meanwhile he was taking stock.

Ange and Luce, with Evelyn Carpenter, had quietly slipped away, obviously aware that this was turning into a family consultation, if not altogether a celebration.

Mr Kent had brought bottles. "I didn't know what the occasion was," he said, rather loudly, but it seemed like a celebration so I've brought champagne, just in case." He handed the bottles to Neil, who whisked them away to the kitchen. "So what's it all about then? You realise that JK Kent is now missing its CEO, two managing directors and an Account Executive, so whatever it is had better be good."

Jack, his arm firmly around my shoulders, drew me towards his father. "Gemma has just agreed to marry me," he announced,

Mrs Kent laughed. "I knew it," she cried. "I knew it, and I'm so glad. Come here Gemma and be welcomed. Imagine! Another Croft marrying another Kent." She turned to my grandmother, who stood silently smiling at everyone. "Did you know?"

"I guessed, that's all, but it wasn't difficult."

Mr Kent had said nothing. Neither had Michael, who seemed as stupified as a professional charmer could ever allow himself to be. Then Mr Kent said "Hmmph," which was apparently his stock answer, or comment, to anything that came his way. Then he patted my shoulder, from which I deduced that while not exactly pleased he was not exactly displeased either. I was suddenly to be seen in a new perspective, from meddlesome, prying journalist akin to the notorious paparazzi, to a new and unexpected daughter-in-law who was not of his own choosing.

I smiled sweetly at him, but privately my thoughts were more of the 'Hard luck' variety. His wife was made of different metal and we smiled approvingly at each other. Neil reappeared with a tray carrying even more champagne glasses.

So there we were, celebrating with mixed emotions, sipping from sparkling gold liquid amid a light dusting of white feathers.

"I hope you have realised," said Jack at last, when all that could be said had presumably been said, "that it is now lunchtime, and if you drink champagne at this rate you won't be able to drive – which includes you, Mr and Mrs Croft, so I suggest we repair to the dining room for the very large casserole Mrs Simmons has been cooking up for us."

"Oh, but..." began my mother.

"Oh but nothing..." Jack smiled down at her, disarming her as I knew tall young men could always do, especially if they were also handsome. I found myself laughing as we obligingly took Jack's advice and followed him into the dining room. Mrs Simmons had laid the table for 10 people, with maybe more to come.

"I think we should invite Mrs Simmons to join us," I said, smiling at her. "After all, we do share a grandfather and if it hadn't been for her uncle Tom and little Billy, none of this would have happened."

Mrs Simmons said thank you, but she would have to get back home to cook her own family's dinner, although she would be very happy to join us while we ate her casserole. So we thanked her and did as we were bid.

We were just approaching the coffee stage when the front doorbell rang again. As Mrs Simmons opened it, a young middle-aged man and a somewhat rotund lady of about 40 stood on the threshold trying not to look as disconcerted as they must have felt. They were both wearing white clerical collars.

My grandmother rose to introduce them and to offer them coffee, which we were about to enjoy in the conservatory. "This is the Rev Jane Whitecross, vicar of Woolcot parish church, and Father Timothy, Catholic priest at St Martins."

There was a moment's hush as we all took in the sudden change in circumstances. Then we all trooped back again to the conservatory, clerics and all, carrying our glasses and obviously deep in somewhat bemused thought. Some of us, I saw, were privately wondering whether we were about to be rebuked for calling down such a multitude of mysterious happenings. Since there was nothing I could usefully say or do, I said and did nothing.

One cleric was to be expected, but two together meant only one thing – they had come to talk 'feathers'. Here we go again, I thought. I took another sip of the sparkling wine and, with Jack beside me, I followed them.

From a position near the door I watched the visitors. The lady vicar had picked up one of the feathers lying at her feet and was studying it carefully. Her dark blue cardigan was stretched tightly over a bulky but still curvaceous bosom and her jeans had been ironed with a decided crease over her knees and down to her shiny shoes. The priest, who was even younger than I had thought at first glance, had also donned jeans and a sweater but his were casual and inclined very slightly to sloppiness. The only point where they properly coincided was in the whiteness of their rounded collars. Both were anxious to establish an identity, however understated they chose that to be.

It was Father Timothy who began. The rest of us seemed to be politely waiting. I felt that, like me, they were all conscious that as there were two of them this was not a parochial visit. They were not after the health and wellbeing of their parishioners. We were all in some way or another preparing our own little speeches.

"Well now," said Fr Timothy, apparently comfortable and at ease. "Thank you for letting us come unexpectedly. We apologise for that, by the way. It was a bit of a spur-of-the-moment decision. We got talking about your feathers and as we were both coming anyway, we thought..."

"We could save your time and ours." Said the Rev Jane.

I gave a small chuckle. "Don't worry about spur-of-the-moment things," I said, "We're getting used to those." I felt small tug at the lock of my hair closest to Jack's fingers, but knew it was a tug of amused agreement.

"I'm quite sure you are. And before I say any more, I am Tim and my colleague here...," He turned to the Rev Whitecross with enquiringly raised eyebrows. She nodded and said "I like to be known as Jane, if that's okay with you?"

Some of us nodded in polite acceptance, but Mr Kent and my mother remained still and silent. They were obviously waiting to see what was coming next, and none too happy at the prospect. I gathered that such informality was not part of their perception of God and His Church – that is, if they had any. I rather doubted that Mr Kent senior believed there was such an entity, in this world or any other. God was a "Thee" and "Thou" and "Verily, verily," idea – or an outmoded myth, dependant upon one's point of view. As for my mother, she had rigidly traditional views on God and the Church which did not coincide with the present gender of one of these 'vicars'.

"Well now," said Tim again, obviously deciding to start again. "We are both really interested in these feathers of yours. They've certainly been hitting the headlines and we're both besieged by questions from just about everyone everywhere. So we've come with a few questions of our own, if you don't mind."

"Don't worry," Michael put in. "We're used to questions too, so fire away, but I'd have thought you had enough answers just by reading the papers. As you say, we have rather hit the headlines."

"Of course, of course," replied Jane soothingly, "but we've all become very sceptical about newspaper reporting, haven't we? So we've come to the source, if you see what I mean."

"What do you want to know?" I asked from the safety of the doorway and Jack's comforting presence. Specifically, I mean. It's a big subject."

"The truth."

"By which I suppose you mean have we made it up? Is it a great big fraud, and is Sarah manufacturing these feathers overnight or conjuring them up with her collection of giant bolsters to be dropped from any nearby handy trees?"

By now everyone was looking at me, the two visitors with slight surprise as if wondering what part I was playing. Then I saw the look of dawning understanding in Jane's eyes and she blinked. "Of course," she said, "I realise now. You are the journalist whose story started the whole thing. Tell me, what inspired you to dig up a village tale from the past?"

"I can answer that," said Sarah, moving her wheelchair a fraction nearer to me. "Gemma didn't start this story. The feathers began before she even arrived here, as I keep telling everyone, but why they don't listen I can't think."

"And the story came from me," my grandmother spoke from her armchair. "I was alive the first time it happened and thought Gemma would like to hear it. As you say, just a little local tale from the past. We neither of us expected it to blossom as it did. Out of all proportion, you might say, so none of us is to blame - or all of us together. The feathers simply – took off, didn't they Peter?"

There was a small ripple of laughter. Peter was sitting in his usual perch on the carpet, industriously comparing one feather from another and tickling the dog's nose with them. Jake sneezed obligingly, which made the boy laugh. Peter looked up and smiled beatifically. "Yes, they just came – whoooooof! - and then they flew into the air, like this," and he spread his arms wide, shaking them up in the air. "It was fun."

Tim and Jane smiled at him, then Jane looked directly at Sarah. "What we'd really like to know is where do *you* think they came from? They come straight to you, right? So who and what sends them to you?"

For the first time, Sarah looked confident of her answer. She had made up her own mind. "Angels, of course."

"But who sends the angels? Where do they come from?"

Michael swiftly intervened. "You don't need to answer them Sarah. They have no right."

"Yes of course they have. Who else is qualified to talk about angels and God than a priest. It's their job, and I shall answer questions if I choose to. So leave me alone Michael."

There was a short, surprised silence. Then Sarah spoke again. "Sorry about that. In answer to your specific question about who sends angels, who else can positively send angels but God? If they send themselves and they are pure spirit, then there must be something outside this world or they would be born and die just like everyone else."

The Rev Jane smiled into her lap and Fr Tim smiled at Sarah. "Perhaps they do," he suggested. "Who are we to say? Now just one more question - why you and why your uncle? Why no-one else?"

"How do we know there aren't others? There may be feathers flying around China or Outer Mongolia only we don't hear about them. But the only connection I can come up with between me and Uncle Billy is that we are – or were – both in wheelchairs."

Jack came to sit on the floor in front of me. He laughed. "It can't be wheelchairs," he said, "or this village alone would have been suffocated by this time. There are so many wheelchairs, walkers and electric scooters around the place it would be like the aftermath of a gigantic snowstorm."

"Only they wouldn't turn to sludge when they melted," I smiled.

"And the refuse men would have a job clearing them up," Sarah nodded.

By this time everyone was laughing. The tension had somehow been released. Mr Kent finally came into his own. "I suppose you're not going to ask the same questions of all of us," he said, "because we'd all have different views, but I think it's time we all had another glass of champagne." He turned specifically to the two priests. "I'm assuming you both drink, or are you like the police, you don't drink on duty? We are or were celebrating the engagement of my son to this young journalist, whom I suppose I must stop castigating for bringing the whole subject of feathers up in the first place. So I hope you stay to share our celebration."

"Certainly we will," Both Fr Tim and the Rev Jane looked delighted and happily accepted the glasses they were handed by Neil. They both turned to me, pleased to wish me happy, and asking me questions about when the Big Day would be, and we were all just taking our first grateful sips when the doorbell rand once again.

We sighed. Who was it going to be this time?

# CHAPTER TWENTY NINE

To my surprise, it was Mr Kent Senior who moved to open the door, although not before hesitating in the doorway and giving Sarah a glance, half anxious and half defiant. "I was about to tell you," he said with the dignity of all miscreants who are not the least bit sorry for what they have done, "that I had a word with a psychiatrist, said to be the best in his field, and he said he'd look in."

With that he was gone, leaving no time for questions or even comments. Only the two clerics moved. They held out hands to Mrs Kent and said they would obviously be *de trop* so would call on us some time later. Meanwhile they wished Jack and myself happy and quietly departed. I personally was a little in awe. I knew the psychiatrist by name and reputation and wondered how Mr Kent had cajoled him into a personal visit, which was so unprecedented that JK Kent's position in the hierarchy of influence must be greater than I had imagined. No wonder the kidnappers thought they were onto a good thing. Unfortunately for them, in any skirmish with Neil's father-in-law, they were always destined to come out backwards. Mr Kent was apparently quite capable of calling out the British Army, the RAF and the Chief of Police if he thought it necessary. I smiled to myself. The Navy would be safe, since we were too far inland for destroyers, but how about Special Forces and/or the Commandos? Would I ever dare to be this man's daughter-in-law?

I glanced at Jack and found he was smiling at me. "What has come into that weird noddle of yours?" he murmured.

"The idea of your father being my father-in-law," I replied, suddenly catching his hand. "If he thought I wasn't treating you well, would he send me straight to the tower or just say 'Off with her head' and be done with it? I'm relying on you to rescue me again if he does."

"Don't worry. He wouldn't dare. Pops and I understand each other."

"I'm glad to hear it," I murmured, just as the door opened, allowing us all to breathe properly again. Until that moment, I now realised, there had been the dead silence of astonishment in the room. My mother had crept closer to my father and clutched his hand – rather as I was clutching Jack's, I thought – and Michael had picked Peter up and was holding him close against his chest. Peter, however, was wriggling to be put down, to continue hugging his feather-chasing partner on the carpet. Both boy and dog were supremely oblivious of adult problems, totally absorbed in each other and in what they were doing.

Sarah, the hub around which we were all revolving, was looking calm but dazed. She had become very white and appeared to be having trouble with her hands, which had tried once or twice to pick up her feather fan. This time she failed altogether and merely sat, apparently deep in thought. "It's the stress," I thought to myself. "The media and all the questions and arguments, it's all too much and it isn't fair."

I was suddenly, fiercely anxious for her. Letting go of Jack's hand I went to kneel by the wheelchair, looking directly into her eyes. Her mother was sitting quietly on Sarah's other side, close beside her and stroking her arm.

"Do you mind?" I asked.

"Mind?"

"About your father calling for this chap? Did you know about it?"

A trifle absent-mindedly she nodded and spoke serenely. "Oh yes, Pops told me yesterday that somebody was interested, but didn't say who, so I forgot all about it."

Her mother frowned, but before she could ask her own questions, Mr Kent and a small, thin man with grey hair and a lined, pleasant face walked across the room and held out his hand to both of them..

"Mrs Kent, I'm sorry to intrude on your family celebrations but I had a word with your husband yesterday and he invited me to come and see for myself. Sarah, I hope you don't mind. You must be sick and tired of being asked things you probably don't know the answer to."

Mr Kent, from his position close to the psychiatrist's shoulder, said: "Sarah, my dear, as I explained to you, Mr Dubois had come to have a quick word with you. This, Derek, is my lovely daughter, who, as you can see, has M S but she is coping amazingly well so far. Perhaps the three of us could go somewhere a little more private," he suggested to the room in general. Only Neil came forward. He looked as possessive as I had ever seen him look and there was a purposeful gleam in his eye. He held out his own hand to this intrusive stranger and introduced himself. As one would hope in view of his profession, Mr Dubois read the situation at once. He smiled at Neil, then, quite charmingly I thought, put Mr Kent firmly his place.

"Just Sarah and me to start with, I think, if that's okay with you, Sarah? Is there anyone you'd really like or need to have with you?"

We all held our breath again. Sarah looked the stranger in the eyes, smiled and nodded. "Just you and me," she said. "I think that would be best."

If I had been hoping, or fearing, that she would choose me, it was also a relief to recognise that family protocol would demand that either her mother or her husband must be her choice. What they thought I could only guess, but neither argued and Neil was allowed to push his wife through the door into a small room opposite. He dropped a kiss on the top of her head. "Tell Mr Dubois the truth and yell if you need anything," he had told her, before the door was closed. Within seconds he was back, to find the rest of us all talking at once. "Oh my goodness, what an awe-inspiring person" my mother said, managing to look charmingly fluttery and feminine and knowledgable all at the same time. Mr Kent was not sure how to reply to this, but was obviously trying to appear as though winkling top medical specialists like rabbits out of nowhere were to him all in a day's work – which I suspected might be all too true. Neil retired once more to the kitchen, to which Mrs Simmons had escaped as soon as she could from what was clearly going to be an intimate family conference. Sarah's mother was accusing her husband of being too darned dictatorial and why hadn't he discussed it with her first? Peter continued playing happily with the dog and I leaned closer to Jack for reassurance.

We were all offered cups of tea or coffee or even more glasses of the fast diminishing champagne but we all declined and simply remained where we were, talking in desultory fashion or sitting in quiet thought.

When it was my turn to present myself, the room I was invited to enter was obviously Sarah's personal study, for it was filled with books and a leather-topped inlaid walnut desk. Two comfortable chairs stood invitingly to the left of the desk, and light, terracotta-flowered curtains moved in the breeze coming from a half-opened window overlooking the rear gardens.

Mr Dubois was seated in one of the armchairs, legs stretched out and crossed at the ankle, flipping through a couple of pages of scribbled notes. He was not at all alarming and pointed in friendly fashion to the other chair. "Please sit down," he smiled, "and make yourself comfortable. I won't keep you more than a minute or two but you might as well be comfortable as not."

He grinned at me and I reluctantly grinned back, aware that putting people at their ease was part of his personal stock-in-trade. My personal interview (if you could dignify it by such a name) was brief and friendly. In fact he merely asked me three questions, all easily answered.

How long had I had known Sarah and how well did I know her now?

I replied to the first question first. "I met her for the first time only about two weeks ago since the beginning of May, in fact, but we became quite close very quickly and now I feel I've known her for most of my life. I would trust her with my own life, anyway."

"Thank you, that's very helpful." He regarded me directly, eye to eye. "Now the most important question - is she making it up – for any reason? Hysteria? Attention seeking?"

I smiled. "Hardly." I said, "If making four feathers multiply into several hundred in a closed and sealed box is making it up, I suppose one could accuse her of magic sleight of hand, but to be constantly living in a small feather storm which turns into clouds at the drop of a hat, I'm not sure a girl in a wheelchair could rustle up that kind of trick – day after day for a long period of time.. So my answer has to be no."

The phychiatrist waved his pen in the air and smiled back at me with a trace of amusement. "Of course there is always the question of an accomplice, is there not? So I think my final should be: 'Where do *you* think these feathers are coming from? You are one of the chief suspects for the role of accomplice, after all."

This time I shook my head, shrugged and lifted my own hands. "No idea," I said, "It's as much a mystery to me as to anyone and I've been asking myself that question for days now without being any nearer to an answer. For what it's worth, I don't think she knows either, or if she does it's a recent discovery she hasn't told me about. Not that she's had the chance. I was off being kidnapped, if you remember, and she's been surrounded by people ever since – not least my mother, who would have prised it out of her if anyone could. So if you're thinking of me as a possible suspect, please remember I was out of action for more or less a day and a half."

"Thanks," he said. "I appreciate what you've told me, but if you were really pressed what would you say? I suspect you have opinions you haven't expressed to anyone yet."

"Not really," I said. "I'm an atheist so find the idea of 'angels' and spiritual causes very hard to take seriously. I think If I really were pressed, I'd say there must be a physical explanation and all we have to do is find it. But so far we haven't."

"Quite. However, if you come to any conclusions, perhaps you could let me know." He handed me his business card. "I don't expect I'll be the last professional person to be asking these things, but I imagine you will be going back to your paper soon. You are on holiday I think?"

I shook my head again. How could I explain in one sentence? "I don't know the answer to that either. I only got engaged last night and we haven't had time to work out details yet. I haven't even had time to advise my paper yet." Then I twinkled at him. "Jack is Sarah's brother and the engagement has come as a surprise to everyone, myself included."

Mr Dubois stood up and held out his hand. "In that case, I hope you will be very happy and I'm even more sorry for intruding on such a momentous occasion." At the door, he bowed slightly and added, "Hopefully you won't spend your entire life in Feather-Feather-Land."

I laughed. "Don't worry, they don't come to me, only Sarah. Is there anyone else's you'd like to see? Neil, or her mother?""

"I have already spoken to Mr Kent, who assures me that his wife is firmly of the opinion that Sarah is right in her view of the situation. It seems she too has a very strong faith. However. I'd like talk to Neil next, if you will be so good as to ask him. He does have a choice, you know, but if you could tell him that his perspective would be extremely useful since, as Sarah's husband, he probably knows her in a way no-one else does. So if you ask Neil to come in. you yourself can now rejoin the happy throng. And by the way, congratulations once again and I hope you will be a very happy woman."

At the door he stopped me. "Before you disappear altogether I should warn you. Multiple Sclerosis is a strange disease and Sarah apparently has the worst kind. People can go for years and then suddenly go downhill, especially if they catch some kind of infection. Her immune system will be very vulnerable, so enjoy her while you can. Now go back to your young man and think happy thoughts about your own future."

# CHAPTER THIRTY

I slipped back into the room and motioned to Neil that it was his turn. He had frowned and looked as unwilling as I guessed he'd be feeling. As predicted by Mr Dubois, he asked if he had any choice, so I relayed the message I'd been given and watched him slip quietly away.

My mother was making fidgety movement, picking up and putting down again the handbag that never left her side, so I went over to sit on the arm of her chair, my own arm curling around the back of it. She looked up at me and I felt a swift moment of pity. Her lovely, ordered world was being shattered and she understood none of it. "Your father and I really ought to be getting on our way. You know I don't like motorways after dark."

"Yes, I do, and I'm really sorry I can't come with you, but there's no need to leave today, you know. Sarah has a spare room and so does Gran. We can find you some nighties or pyjamas and you can relax instead of fretting. Why don't you?"

My mother looked both confused and anxious. "Well, it would be...you'd better ask your father...I don't know...I'm smaller than you, so none of your things would..."

I laughed and squeezed her shoulders. My father was watching us unobtrusively but closely, as was his wont, so I raised my eyebrows at him. "You are being invited to spend the night here instead of trying to beat the motorway rush," I told him, fairly sure he had heard and understood his wife's gentle ditherings.

He smiled benignly at us both. "Sounds good to me." he said. "I assume you do have a proper bed for us. It won't be one of those 'drop in any time' politenessses where we land up on the floor in sleeping bags? Hadn't you better ask my mother? It is her apartment we're talking about, after all."

From his position in the window, staring out at the afternoon sunshine, Mr Kent turned to shake his head solemnly at all of us. "No need for that, Mrs Croft," he said, "Sarah has a very comfortable guest room and the bed can be made up in minutes, so as the official host is temporarily absent, I am acting o his behalf and inviting you to stay for as long as you find it necessary?"

I was not sure whether to clap or frown. Instead I looked across at Sarah, who seemed perfectly content with this arrangement. She nodded happily at me, so I hoped Neil would treat the invitation as a hospitable gesture, not as an attempt by his father-in-law to usurp his authority. My father, equally gracious, bowed his head in appreciation. "That is very kind of you, Mrs Chalmers and Mr Kent, and my wife and I will be very pleased to accept."

I squeezed my mother's shoulders again and bent to kiss her on the top of her newly manicured head. "So there you are," I told her. "All sorted, so you can stop worrying."

"And she can borrow one of my night-dresses," Mrs Kent offered, smiling with obvious pleasure. "I'm small too, you know, although I don't suppose Mrs Croft would know because she's never seen me standing up," and she laughed companionably.

My mother's attention was instantly taken up with this very nice-seeming lady who was offering her own night-dresses to a perfect stranger. I left them talking cozily together when Neil quietly slipped back into the room. This was a closed-up Neil, like a flower beginning to fold just before dusk. I was tired, so he must be too. I raised a questioning eyebrow at him. He nodded, smiled and quietly raised a thumb.

I sighed. Jack was standing close. "Jack," I murmured, "if you only knew how tired I am of being *questioned*."

"Poor Gemma," he whispered back, "I'm so sorry. Let's escape. Leave this rabble behind."

I leaned against him, reassured by the height and presence of him. I vaguely wondered how tall he was but was too exhausted to ask. I moved across to touch Sarah's hand. She was frowning. "I'm so sorry about all this," she whispered. "This is all my fault."

I wrinkled my nose. "Don't be any dafter than you are already," I told her. "Of course it isn't your fault. Even you couldn't empty that many duvets and pillowcases," and on that note I gave a last glance at the assembled families, some of whom were unaware of what was happening around them. After issuing his invitation Mr Kent had said nothing more. He had wandered back to the window and seemed to be communicating silently with the garden, the flowers and the silver birch. I wondered what was going through his mind, having so far been politely but firmly dismissed from the interviews. But too many thoughts were swirling round too small a head and for a moment I felt that my whole body would explode. Instead, with a small wave to Sarah, I went with Jack down through the door and down the steps to the last of the sunshine and the smiling garden.

I took a deep breath.

"This is all so lovely," I whispered, "and we've been missing it. Jack. I am so tired. So tired."

There in the garden he folded me up like one of the flowers at our feet and held me tightly against him. "My darling Gemma, I'm so sorry. Let's disappear – now – and see where fate takes us."

Neither of us spoke again until we were safely in his car and pulling in to the car park, for once unescorted by the usual clatter of clicking cameras, of a pub I had never seen before. It was square and unassuming. There were no mock Tudor additions, just creeper-climbed walls and small diamond-paned square windows, bright now with hanging baskets alight with pansies. We had been driving for almost half an hour, his hand - when it wasn't otherwise engaged in car business – resting lightly on my knee. We entered this new, strange pub and seated ourselves near a glowingly burning wood fire, face to face for the first time. Around us was the muted hubbub of local customers who knew each other but didn't know us, and I was comforted.

Jack touched the tip of my nose with one finger. "I'm guessing you like red wine or brandy. Not exotic cocktails with cherries and fruit and swizzle sticks."

I smiled for the first time, feeling as though I were slowly coming out of a catatonic state, paralysed by shock, confusion and fear but continuing to talk and smile and answer like some newly invented robot.. "Ten out of ten," I said, my voice sounding strange even to my own ears. "Wine for everyday and champagne for specials."

"In that case..." Jack left me briefly, to return almost at once with two full glasses. "There you are, not a swizzle in sight. But I thought we'd all had enough champagne for one day,"

Curiosity was stirring somewhere in the darkest region of my overloaded psyche. "Won't you be breathalysed?"

"No, I didn't drink when you did. I thought someone should keep a steady head."

I nodded gratefully. Then I sniffed, sipped and said: "Mmmmmm!," sitting quietly to study his face. It was a face so familiar that I seem to have known it since childhood, and yet somehow didn't know it at all. I blinked. I was now engaged to a man I had known for less than two weeks – and had disliked for the first part of them. And yet, I thought, I hadn't disliked him at all. To my bemused brain the situation seemed bizarre. If I didn't understand myself, how could anyone else do so?

"Darling Gemma, I have to ask you this. We can't go any further until I have. Do you really, truly want to marry me? I can fully understand why you might not. It's too soon, for one thing, and was a brilliant move on your part to spike your mother's guns. So tell me, please."

I took a deep breath. Words had become difficult. I put my hands on the table, palms up. He laid his own squarely on both.

"At this particular moment," I said at last, "there is nothing I'd like more than to marry you, but my head is so full of thoughts – and fears and questions – I am doubting my own sanity. Until you rescued me the other day, or whenever it was, I was fighting you. Then suddenly I wasn't, and something you said at the roadside stuck in my head. 'You don't know what you've lost 'til it's gone,' you said, and that's when I knew. I knew. I just knew I couldn't bear to lose you." We sat eye to eye for a blink or two, then I added: "Saying we were engaged was a terrible risk, but I was sort of kicked into it. And I wouldn't have held you to it."

Jack kissed both my palms, then fumbled in his pocket to bring out a small box. "Then shall we start again?" He opened the box to reveal a simple but heart-breakingly beautiful ring set with diamonds and sapphires. "Gemma Croft, will you marry me?"

I smiled and my eyes were wet. "Of course."

He put the ring carefully n my finger. "We are now formally engaged," he told me. He leaned across the table and kissed me full on the lips.

The locals didn't even notice.

I gazed at the ring almost in disbelief. The ring was too beautiful and too old, I felt, for it to have come from any village jewellers without immense cost, and if so where and when had Jack found and paid for it? Until that morning he had had no warning that I would pop the question, in public and out of a clear blue sky.

I asked him. "This is just immensely beautiful," I said, "but how did you know you'd be needing it?"

"It was my mother's. It was offered to Ruth, but she likes modern stuff so I was relieved when she refused it.

And of course I didn't know yesterday, but nipped home and fetched it from its hiding place – in my office safe – and since then I've been carrying it around waiting for the right moment. Sorry I didn't go down on one knee then, but I'm quite prepared to do it now."

This time I did laugh. It was a laugh of sheer enjoyment and relief.

"I'm so glad you didn't," I told him, "and if you do it now I shall only giggle. But Jack I love this ring, and the fact that it was your mother's makes it even more special. Doesn't she want it herself?"

"She said she was de-cluttering and never wears it now because it isn't her style any more."

It was some time before either of us spoke again. Then it was to discuss when and where and how we had changed each other's minds from war to surrender. The subject absorbed us both and we spared no details.

Finally, Jack said: "You've had rather a full few days, so I won't press you, but there are one or two questions – but only if you're up to answering them. You must be deathly tired of answering questions by now."

"That's okay, so long as they're not too complicated. My brain has gone scrambled-eggy, so if the answers come out backwards I'm afraid you'll have to work them out. Sorry."

"I'm willing to risk it if you are, so here goes. Question one: Do you intend to go back to London? Your holiday is coming to an end."

"Easy. I am giving up the high-powered media and aim to retire to the country. It's Just that I haven't done it yet. There hasn't been an awful lot of time! What I have done is tell the editor I'm giving the story to someone else to write because I have a conflict of interest and can't be impartial."

Jack leaned forward and kissed me again. "What do you aim to do instead?"

I grinned. "It would be fun to write a column for the local paper, and I'm also well enough known for magazines to receive my offerings with open arms, I hope. Publishers really only like stories from celebrities or war stories – or if all else fails, little country life tales, which is how Little Billy came to be accepted. It was a slow day and there was nothing much else happening. Well that's sort of the plan. Making them is hard at the moment. It's like we're standing on sand at the edge of the sea. Every wave shifts it a bit more and you lose your balance."

"The plan sounds good, as long as it includes me."

I very gently slapped his hand. "Stop fishing, and next question please."

This time Jack frowned, as if he were not too sure how to frame the strands of thought in his head.

"It's these feathers." He said eventually. "Where do you really, honestly think they're coming from, and why now? Why just to Sarah? My mother believes in God – she's a catholic, actually – so she truly believes they are from Him. Angels. A sign of something. She said right at the beginning that there's an old wives tale about if you find a white feather in your house it means an angel has been visiting."

"Yes, I've heard that already. Mrs Simmons quoted it. "

"So how do we account for the thousands of white feathers that have been dropping all around my sister? Why just her and not the whole family? Why does it seem to duplicate the story you wrote about Little Billy? These are things that, as a scientist, I ought to be able to find rational explanations for, but so far I haven't. It's a mystery and I don't like mysteries. Even the research into feathers hasn't revealed anything except that no-one has yet been able to identify the birds. I've trawled the internet and been in touch with the top ornithologists but no-one is any the wiser."

"How much do you agree with your mother, then, secretly. Forget the science part. What do your senses tell you?"

"My senses tell me I trust Sarah absolutely, and I've seen it all with my own eyes, so can't fob myself off with tales of fantasy because clouds of feathers witnessed by different groups of people at different times are, in fact, *facts"*

"So you don't believe in God yet can't get your head around the alternative?"

"Yep. That about covers it. And you...?"

"I don't know. And that's the truth. I simply don't know. My grandmother is a Christian. I think she started off as a Catholic too, but gravitated to Church of England, possibly because she likes the village church. I don't know. She never tries to convert me, which I appreciate, but although she hasn't given a downright opinion on the feathers, I suspect she's waiting to see what's going to happen next. She's very wise, Celia Croft, and I respect her judgement, so when she gets around to telling me what that is I shall listen – albeit sceptically. I don't believe in God either but so far haven't come up with a believable substitute. It's only a few weeks since I would have scoffed at these feather storms, but I have to admit I'm shaken. Turned my back on the question, I think, because I was focussing on Sarah rather than the feathers themselves. So I'm not being much help, am I? All I really know for sure is that her life seems to be draining away and I'm frightened. Billy had the same experience and he died young. Now I'm scared for Sarah, and I don't know what to do." I was silent for a moment then added what the psychiatrist had said. "He told me her M S was very aggressive so we are to enjoy her while we have her. I try not to show it, but this fear is eating me up inside."

"Then we'll talk about our own plans instead and leave the feathers to be feathers."

And over a pub supper and liquid refreshment followed by further mutual discoveries under the trees bordering the car park, that is what happened until it was so late that Jack thought it might be a good idea for him to take me home.

At one o'clock in the morning I climbed the steps to the front door of Croft Court and put myself quietly but happily to bed.

# CHAPTER THIRTY ONE

I woke after a fitful sleep in which fear for Sarah warred with delight for myself, so it was with relief that I finally moved from my room to the kitchen to pour myself a wake-up coffee and drink it seated on a stool at the kitchen table.

I was just rinsing my cup when Mrs Simmons appeared, bringing fresh air and a sense of purpose with her.

"Good, you're up," she said, giving me a fierce hug and a peck on the cheek. "I haven't seen you to say congratulations and I hope you'll be very happy."

I laughed and returned the hug. It felt a little like squeezing a teddy bear. "Did anything happen after we'd gone out?"

Mrs Simmons released me and shook her head, half laughing, half in disbelief. "My dear girl, you missed an uproar. There was such a cafuffle, you wouldn't credit."

I was intrigued. "Why? What had happened?"

"Well, after Mr Dubois had gone – and he had a quick word with me first. I'll tell you all about that later – Mr Kent started to say Sarah could expect more visits now, from scientists and paranormal experts and God knows who, when his wife and your father and Neil, and oh yes, Mrs Carpenter, who had just come to see how Sarah was doing – well, that's what she said, but it's my belief it was just nosiness, and who can blame her? – well, they all started on your Sarah's dad, saying as how she'd had enough poking and prying and making her go through it all again would be sheer cruelty. Inhumanity was what Neil called it. I've never seen him so upset. And your father too, I'd never heard him speak before, but he had plenty to say, apologising for not being a Kent but he had his own opinions and didn't like to see the poor girl harassed, and had Mr Kent thought it through?"

I was amazed and said so. It took a great deal to rouse my father from his usual polite, smiling non-interference since he deeply disliked arguments and avoided them if possible. "Wow!" I said, "So what happened then?"

"My dear, that was only the beginning. In the middle of it Peter's Mum, Ruth, came to fetch him back for tea, which caused another hoo-ha because of course the little chap didn't want to go. He was happy with Jake on the floor, playing with the feathers and rolling over and over, oblivious of everything that was going on over his head. So he had the biggest tantrum and was slapped by his mother, which caused more cries and more tears and Peter pummelled his mum and said it wasn't fair, nobody'd asked *him* and it wasn't fair to smack him for expressing his opinion, only he didn't exactly use those words."

"Oh, poor Peter," I was laughing, but sorry I hadn't been there to pour my own oil on his troubled waters. "I don't suppose the others approved of the smacking either, but carry on, how did they get him away?"

"Oh, she had to promise to bring him back today, first thing, and his dad picked him up and carried him off, sobbing his little heart out on Mike's shoulder. But even then the hoo-ha carried on because Mr Kent was really put out that everybody'd been getting at him, and started the argument all over again. But then Neil's young friend turned up to fetch his dog back, and Jake didn't want to go either and began licking Sarah's face and making a fuss of his own. Your mum looked horrified and I thought she'd be off to the bathroom any minute to get soap and facecloths and towels and things because she said dogs' tongues were unhygienic and Sarah had enough to worry about without having Jake pester the life out of her and give her all his nasty germs."

By this time I was laughing, but Mrs Simmons paused, as if struck. "You know, it's a funny thing but all this time nobody was asking what Sarah thought about it all. Any

214

of it. What she thought of being interviewed over and over again, or whether she wanted the dog to go, none of us had even seemed to think about it. So I looked at her, hard, and she was laughing – quietly and without fuss, just laughing as if she thought we were all funny and it was all a fuss about nothing. I wish you'd been there. She talks to you rather like the sister she never had. You can tell."

"I shall certainly ask her," I promised. "Did it calm down then?"

"Finally. In the end Sarah raised her arm as far as it would go, and it doesn't go very far these days, poor duck, and waved it. We looked at her. It was almost a surprise that she was still in the room. She told everyone to please stop shouting as the noise was giving her a headache and if they wanted to carry on arguing would they please do it elsewhere.

By this time I was almost jumping up and down in glee. "Good for her!" I shouted, "Well done Sarah. Go get 'em, girl!"

At that moment my grandmother opened the kitchen door, her eyebrows raised and with a smile of deep appreciation. "I don't know why you said it, but well done for saying it," she told me. "You can explain later, but right now I'm for coffee, so I hope you've left me some."

"With pleasure," I smiled in deep appreciation. "Gran, you are so *normal*. I do love you."

And I meant it. That there was more to come was certain, but right now I was 'in the moment' and enjoying it hugely.

I poured coffee from the machine into a cup and handed it to her. "Onwards and Upwards," I said.

The three of us toasted 'the moment' and smiled happily at each other

Early next morning I had just showered and pulled on jeans and a sweater when there was an urgent-sounding knock on my door. I opened it to find Neil, clutching at his blonde curls.

"For God's sake, Gemma, please will you come. Peter is distraught and now we've been taken over by a cat."

I didn't even attempt to make sense of this, but simply picked up my phone and followed him through the hall to his own front door, where sounds of wailing and strife reached us even before we had opened it.

I found a melee of one small boy howling his despair and refusing to be comforted by the four adults surrounding him. A few feet away Sarah sat in her wheelchair, half laughing, half sympathetic, but who was the recipient of her sympathy was impossible to guess. And curled up on her lap, seemingly unconcerned and happily receiving her blandishments, was the largest tortoiseshell cat I had ever seen. That Peter was having none of it was obvious to everyone. "I want Jake," he wailed. "Where's Jake? You *promised* me Jake."

Since all the adults were talking at once, the boy was not getting any answers, so continued to kick and wail and fight his tormentors.

I decided to take a hand. This was, after all, why I had been summoned. I closed the door behind me, summoned up all the head teachers I had ever known and clapped my hands loudly – twice – and shouted *"STOP"*. To my amazement (never having been a teacher nor ever desiring to be one), it worked. The noise stopped, Peter stopped wailing and all eyes were turned in my direction. Then the boy broke free from the rest and hurled himself at me, his arms around my waist as far as they could reach and his head buried in my stomach. "Oh please, please, Aunty Gemma, please get Jake back for me, please please *please.*"

As gently as I could, I unwrapped his arms, lifted his face and suggested that it might be a good idea for him and me to go for a walk – maybe even look for the dog. Who knew what we might find? In this I was well aware of the risk I was taking, but after having just taken the greatest risk of all by suddenly making a public announcement of engagement that my fiancé-to-be knew nothing about, what was one risk more? "So come on then, Peter, let's find your coat and get out of all this noise, shall we?"

No-one else uttered a syllable. Michael simply fetched his son's small red coat and opened the door. "Thanks," he muttered to me in passing, with a "Behave yourself," spoken kindly but firmly to Peter. The next minute we were outside in the quiet and stillness of a fresh morning garden.

"Race you to the swing," I said, releasing his hand. "You can have two seconds' start."

He won, of course, and we collapsed squashing together on the wide swing seat, out of breath but satisfied. "I won," he announced firmly.

"Definitely," I said, "but then I'm getting old, and old people don't run as fast as newly hatched people like you."

Peter giggled. "People don't hatch. It's chickens that hatch."

"Certainly, and what are you if not a Spring chicken?"

"I'm not a chicken I'm a boy."

"Okay, a Spring boy. What am I then?"

"An old lady? No, you're not. Your Grannie's that and my Grannie and Mrs Carp-carpen-what her name is, and – I haven't got any more grannies, but they're old. You're just *big*, like Daddy and Mummy and Uncle Jack. So why won't they let me play with Jake?"

The sudden change of subject made me smile but I answered his question seriously all the same. "It's because Jake isn't yours. He isn't ours either. He belongs to someone else and he was only visiting."

"But I want him."

"I know you do, and if I was in your shoes I'd want him too, but we can't keep him when he has a home of his own. It wouldn't be fair, would it? Just imagine – if you had a pet really and truly your own and someone liked him and decided to keep him, you'd be cross and unhappy, wouldn't you? Well, Uncle Neil's friend wouldn't like it if you pinched his dog, and maybe Jake wouldn't be happy either. Dogs like their own homes, and their proper owners, so just think how lucky you were to have him to play with for two whole days while his real master was away on business. He could have been in kennels, couldn't he? But instead he was here to play with you, so weren't you the lucky one?"

"But what about the cat? Whose is he?"

We were interrupted by hands on my shoulders and a voice issuing from above my head. "Actually, Peter, I can't answer that because I've only just arrived so you know more than I do? How about that, then? I didn't even know there was a cat so let's go back and find out and you can explain on the way," he suggested, adding quietly in my ear, "You're going to make a lovely mum."

"Uncle Jack," said Peter, looking up at him from his perch close beside me, and thereby disguising my unexpected (and uncharacteristic) blush. "Do you think a cat has come instead of a dog?"

Jack touched him on the top of his dark curls, "Who knows?" he solemnly. Peter and I stood up and jack came beside me, wanting to know why we were in the garden and what had been happening.

Since I knew little more than he did, I let Peter do the talking, with some breaking off now and again to kick a ball we had just found in the grass. "I want to be a footballer," he told us as we approached the front steps. We told him he would be a very good one, so it was with a relatively happy small boy that Jack and I came home "to find out all about it."

# CHAPTER THIRTY TWO

Sarah's apartment was relatively quiet with only my mother causing a fuss in the sitting room. She was insisting that they leave for home as soon as possible "to avoid the rush on the motorway." I was sorry for her because I knew quite well that the true cause was the cat. She hated and feared them. I found her doing the best she could in her own charmingly mangled way to explain this to her host and hostess. "It's not that I'm allergic," she was saying, apologetically but obviously expecting to be heard and obeyed. "I don't get rashes or puff up or anything, I just don't like them anywhere near me. They get fleas and they're too quiet so you never hear them coming and I don't know why but they frighten me, like witches' cats, and I can't think why this one isn't all black as it should be, so I expect to see broomsticks – only now it's feathers, and I'm not at all surprised this cat has appeared from nowhere, it's exactly what you'd expect a cat to do."

She paused for breath and I kissed her cheek. "Darling Mama," I said soothingly, "Nobody is trying to persuade you to do anything you don't want to do. They are just offering hospitality and of course you're free to go early, to miss the traffic, so please don't worry about it. Honestly, everybody simply wants to make you happy." I didn't even try to put her straight on the subject of witches' cats, or even why this one should be tortoiseshell and not black. She would not have believed me. So I helped her with her suitcase, gave my father a big hug and received a kiss and a pat on my jeans-clad lower regions. He did, however, whisper in my ear: "You're a good girl, Gemma, just be careful and I like your boyfriend."

"Thanks," I whispered back. "So do I."

We both laughed. Within five minutes we had packed them both neatly into the car and waved them off down the drive. I smiled but felt a weight of mixed guilt and relief. I loved my mother. I simply couldn't live with her.

Sarah was where we had left her and I wondered why, until the realisation dawned, properly and for the first time, that she could no longer use her hands. She was now incapable of using them or her lower arms to propel the large wheels. She was also very white and, I saw with rising concern, her frailty was now only too obvious. I went immediately to her side, to pick up her unresponsive hand, stroke it and kiss her softly on the cheek.

"What have we done to you?" I murmured. "Why has no-one noticed? Why didn't I notice?"

"What could you have done? And anyway I'm okay – really, honestly, cross my heart!"

"I could have stopped everyone worrying you."

"Don't be daft, of course you couldn't. But it's all over now. Everyone has gone and it's quiet again and although I don't know where this majestic creature has come from, or even who he belongs to, I aim to enjoy his company while I have it. And yours," she added, leaning her head briefly against my arm.

"It's yours for as long as you want it." I said, stroking the cat's head with one finger. My eyes were wet but Sarah wasn't looking at me so didn't see. There was so much I needed to know, but questions could wait. She had had enough, and, for the moment, so had I.

With a last quietly unobtrusive touch of Sarah's hair and a grateful smile for the carer, who appeared at that moment with a hot drink, a straw and a biscuit on a tray, I fled into the entrance hall and crossed to my grandmother's door. I found her in the kitchen with Mrs Simmons. They stopped talking as soon as I appeared.

"Gemma!" My grandmother was pleased to see me. "What have we been missing?"

I told them about my parents' departure, which they had witnessed through the sitting room window. They had apparently called in to say goodbye while I was in the garden with Peter, so it came as no surprise to either of them that my mother was escaping not only from a possibly flea-encrusted hairy animal but all the embarrassment of a family row which had nothing to do with hers. I asked my grandmother and Mrs Simmons if either of them knew where the strange cat had come from but they denied any knowledge of it. "We assumed it belonged to a resident, one nobody has approached so far." said Mrs Simmons, "We've only scratched the surface here, you know. Perhaps we should all go and knock on a few more doors. There's plenty more on the second floor."

I frowned. "He might have an identity chip. That is, if it's a 'he' but he certainly looks like one to me. Big square face and a sort of male-ness about him. We should have him checked by a vet. Someone may be crying their eyes out looking for him. Meanwhile I'm just off to catch up with the others upstairs. They may know more than we do, and they need to be put in the picture, whatever picture that is. They might be feeling excluded with all the Croft/Kent discussions going on without them."

With promises to be back in time for the next meal, whatever that turned out to be, so disorganised had we become. - "Have we had breakfast or lunch? Do you know I've completely forgotten" - I blew them both kisses and departed for the lift and any view points that might be forthcoming from our nearest neighbours.

I knocked on the Starlights' doorbell first. It was answered at once by Angela. She grinned hugely at the sight of me. "Oh wonderful, come in, come in. We feel so out of things up here. Have your parents gone yet?"

Without giving me time to answer. She persuaded me into an armchair and stood looking down at me. Lucy stood beside her. "Give the poor girl a chance," she said, "and before we do anything else, we're going to toast the newly engaged person in front of us. Is it to be tea, coffee or something alcoholic? We are so delighted, if we had tails they'd be frantic with wagging."

Laughing, I finally said that it was a good job they weren't because I'd collected enough bruises from my last encounter with Jake's tail and preferred not to collect any more.

A grinning Lucy appeared with tall stemmed glasses and three empty cups ready for coffee. "Take your pick," she commanded. "Give Evelyn a ring," she told Angela, "she should be here for this."

"What about the film star?" I asked. "Why is she to be left out?"

Lucy paused in her pouring. "Do we dare? She's the sort of person one doesn't take liberties with, but I'll ask her. She's been a part of it, hasn't she, so she deserves a look-in."

We agreed Eliza might feel hurt if we didn't at least give her the chance to say no, so Angela looked at a scribbled list of numbers – obviously new – and dialled one of them. Within minutes the doorbell rang to usher in not only Evelyn Carpenter but the immensely powerful presence of the Rainbow lady. It seemed right to be all together once again. I told them, fairly briefly, what had happened so far and that conclusions seem to have been reached by the assembled Crofts and Kents, "but mostly Kents," I added, "since they outnumber Crofts by at least three to one."

"Well, you will soon be one of them yourself, won't you?" Ms Redfeld smiled at me and raised her by now wine-filled glass. "But I must warn you that media coverage hasn't gone away. I was caught yesterday, driving out of the gates, and asked if it was true you were engaged to marry one of the Kent brothers, and they wanted my opinion about what's been happening here. I was noncommittal of course, since I don't really know enough myself – but they did ask whether I thought you had invented the whole story for a scoop for your paper and of course, for yourself."

I was not especially surprised. The idea had occurred to me as a likely media perspective, but the Starlights cried out indignantly.

"What did you say to that?"

"The truth. That I haven't known you long enough to comment, but that from what I have seen so far the idea is not only highly unlikely but idiotic. For a start, where on earth could you have procured so many feathers? The thought is bizarre."

The others were looking at me in consternation. I glanced around the room. "What do you all think?"

"The same as Eliza. of course," Mrs Carpenter nodded, and the Starlights added their nods vigorously to hers.

I gazed at them all with a mixture of awe and speculation, but above all with foreboding. "The trouble is," I said at last, "I know how these things work and there's something about all this that's worrying me. We shall just have to wait and see. But meanwhile I'm about to phone my boss to make sure he received my message to give the story to someone else because I am too involved. He's probably already done it, but at least it will show wiling. Not that I want to keep the story. I'm sick of it; it's caused nothing but trouble, and anyway if I hadn't written the first stupid article nobody would have known." I sighed. "Is this ever going to end?" I asked them.

Ange was the first to reply. "You're not stupid," she said. "it started before you ever came here and you didn't invent the story, someone gave it to you.. Meanwhile let's have another glass of wine," She picked up the bottle and flourished it.

"And just to add to it all," I said, sipping thoughtfully, "there's the question of the cat."

Instantly, three pairs of eyes were focussed upon me. "What cat?"

I explained that a newcomer had taken up residence on Sarah's lap. Then, having established that none of those present had any knowledge of this latest acquisition, I took a few more sips, decided I had drunk enough for one day and left them to their own puzzlement while I went back down downstairs to try to make sense of my own.

My grandmother had left Mrs Simmons in the kitchen and was seated comfortably in her recliner chair, feet up and eyes closed. They opened to find me standing next to her. She smiled sleepily at me. "I wasn't asleep," she told me, and held out her hand. "Did you learn anything new?"

"I'm afraid so," I admitted, and relayed Eliza's brief encounter with the press. "And no-one we know upstairs has any knowledge of a cat. We think it may belong to some of the other residents – ones we didn't catch on our first trawl. I'm going to type out a notice and put it through everyone's door, and it's time we took the poor thing to the vet to find out if it's micro-chipped. If so, we can contact an owner. If not, I suppose Sarah can keep it until an owner turns up."

"Good thinking," said my grandmother, "but I'm more concerned about the new press story. What are you going to do about it?"

"I'm about to email my boss to ask him to take me off the story for good, not just for now. I have already compromised not only myself but the paper, so I don't think he'll need much persuading - although one never knows for sure what editors want to do. However, I am now a liability – not a happy position to be in for any of us."

Gran looked hard at me, then said "Go and do it now, then. You won't be happy 'til you have."

I nodded, left for my own room and typed out 10 duplicated 'Cat Found' notices, four to an A4 page, printed them off, cut them into strips on my small, guillotine that was kept permanently in residence ready for my visits, and placed them ready for distribution.

Before beginning the email to the editor, I did what I had avoided doing for the past two days. I tapped into my Facebook and Twitter correspondence. What I read there was so unpleasant that I quickly left the pages and wrote to my boss instead. I had just received enough confirmation of the argument now raging about me, to know that it would be impossible for me to continue in my present job. Other, thicker-skinned reporters might, but I was discovering yet another truth – that the hard and ambitious Gemma Croft was not only thinner-skinned than she had believed but was as vulnerable as anyone else in this world.

The email to my boss took so little time to write that it was composed, checked and sent within the next ten minutes, after which I metaphorically dusted my hands, cleared my brain, told my grandmother I would be next door, and departed once more.

# CHAPTER THIRTY THREE

My real need was to contact Jack, but first it was necessary to talk to Sarah and Neil, so I squashed my first instincts and opened Sarah's door, expecting to find her alone or with Neil or one of the carers. What I found was a roomful or people and a brand new electric wheelchair.

"Oh wonderful!" I said, "just what I was thinking about. What's it like, Sarah?"

She smiled happily and demonstrated how she could manipulate the little knob on the right arm by placing it in the crook of her thumb and forefinger. "Look," she said. "Isn't it clever? And just what I need right now."

I glanced around the room to find both Mr and Mrs Kent gazing at their daughter with gratified pleasure, 'Mission Accomplished' exuding from every pore. Behind the wheelchair, Neil was bending over the workings, examining everything in the greatest detail.

Everyone seemed pleased to see me. Even Mr Kent included me in his welcoming grin. There was, however, someone missing. "Jack not coming today?"

"Been and gone," Neil told me, "He's taken the cat to the vet to see if it's been micro-chipped. He'll be back soon." He looked up at me and winked. "So you haven't missed him. He's bringing today's papers as well."

"That's three of JC Kent's chief officers playing truant," I declared. "The only one missing is Michael – and Peter, of course."

Mrs Kent came over to my side and said no doubt they would be along any minute as well. "It's difficult to keep Peter away from here, although I don't think he'll forgive Neil in a hurry for taking Jake away. Mind you, he did rather take a fancy to the cat in the end, so here's hoping. So where have you been? You look as if you have news."

I flourished the slips of Cat notices to be distributed among the apartments, but said I thought it best if we waited for the papers before saying any more, as our film star had apparently had an altercation with the press on her way out last night.

"Oh, are they still around?" Mrs Kent was surprised. "I thought the nine days' wonder would have died a natural death by now. Sarah hasn't been deluged by feathers as much as she was a few days ago, have you darling? But there's still plenty coming," and she flicked one from her sweater while I retrieved another from her hair. Sarah's lap had received a good many, but they were at least quiescent, causing no real fuss or disruption. I wondered privately how long they would continue to visit Sarah, who in any case seemed entirely unperturbed by them. It had become a family concern rather than a personal one.

At that very moment, when my thoughts were turning yet again to Jack, he came through the door carrying a serene-looking tortoiseshell cat. Unfortunately the cat didn't remain serene. On first sight of the new wheelchair, he jumped instantly to the ground and approached it with the greatest caution, paw by paw, sniffing warily at every part he could reach. Finally, he lifted his chin to Sarah and leapt with surprising agility back onto her welcoming lap, where both appeared to breathe a comprehensive sigh of relief. After two approving licks of Sarah's arm, he turned round twice and settled like a satisfied, purring pillow.

"He's just given you two kisses," I murmured to Sarah, "a sign of high approval, believe me."

Jack's voice from behind me asked if he came in for any of the kisses..

"You'd better ask the cat. They're his kisses. Has he or she got an owner or a name, and has he or she been micro-chipped?"

"No and no. No owner and so far no name although he is definitely a male. Sarah had better give him his name, since he seems to have adopted her."

"Right. The naming is your job then Sarah," I said, "although I suspect you might have christened him already." Then I turned to face Jack and urgently asked the question that had been on my mind since my visit to the Starlights. "Did you bring today's papers?"

"I did. We'll talk about them in a minute, but first on our own, I think, because they're going to make you mad as hell. But fear not, Ginger-knob, together we shall overcome."

With that I had to be content. With the soubriquet of Ginger Knob I quite patently wasn't. I ignored it, however. There were worse things in life than nicknames, and the content of the newspapers was top of my agenda. "Can we go somewhere private, please. I can't wait any longer."

Jack put his arm around me and squeezed. "Does that apply to me or the papers?"

I disdained to reply except to dig him very gently in the ribs. With another squeeze, he led me through the door, waving in valedictory fashion to the rest of the company who were, in any case, too entranced with the new wheelchair to notice, and ushered me through to the entrance hall and the staircase. There he placed me firmly on the second step and wedged himself beside me. Retrieving his arm, he opened the wad of newspapers he had been carrying rolled up inside his jacket and unfolded the first one to show the front page. In hearty capitals, it shouted: "FEATHER- STORM REVEALED AS FEATHER -SCAM." It then went on to describe how "sources close to Ms Croft, who had been 'reporter-on-the-spot' in the so-called feathers mystery, had spoken of their doubts as to its truth from the very beginning. They had also expressed their misgivings at the recent engagement of Croft to the wealthy MD of JC Kent Electronics Ltd, Jack Kent, who was suspected of conniving to produce the feathers in large quantities. "Lucky Gemma," the story continued, "to have landed so firmly on her feet, not only with a scoop for her paper but with a rich fiancé as well."

There was plenty more of the same, repeated over and over in the other papers. I was aghast and turned to stare wide-eyed with horror at this new wealthy fiancé whom I had somehow ensnared into acting as my partner in a full-scale fraud.

Jack stared back then dumped the papers on the next stair and enfolded me in a close and utterly reassuring embrace.

"It's my fault, all of it," I muttered wetly into his shoulder. "If I hadn't written that stupid story about Little Billy..."

Jack stopped me with a kiss. "No it is **_not_** your fault," he said at last, giving my shoulders a gentle shake. Then he planted his chin on the top of my head and gave a small, if ironic, chuckle. "I wonder what they would say if they knew that from either direction our relationship was not Love at First Sight but Hate at First Sight. You can't take any of this seriously."

My voice was muffled against his jacket. "They wouldn't believe you, at least not in public, and they don't take it seriously themselves," I told him. "It's just a rattling good story that they're making the most of before something bigger comes along. But what's bothering me is, who is or are the sources close to me? I would swear it isn't the Starlights or Evelyn Carpetnter, and it was Eliza Redfield who told me about getting nabbed at the gate. Why should she tell me that if she was the source of lies about me. She doesn't know me, for heaven's sake."

"Does that matter? She could make up a long and intimate friendship if she wanted, and get away with it. Could it be one of the carers?"

I sniffed. "If so she's a suicidal fool. She'd be sacked on the spot. In fact I'm afraid they all will be when he reads all this, just in case! Not that that would worry this one overmuch, now I come to think of it. If she was being paid by the paper she wouldn't care about getting the sack, would she? It all depends on who it is and why they did it."

Jack sighed. "You could be right," he said.

"The trouble is," I added mournfully, "Mud like this sticks. People always want to believe the worst. That's what the press relies on. Who wants to read a happy story if they can read a nasty, bitchy one with lots of blood and tears? I had a quick foray into Facebook and Twitter this morning and wished I hadn't. It was vile."

A voice above us said "I hate to disturb Love's Yung Dream" Evelyn said, "but I was hoping to call on you and Sarah to commiserate. No, don't move, I'll squeeze past you."

"We were just going anyway," Jack stood up to make room for us all to descend once more from our second stair perch. The three of us met at the bottom and stared at each other.

"Not good news," Evelyn said, pulling a face, "but Eliza told us earlier about being caught at the gate."

I was surprised. "Was it her blowing the gaff? She gave no indication."

"No, I'm sure not."

"She is an actress after all,"

Jack frowned. "There are plenty of other suspects, so we mustn't jump to conclusions. As you say. She hardly knows you."

"When did details like that stop the gutter press?"

We were silent for a moment then I changed the subject, turning to frown at Evelyn. "You're a crime writer," I said, "what do you personally make of these feathers?"

She gave a small chuckle. "I may be a crime writer, but this is rather out of my remit – more into fantasy fiction than murder, not that I believe it to be fantasy. Fantastic maybe but we've all seen it happen," she replied, "so the question is impossible to answer. The leakage to the press, though, is another matter. That's definitely not fantasy. Somebody is talking out of turn but, more than that, whoever they are they're either getting their facts wrong or are just being malicious. That's the real whodunit."

"I wonder if it's actionable," Jack mused. Could Gemma or her paper sue?"

"Not sure. It might be worth a try, but not until we've found out a bit more."

"I don't think it would help," I said, after a moment's thought. It would only prolong something we all want forgotten." Then I bit my lip and put my last question. "You two are both observant people. Is it my imagination, or is Sarah deteriorating rather fast? I've only been here two weeks but the change is noticeable – and worrying."

It was Jack who answered. "Her M S is aggressive. It suddenly goes downhill then just as suddenly goes into remission and I think that's what's happening now. it's a matter of wait and see. She will certainly be prescribed heavier medication so we have to hope it works."

I sighed, nodded and moved towards the door. "In that case, let's go in and face the music. Got your violins handy? I guess we're going to need 'em." With that, I opened the door and walked through it to the conservatory.

# CHAPTER THIRTY FOUR

The room was calmer, the company seated in their cushioned basket chairs sipping from cups of coffee currently being dispensed by a tray-carrying Neil. He saw us and pointed to the tray. "Dead on cue," he smiled. "I don't know if anyone is hungry but we seem to be missing a meal somewhere along the line. Is Mrs S still here?"

I thought she might still be in Grandmother's kitchen but would fetch her if and when required. Mr Kent scrutinised Jack and myself and glanced questioningly at the newspapers under Jack's arm. "Well? Don't hold back. I've already seen some of the headlines."

Jack nodded. "Thought you might. Here they are. Don't take off. Gemma's been through enough already without adding any more angst."

Mr Kent nodded briefly, opened the front page of one newspaper and read it out in disbelief. "Feather-storm revealed as Feather scam? And who in the world is the source close to home?" He frowned at me. "If I thought for one moment....."

It was Sarah who interrupted. "Pops, don't even think of blaming Gemma. I can prove it wasn't her, and so can Neil and so can Mrs Simmons."

"Ah yes, Mrs Simmons, a member of the Foley family who have no reason to love us."

"And no reason to hate us either."

"Come on, everybody," said Mrs Kent, leaning towards Sarah's chair to stroke the cat, "Mrs Simmons has been a huge support through all of this, so let's enjoy our coffee and think about it sensibly. And it's a lovely day out there, the sun is shining and the garden is looking so beautiful."

Visited by a sudden idea, I murmured "Hang on a second," and walked through to Sarah's now empty kitchen. The original feather box, once again securely taped, sealed, and signed by Angela, Lucy and Evelyn

Carpenter, had been replaced on its shelf. The temptation was strong to open it straight away, to see if the four feathers carefully placed there had multiplied once again. But I resisted. I would be ne rendering three peoples' signatures invalid – a silly thing to do. Instead I lifted the box from its resting place and took it through to the conservatory. I placed it carefully on the table beside Sarah's chair and we exchanged glances. "Just in case," I murmured. She nodded.

At the sight of the box all argument stopped abruptly.

Mr Kent regarded it speculatively. "What's this?"

"It's the box originally sealed and signed by Sarah, me and Neil. As you know, it contained four feathers when we sealed it, but we were all here when we opened it and, if you remember, a huge cloud of them sailed out – several hundred I would have said, at the very least. Well, it was sealed again the other day with four more feathers in, and it's been signed by..." Here I paused to glance at the signatures..."by Angela, Lucy and Evelyn here. Would somebody like to open it?" I glanced at Sarah, who nodded but gestured towards her now practically useless hands. "Mr or Mrs Kent, would either of you like the honour?"

Mrs Kent picked up the box and smiled, rather impishly, I thought. "Yes please. I would very much like the honour."

Mr Kent regarded me with his normal, speculative eye. I wondered how long it would take him to accept me. "You realise you are taking a risk?" he asked me.

"Of course, but isn't everybody? There's a lot riding on this, and not just for me. For the whole family and all the residents."

I handed Mrs Kent the scissors that lay, unused now, on Sarah's worktable. She took them and carefully snipped the tape that criss-crossed the box, preserving as much of the signed label as possible. Then very gently she opened the lid. I held my breath. Any change in feather type would suggest I/we had run out of the original ones, while just four on their own would suggest they had stopped coming altogether.

What I did not expect was what we found.

The box was empty.

I had read the clichéd term "goggle-eyed" but so far had never had occasion to use it. I did now. If a group of people can all be goggle-eyed at the same time, we were that group.

"Where have they gone?" Evelyn was now quietly and unobtrusively panicking. "There were four in there – we all checked the number before we closed the box. So where are they now?"

"Did anyone see any fly out?" I asked everyone in turn. They all shook their heads. Mrs Kent was frowning. "It was me who opened it and I did it slowly, so as not to disturb what was in there."

I began to laugh. "Can we all look around please? There must be four all together somewhere." We all looked and found a great many separate feathers but no four in any one place.

It was then that Mrs Kent stood up to join in the search and saw four immaculate white feathers lying just inside the back of Sarah's collar. For a moment she said nothing, then she picked them all up and held them aloft.

"Guess what I've found!" she cried.

We all stopped what we were doing and stared.

"How in the world did they get there?" Neil scratched his head. "Nothing moved. I'll swear nothing moved."

Mrs Kent smiled her triumph. "'What in the world' is the right question. I was actually leaning over the box when I opened it because I was curious, and I can join Neil in swearing that nothing came out. Absolutely nothing. If it had it would have gone straight up my nose."

Mr Kent was growing more and more frustrated and angry. What is more, he was looking straight at me. "Maybe it was empty when you all signed for it. An obvious conjuror's trick. And who fetched it from the kitchen? Who is the one person who could have tampered with it?"

I stared back. We were eye to eye, his accusatory, mine defiant.

I had had enough.

"If that is what you think of me, Mr Kent, an ambitious liar, a cheat and a fraudster who will go to any lengths to preserve a good story, then you are free to do so. I can't stop you. But will you first get your facts right. I was not present when the box was filled, closed and sealed. I did not sign on the tape because, if you can remember that far back, I was imprisoned in a child's bedroom with Sarah's husband and the only taping was on our wrists. And now, speaking personally, I've had enough."

With that, I kissed the top of Sarah's head, gave her mother a quick hug and walked towards the door. Sarah cried "Gemma, don't. I can't bear this. Please don't leave like that."

I turned at the door to glance briefly around the room. "Sorry Sarah, I can't stay here. If anyone agrees with your father then I'm sorry for it, but until I can prove otherwise I shall make myself very, very scarce. And until then, I am giving Jack his ring back. I refuse to marry into a family that could harbour such horrible, vile suspicions."

With that, I slipped the ring from my finger and handed it to Jack, who shook his head and refused to accept it, whereupon I dropped it, bouncing, onto the carpet by his feet.

As I opened the conservatory door, I was followed by wails from Sarah, her mother and, curiously, from the cat, who stood up and stared at me from his position on Sarah's lap. Cats are incapable of showing emotion in their faces, but I would swear to seeing reproach in his large golden eyes. At the very last minute, Evelyn joined me and we slipped through together.

In the main hall, I turned to Evelyn, unable to contain my combined fury, hurt and exasperation for one moment longer. With my face to the ceiling, I howled with anger and frustration sounding, even to me, like an enraged, caged animal. We looked each other in the eye, then Evelyn put her arms around me. I leaned, sobbing, into her shoulder.

She rocked and shushed me for a minute or two, then held me away so she could speak directly into my face. "Listen, chick," she murmured, "Somebody is out to cause you grief. We'll find out who is doing this, don't worry, and certainly don't take any notice of Mr Kent. He's confused and it's making him feel helpless. He can't control this, you see. We none of us can, but he's used to being in command and this time he isn't. Tomorrow he'll have had time to realise what he's done."

"But Jack..." I began, "I've given him back...I've given him his ring...he'll think I meant it."

This time Evelyn laughed. "Then you'll just have to teach him how to treat a Red Croft."

My response was automatic. "Auburn," I muttered. Evelyn laughed again. "That's my girl," she said. "Now come and sit with me on the stairs and we can talk about Jack. News headlines can wait."

We squeezed together on the very same stair that had cosily held Jack and myself only mnutes before, it seemed. She handed me a packet of tissues, one of which I obligingly blew into, and was just about to launch into a wordy and not very clear description of my situation when the front door opened. Michael came in with a rush and a wad of newspapers. He saw us on the stairs and paused. "What's going on here?"

Evelyn answered for me, since I was sniffing into a tissue and felt no inclination to come out from behind it. "Strictly girl talk," she explained. "If you go through to the conservatory you will no doubt be brought up to date. You might even be in time for one of Neil's coffees."

Mike took no notice. "It's obviously more than that," he accused. "Something to do with these I expect." He flourished the newspapers. "But don't worry, kiddo, Red Crofts are fighting folk. They don't have that hair for nothing."

This time it was Evelyn who frowned at him. "It's not red, Michael, it's auburn."

Mike smiled in appreciation but showed a strong tendency to lean against the wall and chat. "If Gemma is upset, which she obviously is, why isn't Jack here dispensing the old reassuring hug. Shall I send him out?"

"No," I shouted, coming out suddenly from my hiding place. "He'll come when he's good and ready – or when I'm good and ready." The explanation turned into something between a burgeoning wail and a cry of defiance. "You'll know soon enough so I might as well tell you. I've given him his ring back."

Mike was astonished. "You've what? I don't believe it."

"Try." I said.

"If you go in, you'll be told," Evelyn intervened. I caught the warning frown and headshake aimed in his direction and was grateful. I was in no mood for Kents of any description, except of course for a repentant and comforting Jack should he deign to appear. I was more than prepared for his silence. Jack Trent, like the rest of his family, was probably not much given to apologising, although what he would have been apologising for in this case was debatable. It was his father who had hurt me, not he himself. Besides he had told me quite clearly and publicly that he was staying in order to be my advocate. Justice alone had to be on his side in this.

But I was in no mood for justice. Mike took one look at my stormy expression, doffed an imaginary cap and put his hand on Sarah's door knob.

Just as he was about to step through, I suddenly stopped him. Someone was missing and I needed to know why. "Hang on a minute," I said, "Where's Peter?"

Mike pulled a face. "Bad case of chest infection," he said. "Poor little sod, not good at all. Went down with it last night. Ruth isn't pleased; she's having to miss work." And with that he slipped through the door and vanished.

I shivered. "Any infection," the psychiatrist had said. "Vulnerable immune system."

What more was to be visited upon Sarah – upon us all?

# CHAPTER THIRTY FIVE

My mind, already in overdrive since Mike's arrival, focussed on Peter's chest infection and added one more strand to the mix, which had grown into what I was beginning to think of as a ball of muddled knitting wool, all colours and a multitude of ply. There was so much of it. Problem was being added to problem and all I really wanted now was to put my head down somewhere, sleep and forget the lot.

I turned to Evelyn. "Was my grandmother in the room?" I asked her.

"I think she might have slipped out at some point, but you know how quietly she can do things."

I jumped up. "I must go and find her," I said. "If anyone asks I'll be in my own room."

Evelyn nodded, stood up and put a hand on my arm. "She'll be wanting to see you. If she comes looking for you, I'll explain."

"Thanks," I said, "and thank you for being such a sport. You've been terrific." With that, I opened my grandmother's front door and went inside.

She was sitting at a small side table writing in a notebook. The sight of her was enough to let loose even more the tide of frustration and emotion that had been built up over the past few days. I flew across the room, to kneel at her feet and put my head in her lap. I was by now almost too tired to cry. Reluctant tears were accompanied by the frustrated, angry roars of cornered beasts.

Gran stroked my hair but said nothing until the storm had abated.

"Darling girl, "she murmured, "What a time you've been having, and I'm afraid it's all my fault."

I raised my head enough to shake it violently, groped in my pocket for a stray tissue, pulled one out and blew my nose. That small gesture seemed to take all my energy because I instantly collapsed, a balloon pricked and deflated. It was at that point that Mrs Simmons crept through the door, hesitant in case she may not be wanted. She saw me kneeling, apparently comatose with a lifeless head in my grandmother's lap.

"Oh dear, oh dear," she said, laying a hand on my head and gently stroking it. "Poor lamb, we've been asking too much of her – except for you Mrs Croft. You must be the only wise person here right now." Then as a cautious after-thought she asked her if maybe she should fetch Jack. I hardly had the strength to move my head but managed a small shake and a whisper of "no," after which I must have passed into unconsciousness. Life had suddenly become too much and I wanted no more of it.

I awoke in daylight but, since I had apparently fallen asleep in daylight this gave no clue as to which part of the day I was in at that moment. I reached out a reluctant arm to feel for my bedside clock and peered muzzily at it. The result came as a shock. It was half past nine in the morning. At precisely the same moment I discovered that my top clothes had been peeled from me and now lay neatly folded on my bedroom chair. Disconcerted, I just had time to recognise the strong aroma of frying bacon, underscored with the irresistible one of fresh coffee, when my grandmother opened the door and came towards me carrying a cup of something that steamed seductively. I sat up.

Her "Good morning," was said in a perfectly normal voice betraying no especial concern "You're a lazy pup, did you know that?"

I blinked, trying to grope my way through a blur of confusion and ignorance. "What am I doing here and how long have I been asleep, and I assume it was you who undressed me?"

To my surprise she laughed. "Well no, actually it wasn't. More a sort of combined ops, but Jack did most of it."

"Jack did?" I was now thoroughly awake. "For heaven's sake tell me what happened here? Last I knew I was on the floor sobbing into your knees."

"Drink your coffee and come and eat the breakfast Mrs Simmons is cooking, but don't expect this kind of treatment every day, *Mzzzz*Croft, because I consider myself to be owed a return from you at some suitably opportunity. Now I could offer you breakfast in bed, but somehow I think you may want to rise and greet the day."

I took the cup from her and drank from it. It was, of course, Mrs Simmons' special brew of freshly ground coffee beans, hot and stimulating. I raised the cup in salute. "Yes of course I'll get up and please thank Mrs S for her coffee and what I can smell of breakfast. But explanations A S A P please."

"Yes ma'am," She doffed an imaginary cap and left the room.

Breakfast was a cheerful affair, leaving me no chance to focus on the news headlines of the day before, and it was with a feeling of satisfaction that I left the table and strolled to the window. It overlooked the front garden and the drive.

It was as well that I did, for parked at the bottom of the steps was an ambulance, and coming up at top speed, carrying bags of what I assumed to be equipment, were two paramedics.

I turned to my grandmother, all feelings of satisfaction gone at once, and said "Gran. There's an ambulance. I have to go."

My grandmother looked up, startled. "Yes, go," she ordered, hand and finger pointing to the door. "I'll follow."

I arrived in Sarah's apartment. She was in bed. In a small clutch by the door there was a quiet but earnest altercation going on between the carer, Neil, Mrs Kent and the doctor, who must have been called while we were enjoying our 'Full English' in Gran's dining room. The paramedics were obviously prepared. They had their equipment arranged for transport, if not already in use. Sarah herself was saying nothing. She was too busy coughing weakly, obviously distressed because she was unable to hold tissues for herself. She looked flushed and hot and harassed. Occasionally she shook her head in resolute denial but nobody was taking any notice apart from her mother, who was speaking quietly in her daughter's ear. I stood for several minutes unnoticed until anxiety drove me to kneel by Sarah's bed and gaze first at her than at the small, resolute lady on Sarah's other side.

"Chest infection," she mouthed. "Doctor insisted she go to hospital but Sarah said no and Neil's been backing her up."

I frowned. I turned to look at Neil, who was standing rock-like beside the doctor. I raised my eyebrows in a silent question. He shook his head. "I promised her," he murmured. "She made me promise not to send her away. Says she's fine here with her nurses. What do I do?"

I looked back at Sarah, who was by now seemingly in a little world of her own. She was very white, with flushed spots on her cheeks. Her breathing was laboured. I spoke her name but there was no response, even when I touched her hand. Mrs Kent and I gazed at each other then, by mutual and unspoken consent it seemed, we both shook our heads. "I don't think we have a choice," she said.

"You haven't," the doctor nodded briefly in a way that brooked no argument. "Okay you guys," he told the paramedics and gave peremptory orders. Sarah was wrapped in blankets and moved carefully onto a stretcher of some kind. If we had expected some resistance she was obviously beyond the point of making any. Her mother and Neil both declared their intention of going with her. I handed Sarah's mobile phone to Mrs Kent and between us we checked the small suitcase, previously packed and labelled "Hospital" by its forward-thinking owner. We fetched one or two last-minute additions, pronouncing it as complete as we could make it and, with that, Mrs Kent, Neil, the paramedics and the doctor vanished through the doors into the main hall, down the steps and into the ambulance.

In the ten minutes since my arrival, the world had changed. I don't think any of us had realised what a central role Sarah had played and I thought once more of the words culled from who knew where: "You don't know what you've lost 'til it's gone." I had said it once of Jack. How many more times were those words destined to trip me up?

Those were not the words, however, that came at once to change my world yet again. As the ambulance disappeared down the drive my phone rang. I answered it. My father's voice greeted me, calm and slightly amused, but with a note I hadn't heard for some time. He seemed about to apoogise for something.

"Gemma," he said, "your mother would like to speak to you, but as what she's going to say may take a bit of unravelling, I'll be happy to explain it when's she's done. I'm passing you over now."

I took the phone into the quiet little study room and prepared to sit through whatever new drama my mother was about to let loose upon me.

"Gemma darling, I'm so sorry. I haven't slept a wink all night as your father will tell you, especially after those horrid headlines. How could anyone tell such dreadful lies? I mean it's just not *right* and I've been crying all night just thinking about it"

I decided it was time to keep her on track. "But why were you crying? It's just newspapers, for heaven's sake, and a nine day's wonder. Sticks and stones, you know..."

"Yes, but..., you don't understand," and here she sobbed into the telephone, "it's all my fault, but I didn't *know* and the people were so nice and sympathetic and I was only talking to them for a couple of minutes until your father came back and they left."

The truth was beginning to dawn on me. "Okay Mama, you can stop crying. I'm not going to be cross with you, but please will you tell me exactly what happened. At the moment it's all a bit foggy."

"Yes, darling, I am trying to, and to be honest it's all a bit foggy to me too, now, but it seemed such a nice little chat you see. Your father went to the shop and was only gone for a few minutes but these three nice young people came up and asked if I was the famous Gemma Croft's mother? Of course I said yes, and they said I must be awfully proud of you, and I told them how clever you are and how you were really making a name for yourself and how often you had a byline. And I told them you were engaged to Jack and how delighted we all were. So when they asked what I *personally* thought about the feathers and not to worry about what other people said, I told them they must have a logical explanation. I mean, feathers don't drop out of the sky from nowhere do they? They said whoever was behind it must be *extra* super clever, so it couldn't be you, could it, but some kind of superwoman like the film, only she could fly and you couldn't. She laughed at that and said no it couldn't possibly be you then, and I was cross. I told them you were clever enough for *anything* and was just about to tell them the sort of things you'd done but just then your father came back with the shopping, then they all said a really nice goodbye and thanked me for being such a lovely lady. Then they went. It was only after that I realised I might have said too much, so when we drove home I didn't mention it to Bernard, except when he asked who the people were I said they were strangers asking the way. And now I feel *awful* and I know you'll never forgive me, but don't know how to put it right." With that she burst into tears again, so I gritted my teeth and asked to speak to my father.

He was obviously hovering close because he was with me within seconds. "Okay Gemma, you've got the gist. We stopped in Woolcot to fill up with petrol and she asked me to get a few vital things from the shop there. Things for supper, toilet rolls, you know the sort of thing. It didn't take long, but when I came back to the car your mother was enjoying herself, being thoroughly petted and feted by these media people – I've learnt to spot them a mile off now, but these were not the well-meaning kind. I can smell those. And when I asked who they were your mother lied. Then naturally she had a bad night, as I guessed she might, kept crying off and on, so in the end I told her I wanted to go to sleep if she didn't, so would she please confess and give us all some peace. Fortunately, she did. Hence the phone call. Sorry, Tomato-top, but at least we can now identify the 'sources close to the family' and stop accusing other people. Now I'll let you go and wipe up my somewhat lachrymose wife, but I hope I've put your mind at rest. All my love and hugs, babygirl. And don't forget Onwards and Upwards."

I replaced the handset and sat for a while, thinking of too many things at once. We had identified the source of the headline story but Sarah was obviously very sick and was now in hospital. I was still un-engaged to Jack, having had no time to speak to him, and was now quite certain that I was the stupidest person on God's earth.

But was it really God's earth? If not, whose was it? I had had my journalistic good name hauled through muck, had more or less announced my retirement, had by my own hand possibly lost the one man with whom I could live happily forever and was about to lose the closest thing to a friend and sister that I had ever met – all, it seemed to me because of an original little local interest story which had only been published by a fluke. So if there was a God he obviously wasn't on my side.

"Where are you, then?" I asked this non-existent person in whom I did not believe. "If you do exist I don't think I like you very much." And with that parting shot at this questionable creator of our universe, I stood up and returned to the solace of the wisest lady I knew – my grandmother.

# CHAPTER THIRTY SIX

Mrs Simmons was now evidently acknowledged as an official family member because she was sitting comfortably in an armchair dipping the corner of a biscuit into cup of steaming liquid. As I entered she half stood to offer me her chair, but I waved her away. "You stay where you are," I told her "I'm going to get myself a cup of coffee and sit with you for a while. I want to go upstairs later to see the girls, though I guess they'll be down before I can get there."

I was told they had already been to both apartments, finding the bird flown from one and a thoughtful Celia Croft in the other, staring out of the window at an empty drive. They had had no more information to give than we had and Eliza was not answering either her phone or her door. "Are the feathers still coming now Sarah's gone?" Angela had asked. "If not," she had continued, "What fun if they're floating around her hospital bed right now. They'd be a riot."

We considered this in silence. "Where are they now, the Starlights?"

"Gone up to look for ELiza. How was Neil taking it and had either of her brothers turned up?"

"Not before I left," I mused. "Perhaps they've gone on ahead. Neil went with the ambulance and so did her mother. Her father wasn't there, only the doctor and one of the carers. I think she's the one called Shelagh. Maybe the other one is waiting at the hospital."

The full, hideous reality of the situation hit me suddenly. I screwed up my face, hit the arms of my chair with both tightly clenched fists and howled with frustration. "I feel so *helpless!* There's nothing we can do except wait."

My grandmother looked down at her own hands. "You can always try praying," she said calmly enough, although I knew how hard she would find it to suggest such things to me, the seemingly hard and opinionated atheist.

I frowned. "But I don't believe in God?"

Mrs Simmons had been sitting quietly, saying nothing. Now she looked me full in the face. "Why not?" she asked as though it was a perfectly ordinary question to which a perfectly ordinary answer was not only reasonable but expected.

I was disconcerted and fell back on the age-old counter attack of replying to an uncomfortable question with another one.  "Do *you* believe?" I asked.  My grandmother smiled into her hands.  Mrs Simmons raised her eyebrows in surprise.

"The answer to that is I don't know, but that isn't what I asked," she said, quite reasonably. "It's what you believe that counts. You said you felt helpless and your Gran gave you a suggestion. She is a very wise lady, so why not give it a try? I'm a card-carrying agnostic but I'm going to."

"I believe in Science," I said mulishly.  "I'm not wasting my time on meaningless babble."

Mrs Smmmons shrugged and gave a small chuckle. "Okay, okay," she smiled, holding up her hands. "Don't shoot the messenger."

My grandmother evidently felt it was time she took part.  She raised her eyes from her lap and turned them directly upon my face until we were eye to eye, her hands palm upwards, not in supplication but almost in abdication.

"You must, of course, do what you believe in, but you asked and I suggested.  If the obvious door is closed, what's wrong with trying the other? And remember "there are more things in heaven and earth, Horatio, than you have dreamt of in your philosophy."

For the moment I was silenced.  At such a time argument seemed inappropriate.  Besides, she was right in what she said.  There were indeed "more things in heaven and earth" than even Science had so far dreamt of, though, I added to myself, no doubt it would eventually come up with a solution one day in the future.

I stood up. "I'm going to see the girls," I announced, tired of anger, tired of fear and desperately tired of frustration.

I needed Jack but Jack was not there.

I found the Starlights in their flat. Evelyn Carpenter was in their kitchen overseeing the teapot and the coffee machine as it gurgled on the worktop. They were pleased to see me. I asked a question that so far seemed not to have occurred to anyone.

"What happened to the cat?"

Angela spoke up, as she always did, appointing herself, without dispute as spokesperson for the group. Her greying hair in bright pink streaks was tied on top with a purple clip shining with small, costume-jewellery stones of no known composition. For once she was not all in a bustle but was standing at the window, much as my grandmother had been, as though by staring she could conjure up a returning ambulance carrying a restored Sarah surrounded by her ever-present white cloud. Unwontedly still, even Angela's paisley shawl hung limply from rounded shoulders. She exuded helplessness.

Lucy was sitting upright. In some unfathomable way she managed to look expectant and even hopeful. Her thin frame seemed to bristle with energy ruthlessly kept at bay.

Whatever Angela had meant to say was stifled by the sight of Evelyn emerging from the kitchen carrying a tray with four mugs from which steam and the aroma of fresh coffee hit my nose with welcoming warmth. I felt enough coffee had been absorbed into my bloodstream to last at least a month, but the situation demanded even more, so I sank gratefully onto one of the massive cushions that were scattered about the polished wood floor. I realised my question still remained unanswered, so I asked it again. "The cat, what happened to him?"

Then they all spoke at once. "Amazingly, nothing." Angela shook her head. "It simply stayed where it was, curled up on Sarah's bed. I think it's just waiting for her to come back."

"Is anyone feeding it?"

"One of the carers put some food and water out for it but it was ignored. The cat simply stayed put. Quite comfortable it looked, not a bit put out. It's up to the vet or the police – or Sarah – where it goes if the worst comes to the worst."

"Has he been given a name yet?"

"We thought Dusty, but we think it should be Sarah or Peter who chooses his name."

I said I thought Dusty was a good name but as they said, it was the rightful namers who should make the decision. "But how is Peter?" I added. "Has anyone heard?"

"Not a sign so far. He was very poorly yesterday but Michael and Jack have obviously gone to the hospital so we won't know anything until they come back. Michael will know about the boy, for sure, but we don't know how long they'll be."

Let it be soon, I thought. Please let it be soon.

"And what of Eliza?"

I was told she had appeared briefly, then vanished again into the private fastness of her own apartment, which so far non-one had had the courage to breach. "We did wonder, though," said Lucy over her mug, "whether she was the source of the news headlines."

I remembered with a little shock that Sarah's departure had driven my mother's confession out of my mind.

"Oooops!" I said, my finger between my teeth. "We can stop blaming anybody, especially Eliza, as my mother has confessed to the major crime of answering questions from the wrong people. Bless her, she didn't mean to cause so much harm and had a couple of sleepless nights because of it, so I guess she can be forgiven."

The three women grinned, nodded and agreed. They had all met my mother. "Well, thank God for that!" Evelyn cried, "Now let's enjoy our coffee while we can. I have this feeling we haven't got anywhere near the end yet. So here's to Sarah, here's to your mum and here's to all of us." We raised our mugs in salute and that is when the doorbell rang, the door opened and Jack put his head round it.

"Does that include me?" he asked. Everyone shouted "Yes of course, come in." and there was a chorus of mixed voices all asking different questions.

Jack and I said nothing more, but he held out his hand to me. I put down my mug, rose to my feet and went with him through the door, down the stairs and out into the grey early afternoon. At last I was anchored once more to my marker in the mysterious mist that surrounded us all.

I clasped his hand and smiled.

# CHAPTER THIRTY SEVEN

We said nothing but walked hand in hand across the grass to a small copse of trees to the right of the drive. In it we found a tiny private dell, cool and enclosed. Within it, facing the house but not visible from any of its windows, was a wooden bench, green with age but still sturdy. Jack flicked some errant, left-over leaves from the seat and drew me down onto it, his arm around my shoulders. And still we said nothing. Then he leaned towards me and placed his head on my shoulder, his free hand clutching mine.

"She's very bad," he whispered. "They're warning us to be prepared."

I put up my hand to his face and stroked it, kissing the only part of his face visible to me. "Thank you for coming to tell me," I said at last.

"The whole family was there. Nobody really needed an extra body and I needed you. I had to see you, to know you were still here, alive." He raised his head and gave a small, tired chuckle. It was a chuckle full of irony. "I've got to the stage of not wanting you out of my sight. Don't die, please Gemma, and please don't leave me here without you."

"I'm not dying," I told him, running my finger down his cheek, "and as for leaving you, you'll have to kick me out now or put a ring through my nose."

Jack smiled. "A ring on your finger would be better," he said, groping in his pocket for the small box containing the ring I had more or less flung at him the day before. He opened the box and slipped the ring back onto my finger.

"Are you sure you want to be saddled with a redhead?" I murmured. "Especially a Croft one? Do you realise what you'd be taking on?"

He replied with a kiss which was just beginning to turn passionate when he reluctantly broke away and stood up.

"I'm so sorry, my lovely girl, but I must get back there. What are you going to do now?"

"I'd like to stay here," I said slowly. "I need to think. Too much is happening." I looked at him. "I know you must go, but will you promise to let me know if..."

Jack nodded. "Of course," he said. "But don't stay alone too long. Go to your grandmother."

I nodded, then added: "I told her how helpless I felt and she suggested I pray. Me, the fully paid-up atheist?"

Jack smiled, kissed me again, said "Worth a try," and moved towards the lawn. "This is a good place for it. Sarah and I used to play here when we kids. It was 'Our Place.'"

"Give them all my love. Tell them I'm with them in spirit."

"I will," he promised, and with that he was gone.

"Worth a try," he had said. Gran had said much the same. But what did I know of how to go about such things? To pray to someone or something I had always adamantly believed to be the product of mass brain-washing was an alien thought. But both my rocks, which Gran and Jack had now become, were advising it.

It was with a surprised kind of amusement that I realised what I had just said to Jack. "Tell them I'm with them in spirit," were the words I had used. What did 'spirit' mean? Was it all due to whizzing sparks in my brain manufacturing feelings I didn't recognise?

I shook my head, and a tiny whiff of breeze ruffled the trees above me in a sudden stir of gentle movement. I looked up at them. "Are you laughing at me?" I asked, frowning. "How dare you laugh at me!" Then I threw up my hands in despair – or was it surrender? I hardly knew. I simply knew I must kneel down, so I knelt on the damp, leaf-trodden earth and talked to the God who wasn't there.

"Okay God," I began, "I don't think I believe in you, but just in case, I am asking you, no, entreating you, to not let Sarah die. It's too soon, God, it really is. There are things I want to say to her, and questions I have to ask, so please, please, please bring her back to us. Please. Please God don't let her die."

I hardly realised how passionate I had grown and was unaware of the tears pouring down my face until I gave a deep sigh, wiped my cheeks with the back of my hand and rose to my feet.

Tired now, I walked slowly back across the grass to my grandmother. I, the self- proclaimed non-believer, had just succumbed to an emotion I didn't fully understand.

I was only half way across the nurtured and cared-for lawn when my phone brought me instantly back to earth. The name on the monitor was Jack's. I picked it up quickly, afraid of what I might hear.

"Gemma," Jack's voice was strange, held back. "Sarah's dead. She died before I arrived. I was too late."

I froze. "Jack, no. She can't be dead. It's too quick."

"Can't stop. I want to be with you, but I have to be here with the family. My father looks – well, he looks broken. My mother seems calm but somehow as if she's died too. Darling Gemma, please think of us. I'll be with you as soon as I possibly can. Must go. I love you."

He had gone before I could tell him I loved him and I felt bereft, bereft of a friend who had become as dear as a sister and bereft of the presence of the one man who would understand.

Then, quite suddenly, I was fiercely angry. I stood, feet apart, in the middle of the immaculate lawn shaking my fists at the sky and hurling my fury at this God whom I had just been beseeching.

"I knelt down in the dirt," I shouted, "and *debased* myself and asked you not to let Sarah die and you *did*. And I don't care whether you're real or not, I hate you, *hate you!*"

254

I stopped being rooted to the grass and began to run as fast as I could towards the front steps of Croft Court, arriving breathless at the door and falling headlong into my grandmother's arms. She had seen me coming.

Within seconds, it seemed, I was in her recliner chair and she was cradling my head in her arms and breathing "Sh" into my hair. My sobbing grew less until I was left gasping for breath. I blew into the tissues she had held ready, and sat up.

"You know, don't you?" I asked.

"Yes, I knew before you got here. Michael phoned."

I looked directly into her eyes. "I prayed. I knelt down and prayed, and God wasn't there, was he? He didn't answer. Why didn't he answer? I hate him."

My grandmother moved back to sit in another chair as close to mine as possible. She placed her hand over mine and stroked it. "Asking God why he does things is about as much good as asking the sun why it has sunbursts. It isn't going to tell you – although, science being what it is, we'll probably find out about the sunbursts one day."

I frowned. "That doesn't make sense. I can see and feel the sun. I can't see or feel God."

"Okay, brainy-bonce, so I'm not a scientist and I often make mistakes, but then, you see, I'm not God – just a normal human person with a normal-sized brain. So stop blaming someone you've never met."

I sniffed. "Not likely to, am I, because he doesn't exist."

"You need hot chocolate. You've been coffee-d-and-wiine-d out and you need sustenance. And stop thinking so hard. It's a bad habit. You're overloaded already so don't add even more burdens."

With that, she stood up and regarded me with mixed sympathy and resignation. Her look said it all. Finally she shook her head "Once a Croft always a Croft," she mused, "and the red variety are usually their own worst enemies. How long is it since you've eaten anything?"

"Breakfast, and that was huge. I'm not hungry."

"Annie Simmons cut some sandwiches before she left to go shopping. She'll be back soon. Somehow I don't think she wants to go home. Could I tempt you to a nibble of ham and salad?"

"Thank you, but no. Sorry."

And that was the moment when the front doorbell rang and Jack came in, looking stunned.

"It's Sarah," he said, almost in disbelief. "She suddenly sat up. She's asking for you and me. No-one else, just you and me."

I was speechless. Too many thoughts and emotions were racing through my nervous system, flooding me with such a mix of chemicals that all I could do was stare. Jack came, hugged me very tightly then took my hand and helped me out of my chair and towards the door. He looked back at Gran and shrugged, "Don't ask," he mouthed. Then he opened the door and we went through to who knew what.

# CHAPTER THIRTY EIGHT

Neither of us spoke until we were sitting in his car. We merely stared at each other, speechless with a combination of shock, bewilderment and, in my case at least, a grudging kind of belief. But first I had to know the truth.

"Tell me," I demanded.

"I was there. We all were, the whole family except Ruth. She didn't want to bring Peter out. He's better but not really over it. She was afraid he might pass it on."

I nodded. The obvious thought was that Ruth's precautions were all too late. Peter had already passed it on. I was sorry for him but for me at that moment he was irrelevant.

"Sarah was plugged into all these tubes. Completely out of it. She looked dead but she wasn't. The tubes were keeping her alive – but not alive. The family were arguing when I got there. They couldn't agree whether to keep her on the machines or just let her go. She was dying anyway and maybe this was better than going slowly. Only of course in her case it wasn't going to be slow, was it? Frustrating and painful. I took one look at her and remembered how many times she had told me 'no resuscitation, please Jack.' She was always adamant not to be kept artificially alive and that's what we were doing, and I was sure she'd said the same to my father. I told everyone to shush. She was probably able to hear us and the last thing Sarah would want was to have everyone arguing as if she wasn't there. Neil was on one side of her and my mother was on the other. He suddenly said were arguing about her as if she was a dog or a cat. You know, let's put her out of her misery, and we don't want her to suffer, sort of thing. Well she wasn't a dog or a cat and it was up to her and I was right – she might easily be able to hear us. My mother agreed. She said what I'd been thinking, that Sarah had always stipulated "No

Resus." She thought it was a matter of dignity and if it was her time to go she wanted to go."

"So what happened?"

"My father and the doctor agreed that she would be kept alive in order to die a worse death later, and we should honour what Sarah had wanted. Then the doctor asked if we had anything written down and signed by her, and Neil said yes but it would be with her will somewhere. So they pulled the plugs."

Jack was trying not to cry. I fumbled in my bag for tissues for both of us.

"But she isn't dead." I was confused.

"No. I left the room. Didn't want to hang around. That's when I phoned you. Then a couple of minutes later one of the nurses called me back. When I went in everyone was in a state of shock. Real shock. She had suddenly opened her eyes. Neil said she looked around and smiled. She'd said 'Hello everybody' as if nothing had happened. Even the doctor was knocked out by it all. Stunned. Apparently it wasn't possible. That's when she looked straight at me and called my name. 'Jack, fetch Gemma. I want to see her – and you. Just you and her.' I nodded and gave her the thumbs up. It was too much for me, on top of everything else, so I left the room straight away and came straight here."

"Now you've fetched me we can go back together," I said quietly wiping a few errant tears from his cheeks. "I love you, Jack."

He smiled and gave me a quick but fervent kiss before starting the engine and driving round the curving front lawn and out through the gates.

The family was still grouped around the bed, reluctant to give way to Jack and me, but Sarah's greeting to me left us all in no doubt that she meant what she said.

"Sorry guys," Jack said firmly, "but she said me and Gemma for now. Come back in a few minutes."

The Kents moved back slowly, still reluctant, until they had left the room – leaving the door open with nurses well within reach. Sarah opened her hands and we sat, one each side of the bed, holding the outstretched fingers which showed no sign of helplessness. Jack kissed them. I placed them in my own hand and stroked them.

Her face was alight, almost with mischief, and the dimple on her cheek showed strongly. "I saw you," she said to me. Her voice was weak but clear. "You were in the copse and you got your knees dirty and I knew you were praying. Thank you. Then I saw you again. You were crossing the lawn and shouting at God. Gosh you weren't half mad! Now I've seen the Croft fury. Challenge for you, Jack," she chuckled, flicking him a quick glance. "I thought it was quite funny, like an ant stamping little insect feet and telling you he hated you 'cause you hadn't done as you were told. God seemed to share the joke."

I stared at her. "But where were you?"

"Oh, I died, didn't you know? Of course you did. I saw the usual bright light, like most people do, you know, and I wanted to go with it. It was so – so – beautiful. I've never seen anything so beautiful. Gemma you have no idea. No – Idea. I caught a glimpse of light and colour and I could hear music, or at least the sense of it, and knew I was within reach of all that beauty. I knew God, Jesus, was in the light and I didn't want to leave it, but he gave me a message for you. He said to tell you he'd heard you. He always does. And he said if you didn't believe me you were to read Luke chapter 16. verse 31 and Isaiah chapter 49 verse 16.. And especially to tell you he loved you. That's all I remember." She turned to jack and raised his hand to her lips. "I saw you too. You were crying and I didn't want you to cry, and you leaned your back against the door post. You were always my favourite brother. We had such fun together, you and me. I'm so glad you're going to marry Gemma because you're tailor-made and she's the sister I never had. I always knew you would, though."

I laughed, calmer now but very moved. "I always wanted a sister too," I told her. "And I'm so glad to have you back."

She smiled but shook her head. "Only for a few minutes," she said. "I just came back to give you that message. He let me come because you'd asked him so passionately."

I was shocked and not shocked at the same time. It seemed my hopes were being raised and knocked down again in such a series of lightning moves that it was difficult to keep pace. "So you're not staying," I said quickly.

"Don't worry, dying is easy," she replied, the dimple flickering in tell-tale fashion. "Like walking through a door from dim black and white into wonderful technicolour. And you'll love your cottage, you two."

"What cottage?" we both asked.

"Oh sorry, I forgot to tell you. I've seen your cottage. It's a bit run down, well a bit derelict really, but you're going to make it into something lovely."

"Where is it? How will we know it?"

"You just will. Now you can tell the others they can come back again. Tell them I was sorry, but you do see I had to tell you on your own about the message. It's up to you what you do with it. 'Bye Gemma and Jack, I love you both."

Jack went to open the door and found the others waiting. We left the hospital together, just the two of us. We had had our emotions harrowed and uplifted, torn apart and eased, and we needed peace and each other.

With that in mind, we both turned automatically to the copse where Jack and Sarah had played hide and seek and where I had knelt in the dirt and the wet grass to pray, for the first time in my life. What it meant I didn't know. For the present I didn't much care. Yet a certain part of me did care, for I must hunt for a Bible and look for my message. In sudden panic I hunted for the notebook in my bag and wrote the reference numbers down.

"Right," I said at last. "Now what?"

"Now this," Jack muttered, kissing me very hard and hugging me so tightly I was afraid I may never breathe again. When finally he let me go I sighed. For the moment I knew peace.

We sat there comfortably, arms wrapped around each other until Jack said: "I suppose we'd better go and see your grandmother. She'll be wondering."

I nodded against his shoulder. "Yes, she will," I said, feeling just a little guilty because we hadn't gone to her immediately. "Okay, let's go. In any case I've got to find a Bible."

Jack chuckled. "Do you mean to say you don't carry one around in your handbag?"

"How remiss of me." I shook my head clear. "Do you realise Sarah has just died – for the second time – and we're *laughing!* "

"It has occurred to me. Perhaps because she was happy to go,"

"Perhaps." I murmured, privately thinking that her coming back specifically to speak to me was a gift so special I had yet to take it all in. My brain was so full it seemed I had for the moment only enough room for one thing.

My grandmother was in the kitchen, chopping vegetables. I recognised the sign as one of barely contained impatience and frustration. Annie Simmons was with her, busy using a state-of-the-art machine to mix butter and flour in a large yellow bowl. They both stopped what they were doing and looked at us expectantly.

"Well?" they said together.

"Can we all sit down please?" I asked. "It's complicated."

Mrs Simmons nodded but returned to her yellow bowl. "You lot go in," she said. "and I'll finish putting this in the oven then I'll join you – unless of course it's private. Just let me know."

261

"Of course you can join us," I smiled, walking back to the sitting room and falling onto the sofa. Jack settled himself beside me while Gran went automatically towards her recliner. "But first, Granny darling, do you possess a Bible?" I caught her amused glance and added; "Of course you do. Silly question."

She went to a bookcase and extracted a volume bristling with markers. "What exactly are we looking for?"

I fished in my bag for the notebook references which, by some miracle and against all odds, I had remembered, and gave Gran the numbers Sarah had quoted. She sat down to turn the pages until she stopped with a brief nod and read aloud what she had found.

"There are two different ones. The first is '*If they will not listen to Moses and the prophets they will not be convinced even if someone rises from the grave.*' It's the final part of the story of Lazarus and the rich man. Does it mean anything to you?"

I told her yes it did but that I would have to read it for myself in order to digest it. There was no need yet for the whole passage. What she had given me was obviously enough or she would have given me more.

"And what's the second one?" I asked.

"'See, *I have written your name upon the palm of my hands.*' The rest of it is lovely too. Listen, '*Your walls are ever before me. Yours sons hurry back and those who laid you waste hasten to depart from you. Lift up your eyes and see that your children are all assembling and coming to you. As I live says Yahweh, you will wear them all as your jewels. They will adorn you as brides are adorned.*'"

There was silence in the room as Annie entered it carrying a tray. She stood quite still, struck by it. Jack's arm tightened about my shoulders and my grandmother stared down at her hands, immobile and deeply engaged in her own thoughts.

Annie quietly placed her tray on the low table and seated herself beside it, regarding each of us in turn. "I hate to spoil what seems to be a special moment, but anyone for hot chocolate?"

It was a masterstroke of bathos, as though a plug had been suddenly pulled from its socket. We all, at the same time, began to laugh. And we continued to laugh and sip from our mugs for some time, seemingly unable to stop once we had begun..

It had been that sort of day.

# CHAPTER THIRTY NINE

Eventually we recovered and, calmer now, we turned to discuss the mystery of Sarah's dying and the feathers that had appeared from nowhere., but before we were properly into the subject my grandmother said: "I've been thinking a lot about Little Billy and Sarah and I think I may have found a common denominator. At first there didn't seem to be one apart from the wheelchair, but I feel they both knew how to fly."

We waited, knowing an explanation would be given. As the silence continued, Jack asked "Why fly? And in what way fly? Neither of them could walk."

She laughed. "Well I don't mean they took off on broomsticks in the middle of the night," she said, head on one side as though the idea had appealed to her. "I could just as easily have said 'dance', but I was thinking of feathers. They do both, of course."

"Of course," I agreed, but Annie continued to look puzzled. "So what *do* you mean?"

"I mean that their spirits flew – and danced – in spite of everything life threw at them."

I understood. "Sarah twinkled. Did Billy twinkle?"

"He did. He was always fun to be with, even when he couldn't join in everything. That's why we all liked him."

"And why so many people liked Sarah. So we should suggest singing something on those lines for her funeral."

Unexpectedly Jack, in the middle of stroking my hair, made his own suggestion. "How about 'Lord of the Dance'" he suggested. We all knew the song and began to sing it.

> "*Dance, dance, wherever you may be,*
> *I am the Lord of the dance, said he,*
> *and I'll lead you all wherever you may be,*
> *and I'll lead you all in the dance, said he.*"

I clapped. "Perfect," I said, Now all we have to do is persuade the Kent family. And Neil of course. We mustn't sideline him, especially as he's not a Kent and may be over-ruled." I mused for a few seconds then added: "And since they all believe in different things, it could be a battle anyway. Who will have the final say, I wonder?"

Jack said he would put his money on his mother but before we had time to comment, and with perfect timing, Neil knocked on the door, opened it and stepped inside. "Did I hear my name mentioned?" he enquired, "in connection with being sidelined? If so, you needn't worry, I won't be."

"Excellent," we all cried and I clapped again. Then Jack tapped me gently on the hand and whispered into my hair. "Can we go now, please?"

I smiled up at him and we rose from the sofa together. I laughed to myself, thinking this was becoming a habit. Together we walked to the door, said a quick goodbye and descended the steps – crossing the lawn once again to the copse. Half way there, he stopped. "No," he said, "I want to look for our cottage. Sarah said it's got our name on it, so let's have a wander."

"It may be miles away."

"It may, but somehow I don't think so. Sarah loved Little Woolcot. I don't think she would have chosen anywhere else."

We wandered for quite a while, down the Little Woolcot High Street and along side lanes, finally coming to rest again beside an old workman's cottage almost hidden by tall bushes and a mixture of overgrown shrubs and neglected fruit trees. I stopped suddenly. There was a faded For Sale notice, age and weather and a kind of despair turning it into an ancient symbol of hope defeated. And beneath the notice, on the gate that was hanging by one hinge, there was a name.

"Crofters Cottage."

We stared, looked at each other and without another word we squeezed past the gate into a garden with grass waist high, a couple of apple trees and one magnificent magnolia bush just coming into flower. We followed the half hidden pathway to the front door and stopped again.

On the front step, pure white and fluttering a little, lay a single feather.

I picked it up and cupped it in my palms. Breathing was difficult. Then I looked at the sky.

"Thank you Sarah," I said quietly, and gazed down at the beautiful thing that lay there. She had been right. We had found our home.

# FINALE

I still have the feather. It lies very securely in a small Spode saucer on our mantelpiece. But even my feather, as precious as it is, cannot compete with the cloud of them that descended onto Sarah's casket as it was lowered into place in the sweet-soft earth. The feather cloud covered all of us. It raised a muted chorus of amazement and delight from the hundreds of friends, relatives, press and villagers who stood around the grave, and set the reporters' cameras clicking and their pens scribbling furiously into their notebooks. Even the surrounding gravestones and the bouquets that decorated them were covered in the immaculate white, feather storm. But just as we were beginning to move away, the cloud seemed to gather itself up, form itself into perfect wings and sail away over the rooftops. In silence we watched them go. There was nothing anyone could say.

At the last moment, as the wings were gathering strength, I threw onto the casket the Royal Air Force cap with its recently polished wings, together with the DFC medal won by the fighter pilot who had not only given us Billy but also his life during the Second World War and I mentally kissed them goodbye. They had never been mine or even my grandmother's. They had been Billy's but now they were Sarah's and we had no right to keep them.

Jack and I were married three months later, just in time for the first official photographs taken by the new entrepreneur, Neil Chalmers. He had resigned from JK Kent Electronics and with the farewell handshake from his father-in-law plus the legacy which had been held in trust for him by his far-seeing wife, he used his considerable talents on buying all the photographic equipment he could lay his hands on and learning everything possible about becoming a top cameraman. He had kept his original gadgets and simply collected new ones. Our wedding photographs were certainly not only brilliant technically but works of art showing an original talent amounting to genius. He had come a long way in a very short time and I was proud of him.

Being married to Jack, although beset by the usual problems of newly wedded bliss, was the delight I had hoped it would be, and we looked forward to producing our own Red Kent. Moreover, Jack learnt, very quickly, how to contain my occasional forays into fury while for the first time in my life I was prepared to bow to an authority other than my own. We bought our cottage, to the delight of the estate agent who had been unable to advertise it since its previous owner had died intestate and no-one wanted to claim ownership of such a derelict place. As predicted, we 'did it up' until it shone as a beacon of hope and renewal.

The feathers, after their very public display over the rooftops (which of course sparked off yet another frenzy of media activity until another war broke out to divert their attention), were never seen again and so relapsed once more into the realms of fantasy and village mythology, apart, that is, for the owners of the Lamb Inn who quietly changed its name to "The Lamb and Feathers". Generally speaking, however, everyone seemed to be sick of the very mention of feathers for some time to come – and that included me!

Incidentally, Sarah's funeral music did feature "The Lord of the Dance." Even Mr Kent Senior joined in the singing and Mrs Kent was seen wiping her eyes and blowing her nose. Bless her heart! She became the best mother-in-law any girl could wish for.

As for my career, I resigned from my prestigious national paper and spent my time happily writing local human interest stories for the Woolcot Gazette, thereby replacing Ellen who had moved on to greater papers with faster tracks – plus the occasional fictional one for a growing list of magazines.

Ruth, too, that seldom seen and reluctant witness to the whole, threw herself into the wedding festivities with single-minded fervour. Until Sarah's death I had never known what the mysterious job was that kept her rushing hither and thither with nannies and myriad time-commitments. She was the owner of a highly chic and ruinously expensive dress shop in Woolcot Raegis, so my wedding dress and both the top hats and smart dress suits of all the masculine Kents and Crofts were provided by Ruth herself – even to Peter's page-boy outfit, which, seeing that the recipient was not altogether pleased to be "all dolled up", created quite a sensation.

My father having stepped in at the last minute to cancel his wife's order of a dress from Harrods, persuaded her that Ruth's shop was just as chic and much nearer at hand for future ordering. As expected, she looked wonderful and knew it, being secretly convinced in her own mind of outshining the bride.

The cat, however, disappeared as mysteriously as he had come. His body was never found and no-one claimed him. We never saw him again.

If there was one thing, however, I learned from the feathers experience it was the one quoted to me on several occasions and never to be forgotten:

*"There are more things in heaven and earth, Horatio, than you have dreamt of in your philosophy."*

I have also kept, and frequently read, the white Bible given to me by my grandmother, with its gold-tipped pages and exquisitely pen drawn illustrations. In it is a bookmark. It reads:

*"I have written your name upon the palms of my hands."*

*The Wings of Woolcot*

Lightning Source UK Ltd.
Milton Keynes UK
UKOW04f1819120118
316045UK00001B/89/P